Aunt Dimity Slays the Dragon

Nancy Atherton is the author of thirteen other Aunt Dimity mysteries, many of them bestsellers. The first book in the series, *Aunt Dimity's Death*, was voted "One of the Century's 100 Favorite Mysteries" by the Independent Mystery Booksellers Association. She lives in Colorado Springs, Colorado.

✝

Praise for Nancy Atherton and her Aunt Dimity Series

Aunt Dimity Slays the Dragon

"One of the most charming entries in an enduringly popular series."
—*Booklist*

Aunt Dimity: Vampire Hunter

"One of Aunt Dimity's most suspenseful mysteries. Loyal fans will be thrilled by every new revelation."
—*Kirkus Reviews*

Aunt Dimity Goes West

"Just the ticket to ease out of a stressful day."
—*Deadly Pleasures*

Aunt Dimity and the Deep Blue Sea

"The eleventh Aunt Dimity mystery is testament to the staying power of Atherton's cozier-than-cozy premise. . . . Rainy Sunday afternoon reading." —*Booklist*

Aunt Dimity and the Next of Kin

"This is a book entirely without edge, cynicism or even rudeness—this is the way life really ought to be if only we were all better behaved. Put on the teakettle and enjoy."

—*Rocky Mountain News*

"This is Atherton at her coziest. . . . Fans of the series will not be disappointed."

—*Over My Dead Body!* (The Mystery Magazine)

"Cozy mystery lovers wouldn't dream of missing an entry in this series." —*Kingston Observer*

Aunt Dimity: Snowbound

"Witty, engaging and filled with interesting detail that will make the cottage-in-the-English-countryside fanciers among us sigh. . . . Just the thing to veg out on when life gets too much." —*The Lincoln Journal Star*

"The perfect tale for a cold winter's night."

—*Publishers Weekly*

"Fans of this series will be delirious with joy. . . . what a treat!" —*Kingston Observer*

Aunt Dimity Takes a Holiday

"A thoroughly modern cozy . . . The setting is delicious. . . . A very enjoyable read."

—*The Washington Post Book World*

Aunt Dimity Slays the Dragon

NANCY ATHERTON

PENGUIN BOOKS

PENGUIN BOOKS

Published by the Penguin Group

Penguin Group (USA) Inc., 375 Hudson Street, New York, New York 10014, U.S.A. • Penguin Group (Canada), 90 Eglinton Avenue East, Suite 700, Toronto, Ontario, Canada M4P 2Y3 (a division of Pearson Penguin Canada Inc.) • Penguin Books Ltd, 80 Strand, London WC2R 0RL, England • Penguin Ireland, 25 St Stephen's Green, Dublin 2, Ireland (a division of Penguin Books Ltd) • Penguin Group (Australia), 250 Camberwell Road, Camberwell, Victoria 3124, Australia (a division of Pearson Australia Group Pty Ltd) • Penguin Books India Pvt Ltd, 11 Community Centre, Panchsheel Park, New Delhi – 110 017, India • Penguin Group (NZ), 67 Apollo Drive, Rosedale, North Shore 0632, New Zealand (a division of Pearson New Zealand Ltd) • Penguin Books (South Africa) (Pty) Ltd, 24 Sturdee Avenue, Rosebank, Johannesburg 2196, South Africa

Penguin Books Ltd, Registered Offices:
80 Strand, London WC2R 0RL, England

First published in the United States of America by Viking Penguin,
a member of Penguin Group (USA) Inc. 2009
Published in Penguin Books 2010

1   3   5   7   9   10   8   6   4   2

PUBLISHER'S NOTE

This is a work of fiction. Names, characters, places, and incidents are either the product of the author's imagination or are used fictitiously, and any resemblance to actual persons, living or dead, business establishments, events, or locales is entirely coincidental.

THE LIBRARY OF CONGRESS HAS CATALOGED THE HARDCOVER EDITION AS FOLLOWS:

Atherton, Nancy.
Aunt Dimity slays the dragon / Nancy Atherton.
p. cm.
ISBN 978-0-670-02050-8 (hc.)
ISBN 978-0-14-311658-5 (pbk.)
1. Dimity, Aunt (Fictitious character)—Fiction. 2. Women detectives—England—Cotswold Hills—Fiction. 3. Cotswold Hills (England—Fiction). I. Title.
PS3551.T426A93448   2009
813'.54—dc22   2008037297

Printed in the United States of America
Set in Perpetua • Designed by Alissa Amell

For Claudia and Don Stafford,
my next-door angels

One

The invasion of Finch began on a mild Monday evening in late May. By the end of August, my peaceful English village would find itself at the mercy of rampaging brigands, bullies, braggarts, and blundering louts. There would also be an unexpected death.

None of us saw it coming. On the evening in question, my neighbors and I were sitting quietly—some of us somnolently—in the old schoolhouse that had for many years served as our village hall. We were there to attend a village affairs committee meeting, and nearly seventy of us had shown up because the annual May meeting was widely regarded as the most important committee meeting of the year.

The sole purpose of the May meeting was to finalize plans for Finch's many summer activities. It was, for the most part, an egregious waste of time, because everyone knew that the summer fete, the bring-and-buy sale, the gymkhana, the art show, the flower show, the dog show, and the tidy cottage competition would be run exactly as they had been run for as long as anyone could remember.

Innovations might be suggested, discussed, and debated, but they were never adopted. In the end, the same dates would be chosen and the same folding tables would be used, along with the same frayed linen tablecloths, tarnished tea urns, and increasingly shabby decorations. The summer fete would be held, as it had always been, at the vicarage, the gymkhana would take place at Anscombe Manor, and everything else—apart from the tidy cottage competition—would be staged, as per usual, in the schoolhouse. In the eight years since my husband and I had moved to Finch, the routine had never varied in the slightest.

The only thing that ever changed from one year to the next was the assignment of menial tasks to volunteers. The glamorous jobs had been snapped up as long ago as 1982 by women who would defend to the death their right to wear big hats and flowery frocks while opening the art show or graciously awarding ribbons at the gymkhana. Competition was understandably less fierce for the less glamorous jobs. No one fought for the right to iron tablecloths, empty rubbish bins, or pick bits of soggy crepe paper out of the grass on the village green. Since such toil was essential to the success of any event, however, volunteers had to be found.

It was left to our esteemed chairwoman, the all-powerful Peggy Taxman, to delegate the donkeywork, and it was for this reason, and this reason alone, that the May meeting was so very well attended. Peggy had it within her grasp to favor us with the pleasant chore of attending to the tea urns or to condemn us to the noxious duty of scrubbing the schoolhouse floor after the dog show. We were agog to learn our fates.

"The meeting will come to order." Peggy banged her gavel, then pointed it accusingly at the room in general. "And if I catch any of you napping, I'll have you removed from the schoolhouse!"

Mr. Barlow, who had already dozed off, woke with a start.

"We done yet?" he asked sleepily.

"Just getting started," Miranda Morrow murmured from the corner of her mouth.

"Right." Mr. Barlow yawned, rubbed his eyes, and lifted his gaze to the five committee members.

The members sat shoulder-to-shoulder on one side of the long, linen-draped table that had been set up on the small stage at the rear of the schoolhouse. Peggy Taxman occupied the middle chair, a position which allowed her to loom menacingly over the assembled throng. Lesser villagers perched meekly on folding chairs on either side of a central aisle leading to the schoolroom's double doors, through which Peggy would sweep magisterially after she'd made her final pronouncement.

No one would dare to stop her or attempt to dispute her decisions. An empire-builder by nature, Peggy ran two major businesses as well as the post office in Finch. She was a woman of substance, both physically and financially, and her fierce sense of civic duty drove her to rule the village with an iron hand, a steely eye, and a voice like thunder. A reproving glance from behind those pointy, rhinestone-studded glasses was usually all it took to make the bravest among us quail. When the glance didn't work, she employed the voice, and although I'd never seen the iron hand in action, I had no doubt that, if all else failed, she would use it.

The other committee members were much less daunting. Sally Pyne, vice chair and tearoom owner, preferred gossip to governing and was content to let Peggy rule the roost. George Wetherhead, recording secretary and model train enthusiast, was so bashful that he rarely raised his eyes from the laptop computer he used to record the minutes. Mr. Wetherhead would no more think of contradicting Peggy than he would of challenging her to a wrestling match.

Our treasurer, Jasper Taxman, had been a retired accountant before marriage to our chairwoman had forced him to rethink his definition of retirement. No professional career could have kept him busier than his wife did. When he wasn't minding the tills in Peggy's shops or selling stamps in Peggy's post office, he was keeping the books for Peggy's myriad committees.

The last chair on the stage was assigned to the least important member of the committee: me, Lori Shepherd—wife, mother, and hapless draftee. I sat at the long table because, having made the grave mistake of missing last year's May meeting, I'd been appointed, in absentia, to the post of sergeant-at-arms.

All things considered, I'd gotten off lightly. Although my title was impressive, my duties were not. I was assigned to keep order among the villagers during the meeting, and to distribute Peggy's work rosters after it. Since our chairwoman needed no one's help to keep the villagers in order, and since she wouldn't release the rosters until she'd finished reviewing her copious notes, I spent most of the evening staring absently into space.

"Item one," Peggy began. "A few comments on fastening floral swags to the art show tables. Safety pins are considered unsightly and will not be used unless the following conditions apply. . . ."

As if by magic, my eyes stayed open while my mind floated out of the schoolhouse. My first thoughts were, as always, of home. Finch was nestled snugly in a verdant river valley set amidst the patchwork fields and rolling hills of the Cotswolds, a rural region in England's West Midlands. I lived two miles south of Finch, in a cottage made of honey-colored stone, with my husband, Bill, and our six-year-old identical twin sons, Will and Rob.

Although Bill, the twins, and I were American, we'd lived in England long enough to know the difference between crème fraîche and clotted cream, and to develop an incurable addiction to the latter. Bill ran the European branch of his family's venerable Boston law firm from a high-tech office on the village green, Will and Rob attended school in the nearby market town of Upper Deeping, and I divided my time between taking care of my family and serving my community.

Until quite recently, we'd shared our home with the boys' nanny, the inestimable Annelise Sciaparelli, but she'd left us in mid-May to marry her longtime fiancé, Oliver Elstyn, and her room had been vacant ever since. With the twins attending primary school full-time, neither Bill nor I felt the need to hire another nanny, and we agreed that Annelise was irreplaceable in any case.

"Item twenty-four . . ."

Peggy's bellow jerked me out of my reverie.

". . . the proper use of dust bin lids!"

I immediately sank back into a stupor shared by almost everyone in the schoolhouse. I couldn't remember the last time I'd been excited about a committee meeting. My life was in many ways idyllic—devoted husband, healthy sons, happy home—but I'd lately begun to realize that it was also just a tiny bit . . . boring. I loved my friends and neighbors—most of the time—but their faces had started to become a tad too familiar, their habits slightly too predictable. The daily routine of village life, which I'd once found so fulfilling, had recently begun to seem a little too . . . routine.

As I scanned the faces assembled in the schoolroom, I acknowledged sadly that there wasn't much I didn't know about my fellow villagers. Mr. Barlow, a retired mechanic, was in the midst of cleaning the carburetor in a vintage Mustang he was restoring for a wealthy and recently divorced client who lived in Tewkesbury. Although Miranda Morrow was a strict vegetarian, she spent hours every day preparing the choicest cuts of meat for her cat. Lilian Bunting, the vicar's wife, was currently rewriting the third paragraph of her introduction to a book about stained glass. Dick Peacock, the local publican, had taken up pottery as a hobby, but the consensus was that his handmade goblets would do little to improve the taste of his homemade wine.

And so on and so forth. I knew without asking whose dog had fleas, whose roof had sprung a leak, whose grandchildren were angelic and whose were not. If Finch had any surprises left for me, it was keeping them well hidden.

"Item twenty-five: Flower show entry forms. Block letters must be used when filling out . . ."

While Peggy continued to drone, my gaze traveled to the portrait of the queen, hung in a place of honor above the schoolroom's double doors. I usually felt a small, Anglophilic tingle when I beheld England's gracious monarch decked out in royal regalia, but I'd seen the schoolroom portrait so often that it no longer worked its magic.

Sighing, I looked down at my idle hands. If asked, I would have been forced to confess that I had no one but myself to blame for my growing sense of ennui. After the fiasco with the vampire in October, I'd sworn to keep my feet firmly on the ground, and on the ground I'd kept them for seven months, successfully stifling an inborn and nearly irresistible inclination to let my vivid imagination run away with me.

When Sally Pyne's gilded antique biscuit barrel had gone missing in January, I'd clamped down on my desire to nab the thief and left it to Sally to remember—two days later—that she'd loaned her precious barrel to Mr. Barlow, who'd played one of the Three Wise Men in the Nativity play and needed a fancy container for the frankincense.

Similarly, when a stranger spent a cold February morning taking photographs of every nook and cranny in Finch, I *did not* allow myself to envision him as a predatory land developer, a fast-talking film location scout, or a devious foreign spy, and when I learned that he was, in fact, a real estate agent acting on behalf of clients who were about to buy long-vacant Crabtree Cottage, I *refused* to wonder whether or not those clients had sinister ties to the woman who'd died there.

It was just as well, because the clients turned out to be Grant Tavistock and Charles Bellingham, who were sitting just below me, in the front row of folding chairs. The newest residents of Crabtree Cottage were a perfectly friendly pair of middle-aged art appraisers who'd never heard of Prunella Hooper or her tragic demise, and who were so eager to fit into their new community that they'd actually *volunteered* to clean up after the bring-and-buy sale. As I surveyed their shining faces, I thought pityingly, *They'll learn*.

". . . cacti and succulents belong to separate and distinct plant categories and will be judged accordingly, with no exceptions. . . ."

My mind drifted lazily from cacti to flowers to the beautiful bouquet Annelise had carried down the aisle. Annelise's wedding had definitely helped me to keep my treacherous imagination in check. With her mother's permission, I'd thrown myself into every phase of the preparations, attending to each detail with such single-minded devotion that I had no energy to spare for phantom biscuit-barrel thieves or mysterious strangers.

The wedding had taken place on the third Saturday in May—a mere nine days ago, I thought, glancing wanly at the schoolroom's well-thumbed wall calendar—at St. Margaret's Catholic Church in Upper Deeping. Thanks to my impeccable planning, it had gone off without a hitch, but now that it was over, I couldn't help feeling a bit deflated.

What did I have to look forward to, I asked myself, but the summer fete, the bring-and-buy sale, the gymkhana, the art show, the flower show, the dog show, and the tidy cottage competition? A sensible woman would have thanked her lucky stars to live in such a lively community, but when Peggy asked if there was any other business, I could scarcely keep myself from yawning. Everyone in the schoolroom knew that Peggy's question was meaningless because there was *never* "any other business" at the May meeting.

Which was why everyone—except Peggy—jerked to sudden, rapt attention when Mr. Malvern raised a hesitant hand and lumbered slowly to his feet.

Horace Malvern lived next door to me, on a vast estate known as Fivefold Farm. His property ran along the southern edge of mine, and I'd never had the least cause to regret it. He was a model neighbor—a respectable, hard-working, middle-aged farmer whose behavior had, until the moment he'd raised his hand, been as predictable as spring rain. I couldn't imagine what other business he had to offer.

I stared at him incredulously for a moment, then swung around to look at Peggy Taxman, who still had her nose buried in her notes. It wasn't until Mr. Malvern gave a rather pointed cough that Peggy looked up from her clip-board, peered suspiciously around the room, and fixed her gimlet gaze on the burly farmer.

"What is it, Horace?" she snapped waspishly. "Be quick. I can't abide time-wasters."

Mr. Malvern shuffled his large feet uncomfortably, then muttered something gruffly to the floor.

"Speak up, Horace," Peggy ordered. "No one can hear you."

Mr. Malvern cleared his throat and, with a brief glance over his right shoulder, said forthrightly, "My nephew would like to make an announcement."

"Your nephew?" said Peggy, clearly taken aback.

"That's right," said Mr. Malvern, nodding. "Calvin, my brother Martin's boy, would like to make an announcement." Without further ado, he turned toward the double doors and whistled shrilly, then sat down again and ducked his head.

The double doors were flung open, and a lithe figure clad in the belled cap and the diamond-patterned costume of a medieval court jester catapulted down the central aisle in a lightning-fast series of handsprings, backflips, somer-saults, and cartwheels. He came to rest on bended knee at the foot of the stage, just below Peggy Taxman, with his arms outstretched and his bells jingling.

The jester's knee had barely touched the floor when a pair of young men dressed in plumed caps, yellow tights, and bright red tabards took up positions on either side of the doors, raised long, slender trumpets to their lips, and blew an elaborate fanfare. As the last note of the fanfare faded, they turned as one to address the room.

"Arise, gentle folk!" they bellowed in unison. "Hence cometh our excellent and most gracious ruler, the lord of laughter and the monarch of mirth, His Majesty, King Wilfred the Good!"

Sixty-seven jaws dropped simultaneously as King Wilfred the Good strode into the schoolhouse.

Two

King Wilfred paused just inside the doorway, planted his hands on his hips, and beamed benevolently around the room. He was in his late twenties, I guessed, tall and heavyset, with twinkling blue eyes, a full beard, and a cascade of light brown curls that tumbled to his shoulders. I wouldn't have looked at him twice if he'd been wearing a T-shirt and jeans, but the clothes he had on deserved a prolonged second glance. As he stood near the doorway, arms akimbo and head held high, I couldn't help wondering if he'd spent the day ransacking Henry VIII's closet.

He wore a sleeveless, ermine-trimmed surcoat of plum velvet over a gold-shot brocade tunic with long, puffed sleeves, a stiff lace collar, and a belt made of braided silver cord. His stout legs were clad in white tights, with an embroidered garter above each knee, and his surprisingly dainty feet were shod in soft-soled suede ankle boots. Heavy gold rings adorned his thick fingers and a chunky gold chain hung around his neck, embellished with a ruby-encrusted pendant. Set among his light brown curls was a shiny golden crown whose tall points were dotted with gemstones that seemed too sparkly to be real.

The trumpeters doffed their plumed caps and bowed deeply at his entrance, while the jester curled into a ball and rolled to one side of the stage, to crouch beneath an alarmed-looking Mr. Wetherhead. The only villager to "arise" was Sally Pyne, who'd jumped to her feet at the trumpeters' command, then hastily resumed her seat, blushing furiously. The rest of us sat openmouthed and staring, as if we'd been turned to stone.

"All hail good King Wilfred!" the trumpeters chorused, rising from their bows.

"Pray silence, good heralds," the king responded, with a nonchalant wave of his hand. "We see that our magnificence has temporarily robbed our subjects of speech and rendered their limbs useless. We will not, therefore, stand upon ceremony."

The jester rose from his crouch, held an imaginary telescope to his eye, and scanned the room in a sweeping motion that ended at Mr. Wetherhead's startled face.

"Looks to me like no one's standing," the jester announced, "upon ceremony or otherwise."

Mr. Wetherhead twitched nervously and shrank back in his chair.

"Well said, Fool," said King Wilfred, chuckling merrily as he approached the stage. "And foolishly said well, for a fool may well say wisely what a wise man cannot say, and wise man may say foolishly what a fool may—"

"Calvin Malvern!" The name exploded from Peggy Taxman as though it had been shot from a cannon. "Is it you under all that hair?"

King Wilfred removed his crown with a flourish and shook his curls back from his round face. "It is I, Calvin Malvern, at your service, Auntie Peggy."

"I'm not your aunt, you pea-witted nincompoop," Peggy thundered.

"I think of you as my aunt," Calvin assured her. "After the many pleasant hours I spent in your shop when I was but a wee lad—"

"I chased you out of the Emporium more times than I can count, you young rascal," Peggy interrupted.

"But you were always pleased to see me when I came back," Calvin countered, smiling angelically.

"That's as may be," Peggy retorted, "but I'm certainly not pleased to see you now. How dare you disrupt my meeting?"

"Forgive me," said Calvin. "I was under the impression that you'd called for other business."

"Other business does not include prancing in here like a puffed-up popinjay and spouting poetical nonsense," Peggy growled. "What your poor father would think if he could see you strutting around like an overdressed peacock . . ."

"He'd think I was doing something useful with my life," said Calvin.

"Useful?" Peggy snorted derisively. "Run along, Calvin. Take your little friends and play dress-up somewhere else. The grown-ups have work to do."

Mr. Wetherhead gave a terrified squeal as the jester vaulted onto the stage and bent low to peer at the laptop's screen.

"May it please the court," the jester cried, raising a rigid index finger. "I see nothing in the minutes that limits 'other business' to that offered by boring blokes in business suits." He pointed the finger accusingly at Peggy. "You must let the peacock squeak, er, I mean, speak!"

Dick Peacock chuckled and Christine Peacock snickered as a ripple of amusement ran through the schoolhouse.

I was sitting too close to Peggy to risk outright laughter, but I caught the jester's eye and smiled furtively.

"We may as well hear what Cal has to say, now he's here," called Mr. Barlow from the back of the room.

"Hear, hear!" called Lilian Bunting from the front row.

"Let King Wilfred speak," called Miranda Morrow, shaking her strawberry-blond hair back from her freckled face.

Others soon chimed in. While the rest of the villagers spoke up in Calvin's defense, Horace Malvern stared stoically at the floor and said nothing. It was impossible to tell whether he was upset, embarrassed, or simply bewildered by his nephew's antics, but his silence seemed to imply that all was not well between them.

Peggy's silence had a distinctly ominous edge to it, but she was a seasoned politician and she could read a crowd's mood accurately, when she chose to. She waited until the groundswell of support had reached a raucous rumble, then placed her clipboard on the table, banged the gavel twice for order, and folded her arms across her impressive bosom.

"The chair will give you ten minutes," she declared, nodding curtly to Calvin.

Calvin bowed to her, murmuring, "As generous as always, Auntie Peggy."

A titter went through the room, accompanied by a buzz of excitement rarely heard at a May meeting. Lilian Bunting and I exchanged gleefully mystified glances, then gave our full attention to Calvin. I had no idea what he was about to say, but it had to be more entertaining than Peggy's guidelines on stanchion storage.

I expected Calvin to replace his crown and revert to

the persona of King Wilfred while making his mysterious announcement. Instead, he handed the crown to the jester, who won a huge roar of laughter by pretending to put it on Peggy's head before leaping nimbly from the stage to sit cross-legged at Charles Bellingham's feet. Calvin allowed the room to settle down, then began to speak in the artfully modulated tones of a trained actor—or a snake-oil salesman.

"My friends," he said. "Have you ever dreamed of traveling back in time? Have you ever yearned to return to an age when simple folk danced gayly on the green while lords quaffed and knights fought and troubadours sang sweetly of chivalrous deeds? Have you ever longed to submerge yourself in the glories of merry old England?"

Mr. Barlow harrumphed disdainfully.

"Merry old England, my eye," he grumbled. "There's no such thing, Cal, and there never was. The ruling class had it easy enough back then, I'll grant you, but the peasants worked themselves into early graves."

"Lots of nasty diseases in those days, too," Sally Pyne chimed in. "No proper sanitation and some *very* backwards ideas about personal hygiene."

"Rats and lice everywhere you looked," said Christine Peacock, with an expressive shudder. "Not to mention fleas."

"Fleas brought the Black Death to Europe in 1347," Jasper Taxman added learnedly. "In five years, the plague killed some twenty-five million people."

"Nothing merry about the Black Death," opined Mr. Barlow.

"I beg to differ," said Jasper. "The Black Death created a labor shortage, which significantly improved the lot of the common man. A worker could demand a better wage because so few workers were left to do the work."

"Be that as it may," Mr. Barlow riposted heatedly, "no one in his right mind would call the Black Death *merry*."

The debate might have gone on for hours—my neighbors loved a good digression—but Calvin reclaimed the spotlight by using the old actor's trick of shouting very loudly.

"My dear people!" he bellowed. When all eyes were trained on him again, he continued smoothly, "I'm not describing *history*. I'm describing *fantasy*—a dream of England not as it was, but as it should have been. And I'm inviting each and every one of you to share the dream. On the first Saturday in July, at precisely ten A.M., the gates of a new world will be opened to you. And the name of the world will be . . ."

He pointed toward the back of the room and the heralds unfurled a cloth banner upon which were emblazoned the words:

KING WILFRED'S FAIRE

If Calvin expected wild applause or a chorus of awestruck gasps, he must have been disappointed, because his thrilling words were met with dead silence and a general air of incomprehension.

Peggy seemed to speak for the rest of us when she barked, "What in heaven's name are you blathering on about, Calvin?"

"I'm introducing you to an experience you'll never forget," he replied, unfazed by Peggy's bluntness or our blank looks. "For eight consecutive weekends in July and August,

King Wilfred and his loyal subjects will recreate the atmosphere of a great Renaissance festival, featuring musicians, acrobats, jugglers—"

"Like a circus?" Sally Pyne asked hopefully.

"The fair will be far more entertaining than a circus, my lady," Calvin told her, "because you'll be allowed, nay, you'll be *encouraged* to join in the fun. At King Wilfred's Faire, all the world will be a stage. A hundred—"

"Excuse me," Jasper Taxman interrupted. "Who is this King Wilfred you keep mentioning? No British monarch was ever called Wilfred."

"I am King Wilfred," Calvin said, bowing to Jasper. "My kingdom is not fettered by an oppressive adherence to historical fact, good sir. My realm celebrates the imagination. A hundred scintillating performers will roam the fair's winding lanes. They will dress in period costume, speak in period speech, and amuse you in ways too varied and marvelous to describe." Calvin prowled up and down the center aisle, gesturing flamboyantly as he spoke. "Artists will ply their wares, artisans will demonstrate their crafts, wizards will work their magic, and"—he winked broadly—"bawdy wenches will work theirs! Our marketplace will overflow with unique, handcrafted items: jewelry, glassware, pottery, leather goods, and much more. You'll find food and drink, song and dance, pageantry and revelry, and once daily you'll witness the breathtaking spectacle of noble knights on horseback, competing in a joust!"

"And you expect us to participate?" Dick Peacock said doubtfully.

"I'm *not* getting on a horse," his wife stated categorically.

"Perish the thought, good lady," said Calvin, eyeing Christine's ample figure, "but you can bestow your favor upon a gallant knight, if you wish. You can enjoy the varied entertainment and savor the food, and you can most certainly come in costume." He put a finger to his lips and studied Christine critically. "I envision you as a noblewoman of the royal court, with a length of rose-colored silk trailing from your wimple. Or as a pirate maiden in twelve-league boots, with a saber buckled at your waist. Or as a gypsy fortune-teller, with gold hoops in your ears and seven petticoats, each a different shade of red."

Christine herself turned a fairly shocking shade of red, but she did not look displeased. At the same time, faraway expressions crossed the faces of several women sitting near her, as if they were picturing themselves in twelve-league boots with sabers buckled at their waists. Calvin, it seemed, had struck a chord.

"You're free to dress up or to come as you are," he continued jovially, once again addressing the room at large. "If you decide to dress up, don't worry overmuch about historical accuracy. We define the term 'Renaissance' with great liberality. In truth, anything vaguely medieval will do. Creativity is the key, so let your imagination take flight! Did I mention the petting zoo for the little ones?"

Jasper Taxman sniffed. "I'm not entirely certain that young children should be exposed to, ahem, bawdy wenches."

"It's all in good fun," Calvin said reassuringly. "Our performers are trained to provide good, clean, family entertainment with just a hint of spice, and I can tell you from personal experience that the children will be having too much fun in the petting zoo to pay attention to the spice."

"Where are you planning to hold this fair of yours?" Mr. Barlow inquired.

"Not far from Finch," Calvin replied, "which is why I'm here tonight. We want to be on good terms with our nearest neighbors." He stretched an arm toward Mr. Malvern. "Uncle Horace has generously allowed us to lay claim to the northeast corner of Fivefold Farm. King Wilfred's Faire will take place in and around Bishop's Wood. During fair hours, there will be free parking in the pasture adjacent to the wood."

Mr. Barlow's eyebrows shot up and he glanced at Mr. Malvern questioningly, but Mr. Malvern kept his gaze fixed firmly on the floor.

"I collect herbs in Bishop's Wood," Miranda Morrow commented. "I don't recall seeing any winding lanes there."

"There aren't any lanes at the moment," Calvin acknowledged, smiling at her. "Construction will begin bright and early tomorrow morning. I assure you that we will do no permanent damage to the wood. All structures will be temporary in nature. When the fair is finished, they will be removed."

"How much will it cost to attend the fair?" Jasper Taxman asked shrewdly, tapping his calculator.

"There is an admission fee," Calvin admitted, turning to face the retired accountant, "but the cost is trifling compared to the enjoyment you and your loved ones will derive from the fair—nine pounds for adults and four pounds for children aged five to twelve. Children under the age of five will, of course, be admitted without charge."

A peculiar sound filled the schoolhouse, a mingling of disappointed groans with outraged grunts. The groans came exclusively from the women, the grunts from the men.

"Nine pounds?" said Jasper, appalled. "Do you seriously expect me to pay nine pounds to watch people strut about in fancy dress?"

"Indeed not, good sir," Calvin said solemnly. "I expect you to pay nine pounds, and gladly, for much more. Your hesitation is understandable, however. After all, you know not whereof I speak. I will, therefore, make a pact with you and with everyone here tonight." He raised his voice as he turned away from Jasper to face the schoolroom. "If you are not completely satisfied with your day at King Wilfred's Faire, I will personally return your admission fee to you in full."

"Can't say fairer than that," Christine stated firmly.

The women sitting near her nodded eagerly.

Calvin's smile held a hint of triumph as he returned to the foot of the stage, but if he thought he was home and dry, he was mistaken. The villagers were just getting warmed up.

"This all sounds very interesting," Dick Peacock allowed, "but I'd like to hear more about the food and drink you mentioned. Are you trying to put my pub out of business?"

"I could ask the same thing about my tearoom," said Sally Pyne.

"And what about our summer calendar?" demanded Peggy Taxman. "It's hard enough to get people to attend village events. How can we hope to attract a crowd if everyone's gone to your fair?"

Calvin raised a pacifying hand. "Fear not, good people. Neither your businesses nor your events will suffer because of the fair. To the contrary, they'll prosper. King Wilfred's Faire will bring more people to Finch than ever before."

"Which means traffic congestion," Mr. Barlow said gloomily.

Before Calvin could address the traffic issue, villagers began firing a barrage of questions at him. Did he have the proper building permits? Did he have a liquor license? A food license? A sales license? Had the county planning board approved his project? Where would the performers stay once the fair was under way? Although Calvin tried to respond, the questions came so thick and fast that he couldn't get a word in edgewise.

Finally, Mr. Malvern took a deep breath, got to his feet, and shouted, "Shut it, the lot of you!"

"Well, *really*," Peggy Taxman said indignantly.

"Listen up," said Mr. Malvern, ignoring her. "Calvin has the planning board's approval as well as the requisite licenses and permits. The performers will live in caravans while they're working the fair. The caravans will be parked on my property, and yes, we have the county's permission for that, too. The main access road to the fair will run straight from the Oxford Road to Bishop's Wood, so the bulk of the extra traffic will be south of town. Finch'll see more cars than it's used to on weekends, but no more than it can handle."

"Horace Malvern," Peggy blustered, "you have no right to foist this travesty—"

"I have every right," Mr. Malvern broke in. "You may be the queen bee in Finch, Peggy, but my nephew doesn't need *your* permission to use *my* land. Bishop's Wood is on my property and I'll do with it as I see fit, so you may as well stop your whingeing because it won't do you one bit of good. And if you can't see how the fair will benefit Finch, you're blind as well as bossy."

Peggy's nostrils flared alarmingly. "How *dare* you—"

"We will, of course, donate a portion of the proceeds to the church roof fund," Calvin interjected quickly.

"Seems very generous to me," said Christine Peacock.

"Extremely generous," chorused the women sitting near her.

"No, my ladies," said Calvin, kissing his fingertips to them. "It is the village of Finch that is generous. I thank you for welcoming me with such warmth and affection, and I look forward to seeing all of you on opening day—and on many merrymaking weekends thereafter." He snapped his fingers and the jester presented the crown to him. Calvin lowered the crown onto his own head, then raised a hand in farewell. "Adieu, good people of Finch. Until we meet again—at King Wilfred's Faire!"

"All hail good King Wilfred!" bellowed the heralds.

The pair raised their trumpets and played another fanfare as Calvin strode up the aisle, then followed him out of the schoolroom, with the jester tumbling in their wake. Mr. Malvern left his seat to join them, but paused in the doorway to share a parting word.

"It's a done deal," he said gruffly. "Just thought you ought to know." He slapped his tweed cap on his head, spun on his heel, and was gone.

A momentary silence ensued. Some people rubbed their chins, while others peered at the ceiling. A few women fingered their polyester blouses, frowning pensively.

"It sounds good to me," Miranda Morrow said at last. "And it will bring more people to the village on weekends."

"We could do with some new customers at the pub," said Dick Peacock.

"I wouldn't mind filling the chairs in my tearoom," said Sally Pyne.

"They might need fresh meat and produce for their food stalls," said Burt Hodge, a local farmer.

"Fresh eggs never go amiss," said Annelise's mother. Mrs. Sciaparelli's chickens were famously productive.

"Tourists get flat tires, too," Mr. Barlow observed. "And overheated radiators. A mechanic can always find work, but he'd be a fool to complain if the work comes to him."

"It goes without saying that the vicar and I will make good use of the fair's donation to the church roof fund," said Lilian Bunting.

"King Wilfred's Faire could put Finch on the map," Charles Bellingham ventured timidly.

"We're already on the map," Peggy protested. "The fair will compete with our summer events, block our roads, and bring undesirables into our community. Nothing good will come of it."

Jasper Taxman took his courage in his hands and turned to his wife. "The fair might increase the Emporium's cash flow, Peggy. Tourists always need supplies, and you carry a bit of everything in your shop."

Peggy's objections ceased abruptly.

"Do you really think so, Jasper?" she asked. "Do you honestly believe that the Emporium could profit by this . . . this display of childish nonsense?"

"I do," Jasper replied firmly. "What's more, I think that we should have a private meeting with Calvin Malvern as soon as possible. If we can rent a stall at his fair, we might . . ."

As Jasper leaned sideways to have a quiet word with his wife, a torrent of talk swept through the schoolhouse. Everyone was chattering at once, so it was difficult to make out individual comments, but a few words floated above the hubbub.

". . . exciting . . ."

". . . colorful . . ."

". . . petticoats . . ."

". . . boots . . ."

". . . knights . . ."

". . . *jousting* . . ."

While the clamor in the schoolhouse continued unchecked, Peggy listened intently to Jasper. When he finished speaking, she pursed her lips and nodded firmly. She seemed oblivious to the uproar when she turned to face the villagers. Instead of calling the meeting back to order, she brought it to an end with three decisive bangs of her gavel. She then thrust the summer work rosters at me, gathered up her notes, and gestured for Jasper to accompany her as she dashed down the center aisle and out of the schoolhouse.

I wandered among the villagers, dutifully distributing the rosters, and watched in amazement at they were stuffed unexamined into pockets and purses. No one seemed interested in learning whether they'd been assigned to the dog show cleanup crew or to the tea urn polishing squad. Thoughts of present-day Finch had evidently been pushed aside to make room for dreams of merry old England, and the May meeting had ended not on its usual downbeat note, but on a crescendo of giddy anticipation.

We couldn't have known it at the time, but the invasion of Finch had begun.

Three

After eight pleasant but predictable summers in a row, something unexpected was about to happen in Finch. I couldn't wait to share the news with Bill. If I'd driven my reliable Range Rover to the May meeting, I would have shattered all known speed records in my haste to return to the cottage.

Unfortunately, I'd driven the rusty old Morris Mini Bill and I used for child-free trips to the village, so I was forced to putter sedately over the humpbacked bridge and along the hedge-lined, winding lane that led to the cottage, while my brain fizzed with fresh ideas involving sabers, hoop earrings, and rose-colored wimples. I wasn't sure what a wimple was, but I was determined to have a rose-colored one.

It was nearing ten o'clock when I turned into our graveled drive, a good two hours past the twins' bedtime but not necessarily past Bill's. Hoping fervently that my husband had waited up for me, I parked the Mini between my Rover and his Mercedes, and sprinted up the flagstone path, scarcely noticing the early roses that had appeared on the trellis framing the front door or the sweet springtime scent of the late lilacs.

As I stepped into the front hall, I raised my copy of the summer roster high into the air and called out, "All hail good King Wilfred!"

I held the pose, but when Bill didn't emerge from the living room to ask what on earth I was doing, I tossed the roster onto the telephone table, hung my shoulder bag on the hat rack, and went looking for him.

I found him upstairs, in bed, with Stanley, our black cat, curled at his feet. Stanley opened one dandelion-yellow eye when I walked into the master bedroom, but quickly closed it again. He liked me well enough, but he adored Bill, and he would have been perfectly content to spend the rest of his life curled at my husband's feet.

Bill was sleeping so soundly that he didn't stir when I bent to kiss his cheek, and when I accidentally bumped the bed a few times with my knee, he simply rolled over and settled his head more snugly into his pillow. I heaved a disappointed sigh, which also failed to wake him, then tiptoed out of the master bedroom.

I went up the hall to look in on the twins, but they were as deeply asleep as their father. I gazed down at their identical faces and imagined how their dark brown eyes would light up when I described jousting to them in the morning. Smiling, I tucked their blankets in around them, kissed their tousled heads, and returned to the first floor. My menfolk were precious to me, but I wasn't ready to join them in dreamland just yet. I was bursting to tell someone about the fair.

My best friend, Emma Harris, had missed the May meeting because she was tending to a sick horse, but it was too late in the evening to telephone her. A glance at my watch told me that it was too late to call any of my early-bird friends, so I headed for the study, where I knew I would find someone who was always wide-awake.

The study was still and silent. Not a breath of wind

stirred the strands of ivy covering the diamond-paned window above the old oak desk. After closing the door carefully behind me, I turned on the mantelshelf lights, lit a fire in the fireplace, and bowed deeply to Reginald, who gazed down at me from his special niche in the floor-to-ceiling bookshelves.

Reginald was a rabbit made of powder-pink flannel. He had black button eyes, beautifully hand-stitched whiskers, and a faded purple stain on his snout, a memento of a day in my childhood when I'd let him try my grape juice. Reginald had been at my side for as long as I could remember and, as my oldest friend, deserved his place of honor in the cottage. I didn't usually bow to him, but it would have been unthinkable to enter the study without greeting him, and I was caught up in Calvin Malvern's dream.

"What ho, Sir Reginald," I said, straightening. "How farest thee on this marvelous May evening? Art thou well? Dost thou reliveth brave deeds of yore whilst thou sitteth on thy . . . shelf?" I finished lamely, then grinned. "I don't have the lingo down pat, Reg, but I've got a month to practice. Thou wilt be impressed!"

Reginald's black button eyes glimmered with vague understanding, as if he thought I might be crazy but was willing to await further developments. I tweaked his pink ears fondly, took a blue-leather-bound book from a nearby shelf, and sank into one of the tall leather armchairs that faced the hearth. While the fire snapped and crackled in a satisfyingly medieval way, I cradled the book in my arms and called to mind the first time I'd opened it.

The book had once belonged to my late mother's closest friend, an Englishwoman named Dimity Westwood. The two women had met in London while serving their respective countries during the Second World War, and their friendship had continued to blossom long after the war had ended and my mother had returned to the States.

The two friends never met again in person, but they filled the postwar air with a steady stream of letters describing the everyday adventures of their lives. After my father's sudden death, the letters became a refuge for my mother, a private place of peace and calm, an escape from the sometimes daunting challenges of full-time work and single parenthood. My mother told no one about her private refuge, not even her daughter. As a child, I knew Dimity Westwood only as Aunt Dimity, the fictional heroine of a series of bedtime stories invented by my mother.

I didn't learn about the real Dimity Westwood until after she and my mother had died, when Dimity bequeathed to me a comfortable fortune, a honey-colored cottage in the Cotswolds, the extraordinary letters she and my mother had written, and a very special book—a journal bound in dark blue leather.

Whenever I opened the blue journal, Aunt Dimity's handwriting would appear, an old-fashioned copperplate taught in the village school at a time when a woodstove in the parlor qualified as central heating. I nearly fainted the first time her writing streamed across the journal's blank pages, but her kind words steadied me and I soon came to rely on her as a constant source of wisdom and support. I had no idea how she managed to bridge the gap between the earthly and the ethereal, but I knew one thing for certain: Aunt Dimity was as good a friend to me as she'd been to my mother. I didn't want to think of life without her.

Warmed by the memory—and the crackling fire—I

rested the journal on my lap, opened it, and said, "Dimity? Are you there? I have amazing news to tell you!"

The familiar lines of royal-blue ink curled instantly across the page. *As you know, my dear, I'm always eager to hear amazing news. Don't tell me, though. Let me guess. Did Peggy Taxman forget to assign you to the dog show?*

"I should be so lucky," I said, rolling my eyes. "No, Dimity, it's a thousand times more amazing than dodging poop duty."

My goodness. Have aliens landed on the village green?

"Close," I said, "but it's better than aliens." Unable to wait any longer, I blurted, "King Wilfred's Faire is coming to Finch!"

How thrilling! A short pause ensued before the handwriting continued. *Who, may I ask, is King Wilfred? And why is he holding a fair in Finch?*

"King Wilfred is Calvin Malvern," I explained. "And it's King Wilfred's Faire with an *e* tacked onto the end of 'fair,' to make it seem old and quaint. And the fair won't be held in the village, but near it, in Bishop's Wood."

Hold on a moment, Lori. Did you say Calvin Malvern? Are you speaking of Horace Malvern's nephew?

"That's the chap," I said.

I knew Calvin Malvern when he was a little boy. I could have sworn that he came from a long line of farmers. How and when did he acquire royal blood?

"I don't think there's a drop of royal blood in him," I replied. "As far as I can tell, Calvin's the self-appointed king of a make-believe kingdom."

Of course he is. Calvin always liked stories better than real life. His uncle hoped he'd grow out of it, but apparently he hasn't.

"Apparently not," I agreed, laughing. "He showed up at

the meeting tonight tricked out like Henry the Eighth, with a tumbling jester and two heralds in tow. You should have seen Peggy's face when the heralds blew their trumpets."

A moment to treasure.

"I'll never forget it. I doubt if Peggy will ever call for 'other business' again." I couldn't stop smiling as I recounted the evening's events, adding hand flourishes where appropriate, and concluding with, "I think the fair is going to be a kind of medieval theme park."

I'd love to see a medieval roller coaster. I wouldn't want to ride one, necessarily, but I'd love to see one.

"I don't think there will be any rides," I told her. "Just interesting performers, interesting food, interesting things to buy . . ."

You make it all sound very . . . interesting.

"I know," I said, nodding cheerfully. "Isn't it wonderful? Will and Rob will be over the moon when they hear about the jousting. You know how horse-crazy they are, and they love everything to do with knights. I'm going to make costumes for them, Dimity. Did I tell you that Calvin invited everyone to come in costume?"

You did. Several times.

"I'll make page costumes for the twins." I gazed dreamily into the fire for a moment, then frowned and looked inquiringly at the journal. "Pages were the little boys who helped knights prepare for combat, weren't they? Or am I thinking of squires?"

I believe squires were older boys. Rob and Will will make adorable pages. They'll be believable, too, because they really do know how to groom and tack up horses. Are you going to make a costume for Bill as well?

"I doubt it." My smile faded slightly. "Bill's not a costume sort of guy. I can't picture him pulling on a pair of tights, which is a pity, because he has great legs."

Perhaps he could be a friar.

"Like Friar Tuck?" I said, brightening.

Like a tall, well-built Friar Tuck. He wouldn't have to wear hose if he dressed as a friar, because the long robe would conceal his legs. If Bill dressed as a friar, you could dress as a nun.

"A nun?" I said blankly.

Nuns were all the rage in medieval England, Lori. They were often well-bred and highly intelligent women who exercised a great deal of power.

"But they wore . . . habits . . . didn't they?" I said, with a moue of distaste. "Dull, plain, boring habits. I was thinking of wearing something more colorful. Like a wimple. Do you happen to know what a wimple is?"

Nuns wear wimples, Lori, but they're rarely colorful. The kind of wimple you have in mind is probably a tall, thin, cone-shaped hat with a length of fluttery fabric attached at the point.

"That's what I had in mind," I confirmed. "Calvin said that noblewomen wore wimples. I can see myself as a noblewoman, can't you?"

Lady Lori? It has a certain ring to it.

"A pirate maiden would be pretty cool, too," I said. "I've always wanted to be a swashbuckler."

Pirate Lori has a definite ring to it.

"Pirate Lori," I murmured happily. "It'd be fun to brandish a saber and shout, 'Avast, me hearties!'"

I'd urge you to keep your saber safely in its sheath, unless you want to add the sport of ear-lopping to the fair's roster of medieval activities.

"Killjoy," I retorted, putting my feet on the ottoman. "I'm not sure what I want to be, Dimity, but making up my mind will be half the fun. Who knows? Maybe I'll be a noblewoman *and* a pirate *and* a gypsy." I shivered with excitement. "I can't wait for opening day!"

It sounds as though you're anticipating King Wilfred's Faire with a great deal of pleasure, my dear.

"Well," I said reasonably, "it makes for a change, doesn't it?"

Is a change what you need right now?

"I could do with one," I replied, adding quickly, "but it's not just me, Dimity. The villagers were *electrified* by Calvin's announcement. The roof nearly came off of the schoolhouse after he left. If you ask me, *everyone's* a little bored with the usual summer routine."

I sense, however, that you're more than a little bored.

I took my lower lip between my teeth and looked up at Reginald. I didn't want to seem ungrateful for the many blessings in my life, but honesty was almost always the best policy with Aunt Dimity, so I told her the truth.

"I'm glad that something new is going to happen in Finch this summer," I said. "Something unfamiliar. Something that *wasn't* planned by Peggy Taxman. I haven't had anything new and exciting to look forward to since Annelise got married."

Annelise got married nine days ago, Lori. You haven't had enough time to become bored.

"I've had eight years to become bored," I countered. "Eight summers, anyway."

You've had seven summers, to be precise. You spent last summer in Colorado.

"So I did," I conceded. "And I had a grand time. I didn't miss polishing the tea urns or changing the trash bin liners one bit."

I thought you cherished tradition.

"I do, but you can have too much of a good thing." I groaned impatiently. "Nothing ever changes in Finch. I've heard the same people talk about the same things for nearly a decade. It's like being on a conversational treadmill."

May I remind you that another wedding will take place in September? You once described it as the fairy-tale wedding of the century. You can't tell me that you're not looking forward to Kit and Nell's wedding.

Kit Smith and Nell Harris were the most beautiful couple I'd ever known. Kit was the stable master at nearby Anscombe Manor and Nell was the stepdaughter of my friend Emma Harris, who owned Anscombe Manor. Although I'd been instrumental in bringing Kit to the point of proposing to Nell, my matchmaking career had gone into a serious decline after he'd popped the question.

"There's nothing I want more than to see Kit and Nell get married," I retorted, "but September's a long way off, and I won't be involved in their wedding the way I was in Annelise's." I leaned my chin on my hand and went on disconsolately. "Let's face it, Dimity, Kit and Nell don't need my help. They're so flawlessly flawless that they could get married in a telephone booth, wearing burlap sacks and flip-flops, and it would *still* be the fairy-tale wedding of the century. Besides, I think Nell's had the whole thing mapped out since she was twelve years old, and there's nothing I can do to improve on her plans. They'll get along flawlessly without me."

The fair, on the other hand, requires your active participation.

"Exactly," I said. "And the best thing about it is: It'll be a healthy outlet for my imagination! If I see a vampire at the fair—"

Were there vampires during the Renaissance?

"Vampires are timeless," I replied. "And Calvin isn't picky about niggling historical details anyway."

I see. Sorry to interrupt. You were saying?

"I was saying that the fair will be good for me," I said. "If I see a vampire, I won't go off half-cocked and accuse him of stalking my sons. I'll admire his costume and have a good laugh along with everyone else and that'll be it. In other words, I'll behave like a normal human being."

Is that what you want, Lori? To behave like a normal human being?

"I just want to stop making a fool of myself," I said hopelessly. "I want to stop seeing things that aren't there. I want to stop concocting schemes and sneaking around and behaving like a demented twelve-year-old. I want to be grounded and clear-headed and sensible."

Like Emma Harris?

"Emma is my role model," I declared. "When I grow up, I want to be just like her."

An odd thing for a woman in her mid-thirties to say, but I take your meaning.

"I know I shouldn't complain," I said earnestly, peering down at the journal. "I love my life, I really do, but if I don't find a way to shake it up a little, I'll lose my mind. I refuse to be sucked into any more silly mysteries or ridiculous adventures, so I'm going to make the most of King Wilfred's Faire while it lasts, and afterwards—"

Try not to think too far ahead, my dear. You'll only make yourself dizzy.

As I finished reading the word "dizzy," I realized that I was, indeed, on the verge of hyperventilating, so I rested my head against the back of the chair and took a few measured breaths before looking down at the words Aunt Dimity had written in the journal.

I believe you've found a splendid solution to your dual dilemmas, Lori. A summerlong medieval costume party will allow you to enjoy the best aspects of your imagination and at the same time give you a much-needed break from the tedious routine of village life. It was immensely clever of Calvin Malvern to bring King Wilfred's Faire to Finch. I do hope that Bill will be open-minded enough to participate fully in the fair.

"I'll do what I can to persuade him," I said.

I know you will. The mantelshelf clock is chiming midnight, Lori. It's time you were in bed. I look forward to hearing more amazing news whenever you wish to share it with me. Good night, my dear.

"Good night, Dimity."

I waited until the curving lines of royal-blue ink had faded from the page, then closed the journal and returned it to its shelf. After banking the fire, I turned off the mantelshelf lights, bade Sir Reginald adieu, and left the study, envisioning my pink bunny in a miniature crown and a very small ermine-trimmed robe.

"Reginald will be easy," I murmured. "Bill's going to be a much tougher nut to crack."

But as I tiptoed into the bedroom, a game plan was already taking shape in my mind.

Four

The next four weeks were among the most enjoyable I'd ever experienced in Finch. Eye-catching posters appeared in shop windows, touting the fair's many attractions, and unfamiliar vehicles rolled through Finch, causing curtains to twitch, heads to turn, and tongues to wag. Rumors zipped along the village grapevine at top speed, and they weren't the stale old standbys concerning Sally Pyne's neon-colored tracksuits or Christine Peacock's latest UFO sighting, but juicy new tidbits about the construction project going on in Bishop's Wood and the costumes Peggy Taxman had reputedly ordered for herself and Jasper from a theatrical-supply company in London.

No one would admit it openly, but everyone had been bitten by the costume bug. The mobile library was besieged with requests for books depicting Renaissance attire, and there was a run on velvet and brocade at the fabric store in Upper Deeping. Sally Pyne's Tuesday morning sewing class became so popular that she had to add five more to her schedule to accommodate the overflow. Villagers flocked to the tearoom to learn how to stitch leather, hem satin, embroider silk, and, naturally, to sneak peeks at their classmates' handiwork. Scathing murmurs regarding color sense and fabric choices rippled outward from the tearoom and kept the rumor mill spinning merrily.

My neighbors were so busy making doublets, muffin caps, and lace-up bodices that they all but ignored the art show, which took place on the first weekend in June. As a result, only three paintings were entered, and they were so blindingly dreadful that they wouldn't have garnered honorable mentions in previous shows. Since they had no competition, however, they managed to slide neatly—and undeservedly—into first, second, and third place. The paltry submissions made the judging relatively easy, but there was a notable absence of suspense when Peggy announced the judge's final decisions.

The summer fete, too, suffered from a lack of interest. The usual crowd of villagers showed up on Midsummer's Day to sip locally brewed ale, play traditional games, listen to the brass band, and watch the Morris men dance on the village green, but they did so halfheartedly, with the glazed eyes and fixed smiles of people whose minds were elsewhere.

Although the village's first two summer events fell flat, Finch's businesses saw a modest but measurable upturn in sales throughout the month of June. Sawdust-speckled workmen made their way from Bishop's Wood to Peacock's Pub twice a day, with regular side trips to the greengrocer's shop. They paid Mr. Barlow to repair odd pieces of machinery, and kept the register ringing at Peggy's Emporium.

Rumors abounded about the nature of the structures the crews were building in Bishop's Wood. Some villagers confirmed conclusively that the fair would feature a three-tiered, moated castle, while others claimed that the main attraction would be a gigantic fire-breathing dragon. Since I lived next door to Fivefold Farm, I was perfectly situated to spy on the construction site and find out if the tittle-tattle was true, but I resisted the temptation. I wanted the fair to surprise me.

Finch's entrepreneurs didn't care what the fair looked like as long as it kept filling their coffers. They were well pleased with Calvin Malvern for selecting a site so near the village, and they expected profits to soar when King Wilfred's Faire finally opened its gates to the public.

Sally Pyne benefited the most from the fair's proximity to Finch. Her sewing skills were in such high demand that she had to trim the tearoom's hours drastically. I regretted the inconvenience even though I was, in part, to blame for it. I wasn't sure about anyone else, but in my rush to adorn myself with medieval finery I'd forgotten one small but important detail: I didn't know how to sew. A short session with a sharp needle made me painfully aware of my ineptitude and I hurriedly signed up for one-on-one sewing tutorials with Sally, only to discover that I had no talent whatsoever as a seamstress.

I made such a mess of the twins' page costumes that I quietly disposed of them and hired Sally to make replacements. She agreed to make a dress for me as well, but since she was pressed for time, I had to scale down my vision quite a bit. Instead of a wimple-wearing duchess or a saber-rattling pirate, I would attend the fair as a run-of-the-mill peasant woman.

Sally finished our costumes in five whirlwind days, but she never got started on Bill's. Although she'd offered to make a modest, leg-concealing friar's robe for him, he wouldn't even allow her to take his measurements.

My husband had evidently inherited a gene that rendered him immune to the costume bug. He didn't find the notion of role-playing romantic or amusing. He thought it was just plain stupid, and he wouldn't have anything to do with it. I tried every persuasive tactic known to womankind, but he simply refused to countenance the idea of wearing clothes that weren't exactly like the clothes he already owned.

I decided to launch one last, desperate appeal the day before the fair was due to open. After rising early to drop the boys off at Anscombe Manor for their riding lessons, I cajoled Bill into spending the morning at home instead of in the office, and rewarded him with a sumptuous brunch laid out on the teak table beneath the apple tree in the back garden. The weather was glorious and the garden was blissfully free of boy-noise. The stage was set to mount another offensive.

Bill ate his fill of eggs Benedict, smoked salmon, and buttery crumpets, then settled back in his chair, invited Stanley to curl up in his lap, and opened his newspaper. As he perused the morning headlines, I refilled his teacup and took a calming breath. I didn't want to appear overeager.

"Bill?" I said nonchalantly.

"No," he replied, without looking up from his paper. "Definitely and irrevocably no."

"But—"

He silenced me with a look that was downright menacing. Stanley, sensing trouble, jumped down from his lap and trotted into the cottage.

"Listen carefully, Lori," said Bill, laying the newspaper aside. "I'll go to the fair with you. I'll spend an entire weekend there with you, if you like. But I will *not* dress up as a lord, a knight, a friar, an executioner, a wizard, a pirate, a mad monk, a humble woodsman, or anything else your fertile mind may cough up. It's never going to happen. Period. End of discussion. *Finito*."

"So that's a no, is it?" I inquired.

"That's a no," Bill confirmed, and took a sip of tea.

Defeated, I slouched back in my chair and brushed some crumbs from the table. As I did so, I recalled a drawing Rob had made the night before, depicting a mounted knight with an outsized lance in one hand and a flaming sword in the other. It was, according to Rob, a self-portrait, and the memory of it gave me a renewed sense of determination. I would not let Bill disappoint the twins.

"Everyone we know will be wearing medieval clothes," I said. "What will the twins think when you show up at the fair wearing a baseball cap, a polo shirt, khaki shorts, and sneakers?"

"Will and Rob will think that I look like their father," Bill replied.

"But everyone else will think you're—"

"Lori," Bill interrupted. "I stopped caring about what everyone else thinks midway through my first year at prep school. If our friends and neighbors wish to wear feathered caps and pantaloons to the fair, that's their prerogative. I'm not going to cave in to peer pressure at this stage of the game."

"Stick-in-the-mud," I said, scowling. "Fuddy-duddy."

"You've left out spoilsport and wet blanket," Bill said helpfully. "Shall I fetch a thesaurus?"

"I don't need a thesaurus," I retorted, but before I could demonstrate my full mastery of the English language, the doorbell rang.

"I'll go," Bill said brightly, and went into the cottage to answer the front door.

He returned a moment later, with Horace Malvern padding after him. The burly farmer was, for reasons unknown to me, shoeless.

"Mr. Malvern," I said, trying not to stare at his red wool socks. "How nice to see you."

"I left my wellies in the front hall," he explained. "Didn't want to track muck through the house."

"Much obliged," I said.

Bill offered him a chair, then resumed his own.

Mr. Malvern removed his tweed cap and hung it on the back of the chair before joining us at the table. His weathered face was nearly as red as his socks, as if he'd scrubbed it before stopping by, and he accepted a cup of tea gingerly, as if he feared that his powerful hands might inadvertently shatter the bone china teacup.

"You'll have to forgive me," he said, after a sip of tea. "I've been meaning to call round ever since the May meeting, but with the hay making and the milking and all, I've lost track of the days."

"You're always welcome here, Mr. Malvern," Bill told him.

"Am I?" The farmer raised a grizzled eyebrow and placed his teacup carefully on its saucer. "I thought I might not be, after Calvin made his big announcement. You live closest to the wood, after all. I hope the racket hasn't kept you up at night."

"It hasn't," I assured him.

"What racket?" Bill said amiably.

My husband and I weren't merely being diplomatic. If

it hadn't been for the distant sound of hammering and the occasional whine of a table saw, neither Bill nor I would have been aware of the construction work taking place in Bishop's Wood.

"Well, that's all right, then." Mr. Malvern gave a satisfied nod. "You won't have to worry about the performers, either. Their camp will be east of the wood, so they shouldn't give you any trouble at all. If they do, let me know and I'll give 'em a boot up their backsides."

"We'll call you if we have to," I promised, "but I'm sure it won't be necessary."

"What about you?" Bill asked the farmer. "Isn't the fair going to disrupt your operations?"

"I've lots of land," Mr. Malvern replied complacently. "Calvin's welcome to use a corner of it."

"He's lucky to have such a generous uncle," I said. "Is Calvin your only nephew?"

Instead of answering directly, Mr. Malvern rested his massive forearms on the table and asked, "You don't know much about Cal, do you?"

"No," I said. "Bill hasn't even seen him yet."

"I was at home with Will and Rob during the May meeting," Bill explained, "but Lori has described Calvin's performance to me in great detail."

"I'll bet she has. It was quite a performance." Mr. Malvern pursed his lips. "The first thing you ought to know about Cal is: His parents were killed in a car wreck when he was but nine years old."

"I'm so sorry," I said, and Bill clucked his tongue sympathetically.

"It's the way of the world," said Mr. Malvern. "Some folk die before their time and others live long past it. No point in asking why." Mr. Malvern nodded solemnly, then continued, "Cal came to live with me and Mrs. Malvern after he lost his mum and dad, but he wasn't much use on the farm. Always daydreaming. I'd ask him to bring the herd in for milking and the next thing I'd know, my cows'd be stopping traffic on the Oxford Road. He has a good heart, does Cal, but he wasn't cut out to be a farmer. His head was always somewhere else."

"Did he like school?" I asked.

"He liked the school play," Mr. Malvern answered. "He wasn't much of a scholar, but he took to playacting like a duck to water. Joined a theater group in Oxford as soon as he finished school, which is why you never got to know him. He moved to Oxford about six months before you moved into the cottage."

"You must have missed him," I said.

"I did," said Mr. Malvern, "but I was pleased that he'd found a way of life that suited him better than farming. He worked backstage, mostly, rigging lights and painting scenery. He seemed to like it well enough, but he quit the troupe when he turned twenty-one."

"Had he outgrown playacting?" Bill inquired.

"You wouldn't ask such a question if you'd been at the May meeting," said Mr. Malvern with a wry smile. "No, Cal quit the theater group because he came into his inheritance. My brother left him a tidy sum, you see, and the minute Cal got his hands on it, he upped stakes and lit out for America."

"Good heavens," I said, surprised. "Why did he go to America?"

"He wanted to perform in a Renaissance festival," Mr. Malvern replied. "Seems he'd discovered Renaissance festivals online. They're called Ren fests in the States and they seem to go on all year long—up north in the summer and down south in the winter. A lot of them have Web sites with pictures of people wearing crowns and making speeches and sword fighting and such. Cal took one look at those pictures and decided that Ren fests were for him."

"Well," Bill temporized, "at least he had a clear goal in mind when he went to America."

"The missus and I thought he'd lost his mind," Mr. Malvern stated firmly. "We expected him to come running home with his tail between his legs as soon as my brother's money ran out." The farmer chuckled softly and shook his head. "But he proved us wrong, did Cal. He did all right for himself. He spent the first year traveling from one Ren fest to another, learning the ropes and making contacts. Sent us postcards from all over America." Mr. Malvern smiled reminiscently. "He spent the next five summers with a Ren fest in Wisconsin. He started at the bottom, roasting turkey legs in a food stall, but he worked his way up to a starring role as the town crier."

"Did he go down south in the winter?" I asked.

"He did," Mr. Malvern replied. "We had postcards from Texas, California, Florida, Arizona—all of the warm states. He made a go of it wherever he went, apparently. All I know is, by the end of his six years in America, Cal had tucked away enough money to finance his big idea. And his big idea was to bring a Ren fest to England."

"England is stuffed to the gills with historical festivals," I pointed out. "Why did he feel the need to import one from America?"

"The missus and I asked Cal the same thing," said Mr. Malvern. "He told us that the English are . . ." He screwed up his face, as if he were trying to recall his nephew's exact words. "The English are obsessed with reenactments—the accurate recreation of historic moments or periods. Cal doesn't give a flying cowpat—if you'll pardon the expression—about getting every detail precisely right. He doesn't mind if people show up dressed as wood sprites or Viking raiders, as long as they enjoy themselves. As he said at the meeting, his fair is about fun, not authenticity. That's what sets it apart from most English festivals."

"I think it's a brilliant idea." I glanced surreptitiously at Bill before asking, "Will you wear a costume to the fair, Mr. Malvern?"

"I'm going to be a burgher, whatever that is." Mr. Malvern shrugged philosophically. "Cal had the costume made specially for me. I can hardly throw it back in his face."

I smiled. "It sounds to me as if you have a hard time turning down any of Calvin's requests."

"I've a soft spot for the lad, there's no denying it," Mr. Malvern admitted. "He's got something of my brother's look about him. I see it now and again. And he has a good heart."

"He's a breath of fresh air," I declared. "I think King Wilfred's Faire is the best thing to happen to Finch since Kit Smith returned to Anscombe Manor. And I'm not alone, Mr. Malvern. Everyone loves the idea."

"So long as you two do, I'm content," the farmer said. "If you'd said a word against it, I'd've shut the thing down like that"—he snapped his fingers—"but as long as you're not bothered by it, I'll let it go ahead as planned."

I gave him a startled, sidelong glance. While I appreciated his solicitude, I was taken aback by his apparent willingness to close the fair on the eve of its opening. It was almost as if he'd come to the cottage looking for an excuse to call the whole thing off. As he finished drinking his tea, I remembered my first impression of him at the May meeting. I'd sensed then that something was amiss between him and his nephew. I wondered now if I'd been right.

"Forgive me for prying, Mr. Malvern," I said, "but is everything all right between you and Calvin? When the villagers ganged up on him at the May meeting, you seemed to take a long time to come to his defense."

"Everything's fine between me and Cal," said Mr. Malvern. "If I was a bit slow off the mark at the meeting, it's because I was embarrassed by the way Cal engineered his announcement. I'm not as fond of the spotlight as he is." He hesitated, then went on. "But I won't deny that I'm a bit worried about this fair of his."

"Why?" I asked.

Mr. Malvern rubbed the back of his neck and frowned down at the table, then heaved a sigh and said slowly, "As I told you, Cal never was much of a scholar. He barely scraped passing marks in maths when he was at school. After he moved to Oxford, he was so bad at sticking to a budget that he had to borrow money from me more often than not, just to make ends meet. He's never had a head for numbers."

"I see your problem," Bill said, nodding. "It's difficult to run a business if one doesn't have a head for numbers."

"If you ask me, it's damned near impossible," said Mr. Malvern. "How did he manage to save enough money to bankroll the fair? A leopard doesn't change its spots by spending a few years overseas."

"He has his inheritance," I said.

"Yes, but he must have burned through a good bit of it

while he was living in America," said Mr. Malvern. "Now he's paying for permits and work crews and building materials and performers and God alone knows what else. Since he came home, he's been throwing money around like he owns a bank." Mr. Malvern drummed his fingers on the table. "I'd like to know more about his financial situation. I don't understand it, and what I don't understand worries me."

"I wouldn't worry too much," I counseled. "I'm sure the fair will be a huge success and Calvin will earn back every penny he's put into it. I can't wait for the gates to open."

"Nor can I," Bill chimed in. "And Will and Rob are desperate to see the knights on horseback. I have a feeling that the fair will attract a lot of families."

"It'll have to." Mr. Malvern got to his feet, and Bill and I rose with him. "I'd best be on my way. I'm sure you have things to do."

"It's always a pleasure to see you, Mr. Malvern," said Bill.

"Come again whenever you like," I added.

"Thank you, and thanks for the tea." Mr. Malvern donned his cap, shook hands with Bill, and tipped his cap to me. "I'll be off, then. No need to see me out. I know the way."

"What a nice man," I mused aloud after Mr. Malvern had departed. "Do you think he's right to worry about Calvin's business dealings?"

"I have no idea," said Bill. "But I'm not going to let it spoil my enjoyment of the fair."

"Me, neither. Eat, drink, and be merry, that's my motto for the summer." I glanced at my watch and began stacking dishes. "But for now, I'd better clear the table. It's nearly time to pick up Will and Rob."

"Relax," said Bill. "I have to go in to the office to take care of a few things. I'll pick up the boys on my way home."

"You're a prince," I said.

"I'm a dad," Bill corrected. He gave me a quick kiss and walked swiftly into the cottage. A moment later, I heard the Range Rover back down our graveled drive. Since the Rover was equipped with booster seats, we always used it to transport the twins.

I was no longer in a hurry to clear the table, so I sat down and poured myself another cup of tea, to help lubricate my brain while I mulled over everything Mr. Malvern had told us. I'd just taken a large sip when a voice spoke to me from the stile in the tall hedgerow that grew along the garden's southern edge.

"Hullo, neighbor! Mind if I drop in?"

Before I could swallow, a lithe young man clad in torn blue jeans, a tie-dyed T-shirt, and black Wellington boots sailed headfirst over the stile and landed on his knees in the twins' sandbox.

"Jinks the jester," he announced. "At your service."

Five

promptly sprayed a mouthful of tepid tea across the teak table. The young man was at my side instantly, patting my back while I coughed and spluttered.

"Sorry," he said. "Truly sorry. *Immensely* sorry."

"Don't you . . . know how . . . to use a . . . d-door-bell?" I managed, clapping a half-soaked napkin to my dripping chin.

"I'm very, very sorry," he said. "I should have gone to the front door, I know, but the stile was so handy that I—"

"Handy?" I cut him off without mercy, dropped the soggy napkin on the table, and glared at him. "Handy to what? The only thing on the far side of the stile is a cow pasture."

"The cows have been moved to make room for me," he explained.

"And who are you?" I demanded.

"Jinks the jester," he repeated with a bow. "Jinks as in hijinks, by the way, not Jinx as in hex, which, I'm sure you'll agree, would be an inappropriate name for a merrymaking jester. I was at the village meeting last month. I thought you might remember me."

I glanced toward the stile, retraced the arc the young man had followed as he'd soared through the air, and stared at him as realization dawned. "You were with Calvin Malvern. You did handsprings down the aisle."

"Correct," he said.

"I didn't recognize you without your costume," I said ruefully. "But I suppose your grand entrance should have given me a clue."

"I really am *incredibly* sorry." He rocked back on his heels as he surveyed his surroundings. "Lovely place you have here."

"Never mind my lovely place," I scolded. "What are you doing in the cow pasture? Horace Malvern told us that the performers' camp would be east of Bishop's Wood."

"I need room to practice my tumbling passes," he explained. "Since the main camp will be jammed with tents and caravans when the rest of the players arrive, Mr. Malvern very kindly allowed me to park my caravan away from the others."

"I hope you have a good shower in your caravan," I grumbled. "If you're doing handsprings in a cow pasture, you'll need one."

"Mr. Malvern also provided me with a shovel and a rake," said the young man. "I've spent the past two days putting them to good use." He pointed his toe, to display a pristine boot, and fluttered his eyelashes at me. "I come in peace, to build a bridge between our warring nations."

An undignified snort of laughter escaped me, but I was still annoyed with him. I nodded meaningfully at the breakfast dishes and said, "You may as well make yourself useful, as long as you're here. Help me clear the table."

He leaped into action, carrying dishes into the kitchen for me to load into the dishwasher and scrubbing the teak table until he'd erased all evidence of the accident his arrival had caused. Stanley made a brief appearance in the kitchen, drawn, no doubt, by the sound of a male voice, but when he realized that it didn't belong to Bill, he gave a soft hiss and vanished.

I studied Jinks in silence while we worked, and concluded that he wasn't quite as young as his clothing—and his behavior—suggested. To judge by the lines around his eyes and a few telltale strands of gray in his auburn hair, he was closer to Bill's age than Calvin Malvern's—in his late thirties.

He wore his hair in a curly ponytail and he had the lean, muscular build of an athlete, but he wasn't remotely handsome. His eyes were an odd shade of olive-green, his long nose curved slightly to the left, his mouth was crooked, and he had a narrow, pointed chin. He would never be a leading man, I decided as I left the kitchen and returned to the back garden, but he possessed his own brand of attractiveness. His green eyes were large and expressive, and his smile held a hint of mischief that I found endearing.

He waited for me to offer him a chair before taking a seat at the table. I sat across from him and regarded him curiously.

"What's your real name?" I asked. "I can't keep calling you Jinks."

"I'd rather you did," he said. "My parents were going through a very silly phase when they christened me."

"Rainbow?" I guessed, eyeing his tie-dyed T-shirt and his ripped jeans. "Sunflower? Whalesong?"

"It's not as bad as that," he said, laughing. "My given name is Rowan."

"What's wrong with Rowan?" I asked.

"My surname name is Grove," he replied.

"Rowan Grove." I nodded. "I see. Well, it could have been worse. They could have called you—"

"Oak, pine, beech," he broke in. "Yes, I've heard it all before, especially during my formative years. Little boys can be brutal, given a target. I have the scars to prove it. Which is why I prefer Jinks. If I must have a silly name, I'd rather choose it myself."

"Jinks it is, then," I said.

"And you are . . . ?" he asked.

"Lori Shepherd," I said. "And you can't come up with a sheep joke I haven't heard, so don't even try."

"Wouldn't dream of it," said Jinks, shrinking away from me in mock terror. "May I call you Lori?"

"Yes, of course," I said. "It's what everyone calls me. Why don't you use your real name? It's organic, unusual, poetic—just right for a Renaissance fair, I would have thought."

"It may be all of those things," he said doubtfully, "but we're not allowed to use our real names. We're required to assume names that suit our personas. It adds to the fair's ambience and, frankly, it makes our jobs easier. John Smith may be a shy, retiring computer programmer in his everyday life, but when he dons his garb and changes his name to Cyrano"—Jinks raised his arms and struck a fencer's pose—"he becomes a dashing romantic hero."

"Like an actor in a play," I said, intrigued.

"Like an actor in a play without a script," Jinks clarified. "Most of us improvise our parts. It's great fun."

"I imagine it would be," I said. "Why did you choose to be a jester?"

"Isn't it obvious?" he asked. "I have a face only a jester's mother could love." He crossed his eyes and puckered his crooked mouth, then smiled and went on. "I was also a star gymnast when I was at school. And I have a ready wit.

A weedy child with a silly name learns early on to fight with words rather than with fists."

"I think words are *always* better than fists," I said.

"You're not a ten-year-old boy." Jinks allowed his gaze to wander freely over me for a moment, then said brightly, "Nor are you English, if your accent's anything to go by. Where are you from?"

"I'm from the States," I replied. "I was born and raised in Chicago."

"I know it well," he said. "I met Calvin at a Renaissance festival less than an hour's drive from the Windy City."

My eyebrows rose. "Did you work at the Ren fest in Wisconsin?"

He nodded. "I waited tables at a restaurant in Milwaukee during the week and worked the fair on weekends, but I drove down to Chicago whenever I could."

"But you're English," I said. "How did you end up in Wisconsin? Did you discover the Ren fest on the Internet, like Calvin?"

Jinks wrinkled his forehead and squinted at the sky. "It happened so long ago that I can hardly remember. I believe I was studying for an advanced degree at the University of Wisconsin at the time. One fine summer day some friends and I attended a fair we'd read about in a local newspaper. They went home afterwards, like sensible boys and girls, but I stayed on . . . and on . . . and on . . ." He threw back his head and laughed.

I gazed at him uncertainly. "You dropped out of university to become a . . . a jester?"

"I ran away with the circus," he acknowledged cheerfully. "And I've never regretted it. Fantasy feeds my soul. A university degree would have been wasted on me."

"Don't let my sons hear you say that," I said urgently. "I want them to stay in school."

"My lips are sealed," said Jinks, drawing a finger across his lips. "How, may I ask, did a Chicago girl end up living in England?"

Since I had no desire to discuss Aunt Dimity with him or any other stranger, I said only, "A friend left the cottage to me in her will, and my husband and I thought it would be a good place to raise our children."

"How many children do you have?" he inquired politely.

"I have two six-year-old boys," I replied. "They're twins."

Jinks placed his folded hands on the table and said gravely, "If I promise not to ruin their university careers, will you promise to bring them to the fair?"

"I couldn't keep them away if I tried," I said, laughing at his somber expression. "They've spent the past month on horseback, spearing little plastic rings with wooden poles. They wanted to spear other riders, too—purely for the sake of research, you understand—but their riding instructor wouldn't allow it."

"Spoilsport," Jinks scoffed. "Every boy should be allowed to behave like a barbarian once in a while."

"And you have the scars to prove it," I said dryly.

He fell back in his chair, gasping, and clasped his hands to his breast, as if I'd stabbed him.

"Touché," he croaked.

I chuckled appreciatively, then asked, "What brought you back to England?"

"Cal," he replied, straightening. "When he revealed his grand plan to create a Ren fest on the other side of the pond, I asked if I could tag along. Ten years of listening to Americans speak in dreadful, faux-English accents made me long to hear the real thing again. No offense."

"None taken," I said. "Faux-English accents set my teeth on edge, too. Are all of the fair's performers from America?"

"No, indeed," he said. "Our new cast is exclusively from the UK. Cal spent the last six months in England, Scotland, and Wales, recruiting street performers, reenactors, artisans, artists, and food vendors. He's quite a good pitchman, you know."

"I do know," I said, nodding. "My neighbors are a tough audience, but he won them over without working up a sweat."

"Kings do not sweat, Lori," Jinks intoned pompously. "Kings *perspire*. They also stay in rather luxurious caravans while the rest of us camp in less regal style. It is indeed good to be king."

"Why isn't Calvin staying in his uncle's house?" I asked.

"He wants to be in the thick of things," Jinks replied. "A wise king stays in touch with his subjects." He placed an invisible crown on his head, straightened his spine, and raised his right hand in a stiff, formal wave.

I smiled perfunctorily, but my mind was on other things. Calvin's choice of accommodations puzzled me. His uncle's farmhouse was large and comfortable, and close enough to the performers' camp to allow him to be "in touch with his subjects." Why, then, had he felt the need to purchase a luxurious motor home? It seemed like an unnecessary extravagance, unless Calvin was much better off than his uncle thought he was. As Jinks lowered his hand

and leaned back in his chair, I wondered if he could shed some light on the state of Calvin's finances.

"It seems to me that you'd have to be as rich as a king to pay for a Ren fest," I commented. "It must be an expensive proposition."

"A full-blown Ren fest can be expensive," Jinks allowed, "but King Wilfred's Faire isn't going to be full-blown. We'll feature one joust per day as opposed to two, and the stalls and stages have been built to last only until the end of the summer. Temporary buildings cost much less to construct than permanent ones, and the cost will be defrayed by the fees the food vendors and the craftspeople will pay to use the stalls."

"What about the performers' payroll?" I asked. "It must cost a pretty penny to employ so many people."

"Our cast isn't nearly as big as the ones you'll find in the States," Jinks informed me. "We provide our own garb—"

"Garb?" I said.

"Costumes," Jinks explained. "We provide our own costumes, makeup, and props. We're responsible for finding our own digs as well, and I can testify to the fact that our salaries will be modest." He stroked a frayed spot in his jeans and heaved a martyred sigh. "In the States, popular acts can command as much as ten grand for each performance, but we won't have acts like that at King Wilfred's Faire. We're too new."

My eyes widened in astonishment. "Ten grand for each performance? That's a good paycheck for a part-time job. Did Calvin earn that much when he was in America?"

"I've never asked," Jinks said.

"You must have some idea, though," I said. "He was a town crier. Do town criers make a lot of money?"

"I don't know." Jinks studied his fingernails and added delicately, "I'm a player, not a producer. It's not really my business to know how much my fellow players make."

I ducked my head, chastened. "It's none of my business, either. I was just curious."

"You're an American," he said consolingly. "You can't help being curious about money. To me, it's the least interesting thing about the fair. I'm far more fascinated by the intrigue that goes on behind the scenes."

"Do tell," I said, with an encouraging smile.

"I'm afraid I can't," said Jinks, getting to his feet. "I promised Cal that I'd meet him in Bishop's Wood in"—he glanced at his watch—"ten minutes. It was a pleasure to meet you, Lori Shepherd. I must bid you adieu for the moment, but I hope to continue our conversation anon. You will join us tomorrow, won't you?"

"I wouldn't miss it for the world," I told him.

"Until then, my lady . . ." Jinks executed a comically overcomplicated bow, then sprinted for the stile, vaulted over it, and disappeared from sight.

"Anon," I murmured bemusedly.

I was still gazing at the stile when I heard the familiar sound of the Range Rover pulling onto our graveled drive. I gave myself a mental shake, then went indoors to greet my husband and sons. I'd intended to meet them at the front door, but Will and Rob rocketed up the hallway and nearly bowled me over while I was still crossing the kitchen.

"Whoa," I said, catching each of them by a shoulder. "Slow down, and tell me—*one at a time*—what all the excitement is about. Will? You first."

"We're going to ride in the fair," he said breathlessly.

"Just like the knights," Rob continued. "King Wilfred has *costumes* for Thunder and Storm."

"Calvin has costumes for the ponies?" I said, looking up as Bill entered the kitchen.

"He has *caparisons*," Bill said grandly. "They're fancy cloth coverings for horses. Knights used them in battle to distinguish their noble steeds from the enemy's. Calvin has extras and he's going to cut some down to size for the ponies to wear in the jousting arena."

As pleased as I was to add a new word to my medieval lexicon, I couldn't help wondering if the world had gone mad. Will and Rob weren't knights. They were little boys, and little boys had no place in the jousting arena.

"I'm not sure it's a such good idea for you to participate in the joust," I began, trying to remain calm.

"We won't be jousting," said Will.

"We'll be in the parade," Rob announced.

"We'll carry the king's banners." Will held up a grubby finger. "One time a day."

"And one time around the arena," Rob added. "Before the joust."

"What an honor," I said, greatly relieved. "Why don't you kick off your boots in the front hall, then go upstairs—*nice and slowly*—and get out of your riding gear? I'll be up in a minute. You can tell me all about it while you're having your baths."

"Okay," they chorused.

"But *hurry*," Will insisted.

"Five minutes," I promised. I waited until I heard the thumps of their stockinged feet on the stairs, then turned to Bill. "It's not just wishful thinking, is it?"

"Nope." He shook his head and squatted down to

stroke Stanley, who'd followed him from the front door to the kitchen. "Calvin Malvern asked Emma if any of her students would like to participate in the king's procession. Emma made some quick phone calls to parents and ended up with Alison and Billy McLaughlin and, after conferring with me directly, our boys."

"That's half the junior gymkhana team," I said.

"Correct," said Bill. "Emma thinks it'll be good for them to ride in an unfamiliar setting. They've been practicing all morning."

"What about their helmets?" I said anxiously. "Medieval banner-bearers may have gone bareheaded, but our sons—"

"Medieval banner-bearers wore soft caps," Bill interrupted. "But our boys won't. Emma's already laid down the helmet law to Calvin, and if she hadn't, I would have." He gave Stanley a last rub between the ears, then stood. "Emma may add a few ostrich feathers or a touch of gold paint to the helmets, but no one will ride without one."

"Will Emma go along to supervise?" I asked.

"It'll be a team effort," said Bill. "Emma and a couple of stable hands will look after the ponies, while Lawrence McLaughlin and I concentrate on the children and their costumes. King Wilfred will provide lunch for all of us, which is just as well, because we'll be there for most of the day. As usual, Kit and Nell will run the stables while Emma's away. The boys and I have to be at Anscombe Manor by seven tomorrow morning, to load the ponies and transport them to the fair."

"I'll come, too," I offered readily.

"Sorry," said Bill, shaking his head. "You're not wanted."

"Since when?" I said, stung.

"It's the twins' decision, not mine," he informed me. "You're not allowed to see them in costume until they ride in the king's procession."

"Aw," I said, melting. "How sweet. Do we have the most adorable children in the world, or what?"

Our adorable children chose that moment to bellow from the top of the stairs, *"Mummy! Where are you?"*

"They're certainly audible," Bill observed, wincing.

"I'd better go up before they bring the roof down," I said, and started up the hallway.

"By the way," Bill called after me, "I ran into Sally Pyne while I was in Finch. According to her, no one from the village is going to wear a costume tomorrow."

I swung around to face him. "No one?"

"No one," he repeated. "Apparently there's been a general change of heart. Sally told me that her sewing students have agreed to take a look at the fair before deciding whether or not to wear their new outfits."

I blinked at him, nonplussed.

"I thought you'd want to know," he said.

"Thanks," I said faintly, and made my way upstairs

I felt somewhat dashed. Nearly everyone in Finch had taken one or more of Sally's classes. They'd worked their fingers to the bone to produce elaborate garments for the fair. I couldn't understand why they were having second thoughts about using them.

I pondered the question while I ran the boys' bath, and gradually began to have my own second thoughts. My neighbors weren't stupid, I told myself. Perhaps it would be wise to follow their lead and attend the fair as an observer before jumping into it with my usual abandon. The twins and their ponies could get away with wearing costumes because they would be part of the official pageantry, but until we tested the waters, Bill and I might be better off in civvies.

"Dimity," I murmured, reaching a decision, "I'm going to make you proud of me. For once, I'm going to look *before* I leap."

As I tossed two rubber ducks into the tub, I could almost feel the warm glow of her approval.

don't know who was more excited the following morning—the twins or me. I rose at the crack of dawn to get a jump start on the day, and the twins bobbed along in my wake. We'd already finished our porridge by the time Bill came downstairs for breakfast, and we could scarcely conceal our impatience as we watched him eat his. To keep Will and Rob from force-feeding their father, I hustled them out of the kitchen and into the front hall to help me load the Rover.

I sent them out to the car with Bill's day pack, which I'd filled with everything I thought he and the boys might need while they were away from home: sunblock, rain ponchos, warm sweaters, snacks, bottled water, a change of shoes for the twins, and a few other odds and ends. A glance at the brilliant blue sky told me that the sunblock would probably be more useful than the sweaters, but I'd learned through hard experience that a fine English day could turn fiendish at the drop of a hat, so I left the sweaters where they were.

While Will and Rob dragged the bulging pack to the Rover, I stowed their costumes in a garment bag, where they would remain until the boys changed into them at the fair. I'd decided the night before to pair their everyday black riding breeches and boots with the tunics Sally Pyne had made for them. Tights and soft leather shoes would have been more authentic, but breeches would be more comfortable, and riding boots, safer.

Sally had done a superlative job on the tunics. Rob's was a deep sapphire-blue, with exquisite Celtic interlace embroidery done in silver thread on the belt, the stand-up collar, and the wide cuffs, while Will's was crimson, with gold embroidery. The boys had refused to model their costumes for me—they wouldn't dress up until their ponies did—but Sally had assured me that the outfits were appropriate for the young sons of a noble family. Her words pleased me no end. My sons had always been little princes in my eyes, so I thought it both fitting and proper that they should dress the part.

I took one last, satisfied look at the tunics, then closed the garment bag and hurried out to join the twins, who'd managed to haul the day pack as far as the Rover's rear cargo door. They were on their way back to the kitchen, intent on removing their father bodily from the breakfast table, when the man himself emerged from the cottage, clad in baseball cap, polo shirt, khaki shorts, and sneakers.

"Why aren't you in the car?" he asked the boys, feigning astonishment. "You don't want to be late, do you?"

Will and Rob scrambled into the Rover. I buckled them into their booster seats, kissed them good-bye, and reminded them to mind their manners. I was about to add a brief lecture on riding safety when I heard Bill give a low whistle. I looked up to see him standing at the cargo door, hefting the day pack.

"I hope you remembered to put the kitchen sink in here," he said. "We may have to wash King Wilfred's dishes before the day is through."

"I *knew* I forgot something," I said, snapping my fingers. "Wait here. I'll run in and get the sink."

"Never mind," Bill said, laughing. "Milords and I must make haste. We'll see you"—he glanced at his watch—"in approximately three hours." He closed the cargo door, climbed into the driver's seat, and pulled out of the driveway, bellowing, "Onward, knights of the realm! Your steeds await!"

I ran to the mouth of the drive and waved to them, feeling like a damsel left behind to dust the castle while her men galloped off on a crusade. When the Rover vanished around the first curve, I returned to the kitchen to wash the breakfast dishes, then wandered into the back garden to peer longingly in the direction of Bishop's Wood.

The air was filled with the familiar sounds of birdsong and rustling leaves, but silence reigned on the other side of the stile. Unlike my sons—and, to be honest, myself—Jinks recognized the virtues of sleeping past dawn.

The builders were awake, though. As I turned toward the cottage, the faint buzz of a solitary handsaw drifted to me on the morning breeze. Someone, it seemed, was finishing a last-minute project at the fair. I wondered if he was working on the three-tiered, moated castle or the gigantic fire-breathing dragon, told myself I'd find out soon, and went into the cottage, tingling with anticipation.

You must be very proud of yourself, Lori.

I smiled down at the blue journal. I'd decided to spend a few minutes in the study before leaving for the fair, and

Aunt Dimity's praise made me feel as though I'd made the right choice.

You've exercised an unprecedented amount of self-restraint over the past month, my dear. The old Lori would have clambered to the top of Pouter's Hill twice a day with a pair of high-powered binoculars to monitor the building site in Bishop's Wood, but the new Lori has successfully quelled her curiosity.

"Yes, she has," I said, preening.

You've also resisted the urge to peer over the stile at your interesting new neighbor.

"I'm not a Peeping Tom," I protested.

Of course you're not. You are, however, a trained and talented member of the Finch Busybody Society. As such, I would have expected you to keep abreast of Mr. Jinks's activities. You have, however, defied my expectations.

"Thank you," I said.

Finally, while the old Lori would have worn her medieval finery without pausing to consider the consequences, the new Lori refuses to behave impulsively.

I glanced down at my sandals and my apple-green summer frock and felt a distinct twinge of regret for the costume I'd left hanging in my wardrobe. I'd tried it on a dozen times, after Sally had given me instructions on how to wear it. The long-sleeved cotton chemise came first, then the underskirt, the overskirt, and the apron, after which I would lace myself into the tight-fitting bodice, wrap the leather belt around my hips, and pull the floppy muffin cap onto my head at a becoming angle. A pair of knee-high white socks and brown suede flats completed the ensemble. I'd practiced the routine so often that I could don my garb in less than fifteen minutes, but I hadn't shown the end result to Bill yet. Like the twins, I wanted to wait until I was in the proper setting to reveal my new look.

"I'm not ecstatic about going to the fair dressed as my-self," I admitted. "I love my peasant clothes."

The colors Sally had chosen were fairly dull—the chemise and the apron were off-white, the underskirt was hunter-green, the overskirt was rust-colored, and the bodice was a dusty blue—but the costume she'd created wasn't exactly boring. Although the full skirts were long enough to hide my ankles, the bodice gave me a shape I hadn't had since the twins had started eating solid foods, and the chemise's neckline was so low that I'd discovered brand-new places to put sunblock. I wasn't sure how Bill would react to seeing so much of his wife on display, but I thought I looked rather fetching.

I admire your determination, Lori. While I'd been day-dreaming, Aunt Dimity's handwriting had continued to scroll across the page. *It may be vexing to postpone the pleasure of wearing your period attire until you know more about the fair, but your decision to do so is indisputably sensible. I can say without reservation that your cautious, levelheaded approach to the matter is one I would expect from Emma Harris.*

"Really?" I said, delighted.

Really and truly.

"You've made my day, Dimity." I looked at the man-telshelf clock and smiled. "I'd better be going. I don't want to miss the grand opening."

Have a wonderful time, my dear.

"I intend to," I said.

I closed the journal, returned it to its shelf, and curt-syed to Reginald. Then I scurried into the hallway, called a hasty good-bye to Stanley, and grabbed my shoulder bag as I dashed past the hat rack. I climbed into the Mini at precisely nine-fifteen. Although it would take me no more than ten minutes to drive to Bishop's Wood, I didn't think it would hurt to get there early. Apart from that, I was fed up to the back teeth with waiting.

Unfortunately, I had to wait a little longer than usual to back out of the driveway, because I was held up by a string of cars cruising along my lane. Most were driven by neighbors, who waved as they drove past, but at least a dozen were driven by sunburned strangers with screaming children in the backseats and loud music on the radios. Since my lane wasn't even included on most road maps, I was surprised to see so many unfamiliar drivers using it. Perhaps Mr. Barlow had been right, I told myself. Perhaps the fair *would* cause traffic problems in the village. I experienced a moment's concern, then began to laugh.

"You've lived in the country for too long, Lori Shepherd," I said to my reflection in the rearview mirror. "Six cars *do not* constitute a traffic jam."

I shook my head at my own foolishness, backed cautiously into the lane, and gave the Mini a little extra gas. I didn't want to be the last one to arrive at the fair.

My cheerfulness increased tenfold when I saw the sign on the Oxford Road marking the turnoff to the fair. The billboard was ten feet tall and at least twelve feet wide, and its bright red Gothic lettering was bracketed by delightfully lurid paintings of a fearsome black dragon and a rearing unicorn.

I smiled at the Web site address, knowing that Calvin Malvern would take particular pride in adding his Ren fest to the list of those that had inspired his dream, but the lurid paintings turned my smile into a broad grin. I felt as if I were being rewarded for my patience, as if the ferocious dragon and the noble unicorn were mere hints of still more splendid surprises to come.

I followed the arrow directing me onto a newly graded dirt road to my left and drove along it until a spiky-haired young woman in disappointingly modern blue jeans and a boring white T-shirt waved me into the pasture that had become a parking lot. When I saw the number of cars that were already parked there, I wished I'd left the cottage earlier.

I was in such a hurry to catch up with the rest of the fairgoers that I almost forgot to lock the Mini. I never locked it when I was at home or in Finch, but the sight of unfamiliar cars on my lane served as a salutary reminder that I was no longer surrounded by people I knew and trusted.

I could see from the car park that Bishop's Wood had

been enclosed by a ten-foot-tall wooden security fence intended, no doubt, to keep freeloaders at bay. The most dramatic piece of construction wasn't apparent until I'd joined the hundred or so onlookers who were waiting for the fair to begin. Calvin Malvern's builders hadn't created a moated castle or a fire-breathing dragon, but they'd done a marvelous job of recreating a grand, medieval gatehouse.

The imposing structure was hung with colorful banners, surmounted by a crenellated walkway, and flanked by two square, battlemented towers that were at least thirty feet tall. A small door halfway up each tower gave access to the walkway, and flags flying from the tops of the towers suggested that their roofs were accessible through trapdoors. The gatehouse was pierced at ground level by three wide, round-headed wooden doors placed side by side beneath a large gilded wooden sign whose red and blue Gothic lettering spelled out the words: MAYNE ENTRANCE.

I suspected that the gatehouse had been constructed out of plywood and plaster, but the surfaces had been skillfully shaped and painted to resemble rough-hewn stone, and each door looked as if it were made of solid oak. The smell of fresh paint and sawdust lingered in the air, testifying to how recently the building work had been completed.

Although the three "Mayne Entrance" doors were still firmly shut, the entertainment had already begun. A juggler, a lute player, and a woman with a large snake draped across her shoulders stood on the gravel apron before the gatehouse. Each was suitably attired in period clothing and each kept up a steady patter of witty repartee that caused the onlookers to erupt in repeated explosions of laughter. I was gazing at the snake and thinking of how much Rob and

Will would enjoy petting it when Lilian Bunting appeared at my elbow.

"Isn't it exciting?" she asked, her gray eyes shining.

"So far, so good," I replied. "Calvin must have mounted a strong publicity campaign. I didn't expect to see so many people here on opening day."

"Did you notice the extra motorcars on your lane this morning?" said Lilian.

"It was hard not to," I said. "I'm not used to looking both ways before I back out of my driveway."

"You'll have to get used to it," said Lilian. "I've no doubt that day-trippers will use your lane as a shortcut. Apart from that, several performers are staying in the village, so they'll be passing your cottage on their way to work on weekends."

"When did performers move into the village?" I asked, surprised.

"Yesterday," said Lilian. "Sally has a wizard in her spare room, the Peacocks have a magician and two jugglers in the rooms over the pub, and the new people in Crabtree Cottage are playing host to a mime."

"If you ask me, Grant and Charles made the best choice," I said. "A mime would be an ideal houseguest. You'd hardly know he was there."

"True." Lilian paused to watch the juggler take bites out of the apples he was juggling, then added wistfully, "There are times when I wish I'd married a milkman instead of a vicar. I don't know how I'll be able to concentrate on Teddy's sermons tomorrow, knowing what I'll be missing here. I'm afraid we may see a decline in church attendance this summer, which will mean a corresponding decline in the offerings on the collection plate."

"Maybe King Wilfred's donation to the church roof fund will make up for it," I said.

"One can only hope. Have you bought your ticket yet?" she asked, and when I shook my head, she pointed to a counter built into a windowlike opening in the security fence to the left of the gatehouse. "The ticket booth," she explained.

I thanked her and hastened over to pay my entry fee to a buxom girl wearing a costume not unlike the one I'd left at the cottage.

"Well come, my lady," she said. "Have you traveled far this fine morning?"

"I live just around the corner," I told her.

"May all of your journeys be short and free from care." She handed over my change and what appeared to be an advertising leaflet. She nodded at the leaflet and explained, "A program book with a map of the grounds, my lady, for those who wish to know where they are and where they have been and where they may be going. If you'd rather not know, you may tuck it into your pouch"— she indicated my shoulder bag—"and banish it from your thoughts."

"Thanks," I said, and as I turned away from the ticket booth, I slipped the program book into my bag along with my change.

By the time I rejoined Lilian Bunting, a knot of neighbors had gathered around her. As Bill had forewarned, they were wearing ordinary, everyday clothing, but the looks on their faces suggested that the next time they attended the fair, they'd be dressed less conservatively.

"Do you have a costume in mind?" I asked Lilian.

"I have one hanging in my wardrobe," she replied. "I'm

to be an abbess. I want to pay tribute to the intelligent, powerful women of the Middle Ages. And you?"

"A peasant," I said. "I'm paying tribute to Sally Pyne for fitting me into her overbooked sewing schedule."

"I believe peasant women are known as wenches at the fair," said Lilian. "Isn't it delightful? I've tried to convince Teddy to come as a monk, but he won't cooperate."

"Bill's the same way," I said, and we sighed in unison.

A blare of trumpets interrupted our sighs and silenced the chattering mob, which had grown considerably since I'd arrived. The three entertainers—four, counting the snake—promptly withdrew through the three doors and a hundred faces turned upward as King Wilfred's heralds appeared atop the east tower, proving to my satisfaction that there was, indeed, a way to reach the tower's roof.

The heralds wore the same red tabards they'd worn to the May meeting, and they blew the same fanfare. I wondered briefly if it was the only tune they knew, but my attention was diverted to the top of the west tower, where Jinks stood, clad in his jester costume and mimicking the heralds, though he played his imaginary trumpet as if he were a crazed jazz musician. He snapped to attention as the heralds lowered their horns.

"Attend, good people!" they shouted. "Lord Belvedere, the king's steward, approaches!"

A gray-bearded man in a gold-trimmed, emerald-green velvet doublet and dark blue pantaloons emerged from the small door in the west tower and walked to the center of the crenellated walkway, accompanied by six equally well-dressed courtiers, who arranged themselves in various poses behind him.

Jinks, standing well above them and therefore out of

their sight, proceeded to imitate the movement and posture of each in a way that was both remarkably accurate
and unmistakably ridiculous. Although they must have
heard the jingling of his belled cap, they acted as though he
weren't there, which made his mimicry even funnier.

"I bid you good morrow, gentles," said Lord Belvedere,
raising his voice to be heard above the crowd's tittering. "I,
Lord Belvedere, thank you on behalf of our beloved monarch, King Wilfred the Good, for gracing us with your
presence today. Within you will find marvels and amuse-
ments such as you have never seen before, as well as boun-
teous food and drink fit for a king—or a queen!"

A few women let out hoots of approval and everyone else laughed.

"At two of the clock," Lord Belvedere continued, "a
tournament of arms will be held in His Majesty's joust
arena. Hearken to my words, I pray you, as I present the
puissant warriors who will face the perils of mounted
combat. Pray bid a hearty well come to . . ."—he turned
to his left and flung an arm toward the small door in the
east tower—"Sir Peregrine the Pure!"

A tall, broad-shouldered man with a handsome,
clean-shaven face and shoulder-length white-blond hair
strode onto the walkway. He was clad in a chain-mail shirt
and a breastplate, he carried a shield on his left arm, and
his right hand rested on the hilt of his sword. His breastplate gleamed in the morning sun and his shield bore the
image of a rearing unicorn. As he struck a manly pose beside Lord Belvedere, Jinks broke into loud hurrahs, which
were instantly reinforced by cheers from the crowd. Sir
Peregrine acknowledged the acclamation with a sequence
of suave nods.

Lord Belvedere waited until the cheering began to flag, then flung his arm toward the west tower. "I give you . . . Sir Jacques de Poitiers, the Dragon Knight!"

A short, stocky man with coal-black eyes, long, dark hair, a thin mustache, and a pointed goatee stepped out of the tower's shadowy doorway and onto the walkway. His breastplate was pewter-colored, and his shield featured a fearsome black dragon. As he strode to his place opposite Sir Peregrine, Jinks emitted a loud boo, which was echoed with great enthusiasm by the crowd. Sir Jacques snarled, shook his fist, and eyed the fairgoers pugnaciously, which only made them boo louder.

"At two of the clock," Lord Belvedere reiterated, "these gallant knights will face each other in the joust arena. Will Sir Peregrine prevail? Or will the Dragon Knight conquer? Come to the arena to cheer on your champion!"

The knights bowed—Sir Peregrine with an elegant swoop, Sir Jacques with a brusque jerk—and exited the walkway to the mingled boos and cheers of the crowd. The heralds raised their trumpets to blow another fanfare—which sounded very similar to the one they'd blown already—then bawled a familiar refrain from the top of their tower.

"Arise, gentle folk! Hence cometh our excellent and most gracious ruler, the lord of laughter and the monarch of mirth, His Majesty, King Wilfred the Good!"

"Bow in the presence of the king, you scurvy curs," Jinks bellowed down at us, but as soon as a few people followed his order, he held up an admonitory finger and said fussily, "*Tsk tsk*—Simon didn't say!"

A rumble of laughter rolled through the crowd as Calvin Malvern, wearing his gem-encrusted crown, his plum-colored surcoat, and the rest of his King Wilfred regalia, strode to the center of the crenellated walkway. Lord Belvedere and his retinue bowed deferentially, then formed a half circle behind the king, but Jinks dropped all the way to his knees and groveled pathetically, eliciting still more laughter from his audience.

"We bid you well come, gentle folk," said King Wilfred, beaming down at us benevolently. "And we hope you will find pleasure in every moment you spend at our great fair."

Jinks had risen to his feet and was now lip-synching the king's speech while mimicking with exaggerated pomposity the king's facial expressions and gestures. The crowd tried to pay respectful attention to King Wilfred, but individual giggles kept breaking through.

"While you rove the lanes, passages, and alleyways of our fair," the king continued, as if unaware of his jester's existence, "we command you to be merry. Let sorrow and toil be forgot! Eat, drink, sing, and dance to your heart's content. Above all, laugh, and with laughter drive back the tides of darkness and woe. We, your sovereign monarch, declare this day to be . . ."

As King Wilfred placed his beringed hands on the parapet and leaned forward to emphasize his words, several things happened in quick succession. The section of parapet upon which he was leaning broke away from the wall and fell to the ground with a crash of splintering two-by-fours and shattering plaster. A cloud of plaster dust billowed into the air.

And the king lost his balance.

Seven

F cried out in alarm as the king fought to keep himself upright. His arms windmilled wildly, his crown slipped sideways on his head, and for one heart-stopping moment it seemed certain that he would fall through the ragged gap in the wall and plummet headfirst to the ground. He was within a scant hairsbreadth of losing his battle with gravity when Lord Belvedere leaped forward, seized him by the collar of his plum-colored surcoat, and hauled him backward into the courtiers' outstretched arms.

The crowd emitted a collective moan of relief, and Lilian and I leaned limply against each other, our hands to our breasts. A few people began to applaud, but I couldn't tell whether they were saluting the king's survival or showing their appreciation for what they perceived to be a marvelous stunt. King Wilfred certainly behaved as though the incident had been arranged for our amusement. He allowed his courtiers to set him on his feet, smooth his rumpled garments, and straighten his crooked crown, then stepped forward and planted his hands on his hips.

"If we weren't a *merry* monarch," he roared, "heads would roll!"

I chuckled along with everyone else and the tension in the air dissipated, but I couldn't help noticing that Lord Belvedere looked as rattled as I felt. While Jinks led the crowd in three rousing cheers for Good King Wilfred, Lord Belvedere muttered something to a brawny courtier. The courtier nodded and quickly exited the walkway through the east tower.

Lord Belvedere then stepped forward and said, "If I may address your subjects, Your Majesty?"

"But of course," said King Wilfred, and stepped aside.

"Lord, ladies, and gentles all," said Lord Belvedere. "Be assured that no harm will befall you as you enter our great fair. I bid you use the side entrances"—he gestured to the right- and left-hand doors in the gatehouse—"until His Majesty's minions clear away all sign of our ill-fortuned incident. Your Majesty . . ." he concluded, and bowed the king to the center of the walkway.

"The time draws nigh, gentles." King Wilfred looked up, as if he were judging the hour by the position of the sun, and raised a pudgy hand. When he let it fall, a cannon blast rent the air, making Lilian and me jump.

"Let the revels begin!" shouted King Wilfred.

The heralds blew another fanfare as the king and his court exited the walkway through the east tower. Tantalizing strains of lilting music floated over the walls as the milling throng followed Lord Belvedere's advice and formed two more or less orderly lines. A moment later, two of the main entrance doors opened, a pair of costumed ticket takers appeared, and the lines began to move through the gatehouse and into the fairground.

"Are cannon medieval?" I asked Lilian, as we took our place in the left-hand line.

"They certainly are," she replied. "Cannon have been used in Europe since the mid-fourteenth century. Frankly, I think we could have done without one this morning. The plunging parapet was quite enough drama to be going on with." She scanned the gatehouse apprehensively. "Do you think the rest of the structure is sound? Perhaps we should have worn hard hats, to protect our heads from loose bits of wall."

"A knight's helmet would be more suitable than a hard hat," I pointed out. "But I wouldn't worry about the rest of the wall coming apart. King Wilfred isn't leaning on it at the moment."

"I take your point," Lilian conceded. "Calvin is a portly young man. I suppose it was asking too much to expect a mere set decoration to support his weight. I do hope he won't lean on it tomorrow."

"I suspect that Lord Belvedere will advise him to avoid leaning on anything from now on," I said.

The center door swung open and a lanky, dark-haired young man emerged from the gatehouse. He was in his early twenties, dressed in faded blue jeans, a short-sleeved cotton shirt, and work boots, and he was pushing a wheelbarrow. He parked the wheelbarrow next to the biggest pile of debris, stood back, and peered upward at the spot where King Wilfred had so recently teetered. The young man scowled, then bent to his work, tossing chunks of plaster and pieces of broken wood into the barrow with such force that he reduced most of the plaster chunks to powder.

"Someone didn't get the memo about dressing in period garb," I murmured to Lilian.

"Oh, I don't know," she murmured back. "Those blue jeans look as if they could be a few hundred years old. As will his tools, if he doesn't take better care of them."

I glanced over and saw the handle of a broom protruding from the wheelbarrow, along with a crowbar, a shovel, a small sledgehammer, and a handsaw. The sight of the handsaw stirred a memory in the back of my mind, but it wasn't until Lilian and I had almost reached our ticket taker that the memory clicked into place.

"A saw," I whispered, and came to a standstill as the recollection triggered an avalanche of unsettling thoughts.

Only a few hours before Calvin Malvern's near-fatal accident, I'd stood in my back garden and heard the rhythmic buzz of a handsaw drift toward me on the morning breeze. The sound had come from the direction of Bishop's Wood. I'd assumed at the time that someone was finishing a last-minute project at the fair, but what if I'd been wrong? What if someone had instead been engaged in a last-minute piece of *sabotage*?

Startled, I swung around to stare at the young man. He was still scowling, still flinging debris into the wheelbarrow. Was he angry because the parapet had fallen, I wondered, or because Calvin Malvern hadn't fallen with it?

"Lori," Lilian called. "You're holding up the queue."

"What?" I blinked stupidly for a moment before I remembered where I was and what I was supposed to be doing, then scurried forward, handed my ticket to a full-figured young woman in peasant garb, and followed Lilian Bunting through the gatehouse.

"Are you all right, Lori?" Lilian asked, pulling me away from the stream of fairgoers pouring through the entrance. "You seem distracted."

"I'm fine," I said, glancing uneasily over my shoulder.

"Good." Lilian consulted her program book. "I'm going to find my way to something called the Farthing Stage. According to the schedule, Merlot the Magnificent will perform his magic show there at half past ten. I'm exceedingly fond of magicians. Will you join me?"'

"I'd rather explore," I said. "I'm sure we'll run into each other again before the day is through."

"I'm sure we will," Lilian agreed. "I'll see you later, then."

As soon as she left my side, I turned to examine the gatehouse. When I spotted a small door at the base of the west tower, I started toward it. I intended to climb up to the walkway and take a closer look at the broken parapet, to see if I could detect any sign of tampering, but as I approached the door, it swung open and a familiar figure stepped into the sunlight, his belled cap jingling merrily.

"Hullo, neighbor." Jinks closed the door behind him, locked it, and tossed the key to the nearest ticket taker, who tucked it into her ample cleavage. Then he faced me, smiling broadly. "Have you been waiting for me? I've been hurling abuse at unsuspecting patrons, to help them pass the time while they're queuing up. I love my job!"

I smiled weakly and Jinks peered at me more closely.

"You weren't waiting for me," he said flatly, reading my expression. "You weren't thinking of leaving, were you? You've only just arrived."

"I'm not leaving," I assured him. "I, uh, thought I'd go up to the top of the tower and, um, check out the view."

"Sorry," he said, cocking his head toward the door. "Cast members only, for insurance reasons. Until the damage is repaired, we won't be allowed up there, either." He pursed his lips and regarded me quizzically. "Why on earth would you want to see a view of your own familiar countryside when you have Gatehouse Square to look at?"

"Gatehouse Square?" I echoed, perplexed.

"Lori," Jinks said gently. "Turn around."

I turned away from the gatehouse and felt my jaw drop as tumbling waves of sound, color, and scent slammed into me. It was as if sensory dials in my brain had suddenly been turned to full blast. I nearly reeled from the impact.

The gatehouse opened onto a large square bordered by roofed shop stalls made of rustic wood and hung with gaily colored banners that fluttered prettily in the breeze. A team of Morris dancers hopped and stomped in the center of the square while a frisky hobbyhorse patrolled its borders and a fiddler played a jaunty tune. A cluster of bright-eyed children gazed in wonder at a wizard who seemed to be making coins appear out of thin air, and chuckling adults steered a wide path around a juggler armed with water balloons. Costumed vendors shouted out descriptions of their wares, which ranged from ornate blown-glass ornaments to souvenir T-shirts, and clouds of incense wafted from burners placed at the curtained entrance to what appeared to be a fortune-teller's booth.

"Wow," I said faintly.

"You seem surprised," said Jinks. "Did you somehow fail to notice that you'd entered Gatehouse Square?"

"My mind was on other things," I confessed. "The accident startled me."

Jinks's green eyes narrowed shrewdly. "And in a rush of civic-mindedness, you decided to inspect the rest of the gatehouse, to make sure it's safe."

I confirmed his guess by blushing furiously and looking down at my sandaled feet.

He smiled. "It's perfectly safe, I promise you. Lord Belvedere wouldn't have allowed us to open the doors if he'd thought the public was in danger. The bit that fell off was finished in a rush this morning, by someone who must not have known what he was doing. Once Edmond repairs it, it'll be strong enough for Cal to dance on it."

"Who's Edmond?" I asked.

"Edmond Deland, the royal dogsbody," Jinks replied, and when I continued to look blank, he explained, "The surly chap with the wheelbarrow. A minion if there ever was one."

"Oh, *him*." I glanced at the gatehouse. "What's his problem?"

"Backstage intrigue," Jinks said, waggling his eyebrows. "Fear not. All shall be revealed when you and I have time to talk. Perhaps I'll pop over the stile tonight and fill you in." He touched my arm. "I'm sorry you were frightened."

"I overreacted," I said sheepishly. "I'm okay now."

"How could you be otherwise? You're at King Wilfred's Faire!" Jinks executed a low bow. "Pray excuse me, my lady. I must away to join my king. May the rest of your day be filled with boundless merriment!" He shook his cap at me and jogged off across the square, pausing to walk on his hands as he passed the bright-eyed children.

I watched him go, then ducked my head and groaned. I couldn't believe that I'd slipped back into my old habits so easily. Anyone with a particle of common sense would have blamed King Wilfred's accident on shabby workmanship, but I'd taken my usual detour around rational thought and driven smack-dab into an absurd assassination plot. If Jinks hadn't intercepted me, I would have spent half the morning crawling through plaster dust instead of savoring the sights and sounds of the fair. I was thoroughly ashamed of myself for letting my imagination run amok yet again.

"It stops here," I muttered determinedly, and pushed all thoughts of sabotage from my mind.

For the next three hours I gave myself up to the fair's enchantments, exploring the grassy lanes that ran outward from Gatehouse Square. When I saw a neighbor approaching, I gave a friendly wave, but quickly walked the other way. I wanted to be surrounded by unfamiliar faces, for a change, and overhear gossip I didn't already know by heart.

The lanes were lined with shop stalls, which gave the fair the air of a vibrant village. Some of the stalls were no bigger than closets, but others were split-level affairs as large as my living room. All of them had awnings or small roofs jutting over the lanes, presumably to shelter fairgoers from the inevitable summer showers. The vendors wore costumes made of cotton and linen rather than velvet and satin, and they spoke a semimedieval patois that was occasionally difficult to understand, but always entertaining.

The lanes wound through the woods and crisscrossed one another unpredictably to form a delightful maze that guaranteed surprises around every bend. I would have willingly lost myself in the labyrinth, but the fair's layout was more orderly than it seemed: All of the side alleys eventually took me back to Broad Street, a wide thoroughfare that formed the fair's main boulevard, where larger and more elaborate stalls could be found.

Strolling performers popped up everywhere I turned. I encountered the juggler and the lute player I'd seen outside the gatehouse as well as a pair of singing pickpockets, a troupe of belly dancers, a flock of winged fairies, miscellaneous beggars—who whined and groveled amusingly until coins were flung at them—and a stilt walker dressed as a tree, who'd clearly taken his inspiration from the ents, J. R. R. Tolkien's imaginary shepherds of the forest.

Other acts performed on small, open-air stages before audiences seated on long wooden benches. Penny Lane ended at the Farthing Stage, where Merlot the Magnificent performed dazzling feats of legerdemain five times a day. Harmony Lane led to the Minstrels' Stage, which featured singers, musicians, and dancers, and Ludlow Lane led to the Shire Stage, where acrobats, jugglers, and comic acts held sway. The modest petting zoo was very near the Shire Stage, and the animals' varied grunts, squawks, and aromas prompted predictably earthy but nonetheless amusing improvisations from the nimble-witted performers.

The Great Hall turned out to be yet another stage, but the entertainers who performed there didn't sing, dance, juggle, or tell jokes. Its gilded sign proclaimed that it was used exclusively by King Wilfred during royal ceremonies, such as weddings and the conferring of knighthoods. Its main feature was a red-carpeted dais upon which sat a magnificent gilded throne.

Pudding Lane was populated by food vendors selling savory meat pies, sausage rolls, chips, fruit tarts, chocolates, honey cakes, and other goodies, as well as cider, ale, herbal teas, and the usual soft drinks. I sampled a honey cake, found it delicious, and immediately asked for the recipe, but the vendor informed me regretfully that it was the king's privilege to hand out recipes, not hers.

Pudding Lane petered out, appropriately, at a large picnic area on a gently sloping hillside overlooking the oval joust arena and the adjacent archery range. A simple two-bar fence encircled the arena, and a giant white marquee stood at its western end, opposite Pudding Lane. I could see the twins' ponies grazing with other horses in the pasture beyond the marquee, but there was no sign of activity in the arena. I assumed that the knights were taking their ease in the big white tent while my sons and the rest of Emma's junior gymkhana team polished armor, fluffed plumes, and cleaned tack.

The archery range was bustling. A dozen William Tell wannabes stood on the firing line, drawing bowstrings and letting arrows fly at bull's-eye targets mounted on hay bales. It looked like an enjoyable challenge, but I was too excited to stay in one place for more than a few minutes, so I strode back down Pudding Lane and continued to explore.

At various stalls throughout the grounds, potters, spinners, weavers, wood carvers, metalsmiths, leatherworkers, and other artisans demonstrated their crafts. After watching a potter turn a glob of sticky clay into a graceful goblet, I decided that the fair would be a wonderful educational opportunity for Will and Rob. I had no doubt that my sons would be as fascinated as I was to watch raw materials transformed by hand into useful and beautiful objects.

If I'd wanted to weigh myself down, I would have shopped till I dropped, but since I'd brought a shoulder bag instead of a day pack, I merely ambled from one stall to the next, making mental lists of the Christmas and birthday presents to be purchased when I was better prepared to carry them. The choices seemed endless: soaps, lotions, perfumes, pottery, jewelry, swords, staffs, leather tankards, hooded capes, woven throws.

When I stumbled upon a stall filled with tiny costumes, I realized that I wasn't alone in wanting to dress a cherished childhood companion in a crown and an ermine-trimmed robe. A short conversation with the vendor confirmed my guess that I was surrounded by people who would smile benignly upon my relationship with Reginald. It was a comforting thought, but I'd absorbed so many thoughts by then that I had to retreat to a quiet alleyway, to give my overloaded brain a chance to settle down.

The alleyway didn't remain quiet for long. As I stood smiling vaguely at a marvelous display of crystal balls, five young women spilled out of a stall filled with bronze dragons and took up a position a few yards away from me. They appeared to be in their early twenties, and each was dressed in what a vendor had described to me as the standard wench uniform—laced bodice, peasant blouse, and flowing skirts. They'd set themselves apart from the standard wenches, however, by wearing flowered circlets on their heads, with curled ribbons trailing down their backs.

The smallest member of the group, a pretty young woman with hazel eyes and long brown hair, placed an empty basket on the ground before her, then straightened. She hummed a note, the others harmonized, and the group began to sing a madrigal. I listened, entranced, as their sweet, pure voices wove in and out of the intricate song, and when they finished, I was the first to step forward and drop a handful of coins into their basket.

I wasn't the only one to witness their performance. As I turned away from the basket, I caught a flicker of movement from the corner of my eye. Glancing toward it, I spied Edmond Deland lurking in a narrow gap between two stalls. I pretended not to notice him, but when I returned to my vantage point near the crystal balls, I shifted my position slightly so that I could keep an eye on him.

The surly young handyman kept to the shadows, as if he didn't wish to be seen, and gazed fixedly at the tiniest madrigal singer. When she led the group into the next madrigal with a solo introduction, his chest heaved and his expression softened, as if the sound of her voice had pierced his heart. It took no imagination whatsoever to see that he had feelings for her.

The distant sound of trumpets pulled Edmond from his pleasant reverie and put the scowl back on his face. The girl, by contrast, lit up like a Christmas tree and peered eagerly toward Broad Street. The other madrigal singers exchanged knowing glances and, after retrieving their basket from the ground, began to move en masse toward the main boulevard, singing as they went. A knot of appreciative listeners followed them, but Edmond frowned angrily, spun on his heel, and disappeared behind the stalls.

"What's happening?" I asked the woman in the crystal-ball stall.

"'Tis one of the clock," she replied. "The king's procession cometh forthwith."

"Where does it, um, cometh?" I asked awkwardly.

She smiled. "If you make your way to Broad Street right quick, my lady, the procession will pass before your very eyes."

"Thanks." I was fairly certain that I wouldn't be allowed to return home if I missed Will and Rob riding in the king's procession, but I couldn't stop myself from asking one more question. "Do you know the name of the lead madrigal singer?"

"Mirabel," she replied. "Little Mirabel. She has the voice of an angel, does she not?"

"She does," I said, and hurried to catch up with the

singers. They'd stopped at the edge of Broad Street, and I elbowed my way through the jostling crowd to stand beside them. The taller girls had formed a protective pocket behind Mirabel and regarded her with tolerant amusement as she craned her neck and stood on tiptoe to watch for the oncoming procession.

I studied her with frank curiosity. She looked like a besotted groupie waiting for a rock star to appear. Was she anxious to see the king's procession, I wondered, or was she longing for a glimpse of the king himself? Could it be that little Mirabel was, for reasons beyond my understanding, infatuated with her king?

It was hard to picture Calvin Malvern as a Don Juan, but Jinks had told me that people's personalities changed when they took on roles at a Ren fest. As King Wilfred, Calvin might very well enjoy a spot of dalliance with a humble but adoring young maiden. He might even attempt to exercise his droit du seigneur. As far as I could tell, King Wilfred had no queen, so there was nothing to keep him from making a royal pass at every pretty girl who crossed his path.

Or was there?

Though the sun was warm, a chill crept down my spine. Edmond's furious scowl flashed before my mind's eye, followed by the stark image of a handsaw protruding from a wheelbarrow.

"*Regicide,*" I whispered.

Eight

*T*he sun seemed to darken and the crowd seemed to recede into the background as I recalled how easily the parapet had given way and how close Calvin Malvern had come to losing his balance and, perhaps, his life. There was no denying that Edmond Deland had the tools and the skills needed to make such an accident happen. If Mirabel had spurned his love and bestowed hers on the king, he would also have had a motive.

"Slow down," I muttered under my breath. "Don't get ahead of yourself, Lori. You don't *know* anything yet."

An earsplitting blare of trumpets interrupted my uneasy meditations. I winced, glanced around, and saw the king's heralds striding past me, blowing their usual fanfare and crying, "Make way! Make way for the king!"

The few stragglers still crossing Broad Street scuttled to the sidelines to avoid being trampled by what turned out to be a formidable procession. The heralds were followed by a collection of entertainers who strutted, danced, banged tambourines, twirled ribbons on wands, and exchanged good-humored badinage with the onlookers lining the route. People cheered for their favorites as they passed by. Some showed their appreciation by tossing coins, which were expertly caught, though not always by those at whom they'd been aimed.

A phalanx of bearded men dressed in studded leather jerkins came next. Each bore a longbow, a spear, a poleax, or a halberd. The weapons looked deadly enough to be used in battle, but the men who carried them were too soft in the belly and smiled too genially to be mistaken for hardened warriors.

The soldiers were followed by a gap in which Jinks performed a breathtaking sequence of acrobatic maneuvers. As he sailed by, I remembered his offer to pop over the stile for a visit after he'd finished his day's work. I hoped he would make good on his offer. I had a sudden, urgent need to know everything he could tell me about the fair's backstage intrigue.

After Jinks came the moment I'd been waiting for. King Wilfred and his court strode into view, led by the gray-haired Lord Belvedere, flanked by Sir Peregrine and Sir Jacques, and accompanied by a dozen noblewomen, all of whom wore lustrous gowns and splendid wimples. My heart ached with envy when I saw the wimples, but I thrust my feelings aside and concentrated solely on the king.

As the merry monarch approached, he raised a plump hand to his lips and blew a kiss toward my section of the crowd. I heard Mirabel's delighted squeal and turned just in time to see her blush adorably and sink into a picture-perfect curtsy. The other madrigal singers giggled and nudged one another approvingly, then the tallest one, who seemed more mature than the rest, spoke to Mirabel.

"'Tis time for us to return to our labors," she scolded good-naturedly. "Thou hast seen him and thou shalt see him again anon."

"And anon and anon," another girl added mischievously.

The girls then edged their way through the crowd, towing a reluctant Mirabel in their wake. I peered at them pensively until a pair of piping voices reminded me of my original reason for watching the king's procession.

"Mummy! MUMMY!"

The sight of Will and Rob astride their gray ponies chased all thoughts of sabotage from my mind. Alison and Billy McLaughlin, their gymkhana teammates, rode in the procession as well, but I couldn't take my eyes off of my sons. As Sally Pyne had promised, they looked like little princes in their gorgeous velvet tunics, and Thunder and Storm looked equally noble, draped in white and gold caparisons supplied by Calvin Malvern. When the boys finished waving giddily at me, they resumed the dignified demeanor they'd been taught to display at horse shows.

The four children rode their ponies at a sedate pace at the rear of the procession. They were followed by an older rider, also in costume but riding sidesaddle. She wore a beautiful pair of suede gloves, an elegant leaf-green gown, and a tall wimple adorned with the daintiest wisp of silk. I was so busy checking out her garb that I didn't realize who she was until she passed directly in front of me.

"Emma?" I said, my voice squeaking with disbelief. *"Emma?"*

Emma Harris, my levelheaded, unromantic, unimaginative best friend, turned her wimpled head to grin at me, then raised a gloved hand and favored me with a regal wave as she followed my sons down Broad Street on her mare, Pegasus. I was so shocked to see her decked out in damsel gear that I nearly missed the procession's denouement.

The crowd trailed after the king and his cohorts as they turned up Pudding Lane toward the joust arena, but one member of the procession lingered. Alone, unsung, armed with a wheelbarrow, a shovel, and a large sack of sawdust, Edmond Deland moved silently through the noisy throng, clearing Broad Street of the messes left behind by the ponies.

As I watched him bend to his task, I felt a sudden rush of sympathy for him. How could a young man who scooped pony poop for a living hope to compete with a king? I didn't forgive or condone his violent tactics, but I thought I understood his desperation. I wanted to reach out to him, to offer words of consolation that might calm the fire of jealousy that was burning in his breast, but before I'd taken more than a half step toward him, a hand on my elbow stopped me.

"Lori?" said a voice.

Lilian Bunting had caught up with me. I stared at her abstractedly for a moment, then realized with a sinking heart and a flaming face that I'd done it again. I'd thrown myself, body and soul, into a drama that didn't exist outside of my own head. With almost no effort at all, I'd turned a few glances and a blown kiss into a love triangle and a murder plot. If Lilian hadn't happened by, I would have accosted a total stranger and accused him of a heinous crime. When I thought of the embarrassing scene my impulsiveness might have provoked, I wanted to take a scrub brush to my brain.

"You look as if you're a million miles away," said Lilian.

"I was," I admitted. "But I'm back now. How was Merlot the Magnificent?"

"Magnificent." Lilian slipped her hand through my arm.

"Come along. I'll tell you all about him on the way to the arena. We don't want to miss the joust! Did you see Emma in the procession? I thought she looked wonderful, didn't you? Will and Rob were simply charming, of course. Did you stop at Jasper Taxman's stall? I couldn't believe my eyes when I saw him in a velvet doublet and hose. He told me that Peggy stayed behind at the Emporium because she didn't care for the costume she'd ordered from London, but I heard a different story from Sally Pyne. According to Sally, the bodice was so small that Peggy popped out of it in a most immodest manner. Naturally, Peggy asked Sally to alter the bodice, but Sally told me that she'd have to add so much material to the old bodice that she might as well make a new one from scratch. . . ."

My friend's gossip washed over me like a soothing balm, anchoring me in a world I knew and helping me to regain a firm foothold on the slippery shores of reality. I promised myself that, as soon as the joust was over, I would look for Jasper's stall and seek out Sally Pyne. I wanted to get the lowdown on Peggy's costume malfunction, of course, but I also needed all the anchoring I could get.

Lilian and I bought spinach pies, fizzy lemonade, and honey cakes as we strolled up Pudding Lane. By the time we reached the picnic area overlooking the joust arena, all of the tables were taken, so we sat on the ground with many other spectators and spread our al fresco lunch between us.

While most participants in the king's procession had dispersed to other parts of the fair, the king and a few select members of his entourage had seated themselves in chairs on a sturdy raised platform on the far side of the arena. The platform was hung with festive banners and shaded by a striped canopy whose four stout wooden posts were wreathed in bright ribbons and fresh flowers.

The king sat in a high-backed, gilded throne close to the platform's front railing, where he could see and be seen by his subjects. The throne on the platform was less ornate than the one I'd seen sitting on the Great Hall stage, but it was still pretty stately. Gray-bearded Lord Belvedere stood beside the throne. He appeared to be fiddling with a pair of speakers mounted on the canopy's foremost posts.

"Anachronism alert," I said, nudging Lilian. "The stage is wired for sound."

"I suppose we must make some concessions to modern times," she commented. "I, for one, was relieved to see that chemical loos had been provided for our convenience, rather than their medieval equivalents. And it isn't a stage, Lori. It's the royal gallery. I've been reading up on jousting, which, I discovered, is also known as tilting. The joust arena can also be called the tiltyard, the lists, or the list field."

"Fascinating," I said. "Speak on, O learned one. It'll give me a chance to finish my spinach pie."

"Mock if you will," said Lilian. "I will not be daunted."

She was stating the simple truth. Lilian Bunting had a scholarly turn of mind. If she was determined to dispense knowledge, it would take more than gentle teasing to divert her from her course.

"The earliest tournaments sprang from rather bloody affairs called melees," she began. "A melee was a mock battle in which foot soldiers and mounted knights clashed violently with opponents. Melees usually continued until one side beat the other into submission."

"Why did they go to such extremes if it was only a mock battle?" I asked.

"Practice," said Lilian. "The knights wanted to maintain their fighting skills between real wars, but so many of them were killed or injured in the process that tournaments were eventually banned. They were later revived as a form of royal entertainment as well as a source of income for the knights. Prize money was awarded and a new set of rules was generally followed, with a points system that discouraged outright slaughter."

"How civilized," I said.

"Jousting is much safer nowadays," Lilian said confidently. "Modern knights use breakaway lances and carefully choreograph any hand-to-hand combat that might take place. I'm sure Calvin's hired competent performers. King Wilfred wouldn't want his fair spoiled by bloodshed."

"I should think not." Thoughts of sabotage flickered in my mind, but I doused them by asking a question that had been puzzling me for some time. "Do you happen to know the difference between a page and a squire?"

"Age," Lilian replied, unwittingly confirming Aunt Dimity's guess. "The young sons of noble families became pages in neighboring households, where they learned gentlemanly skills such as deportment and riding. When a page reached the age of fourteen or thereabouts, he could become a squire and serve a particular knight. Squires in turn could become knights, if they could afford the expense, which was considerable. If they couldn't afford it, they might remain squires for the rest of their days. Oh, look!" She pointed to the white marquee. "Squires!"

Two teenaged boys in matching tunics, tights, and feathered caps rolled back the flaps of the huge tent and tied them in place with ropes. At the same time, Lord Belvedere's voice crackled unintelligibly through the speakers.

"Ah," I said, nodding wisely. "It's a *medieval* sound system."

"It sounds quite modern to me," said Lilian. "These honey cakes are delicious, by the way," she added. "Did you, by any chance, acquire the recipe?"

I smiled wryly. "I have to ask the king for it. Apparently he's in charge of the fair's recipe box."

"I'll have a word with Horace Malvern after church tomorrow," said Lilian. "The king's uncle should be able to procure a recipe for us."

Our conversation was cut short by a sudden burst of applause.

"Hooray," said Lilian, her face brightening. "Here come the twins!"

She remained seated and silent, as befitted a vicar's wife, but I jumped to my feet and cheered boisterously as a mounted procession emerged from the marquee and circled the arena at a snappy trot. Rob and Will led Sir Peregrine the Pure onto the field of battle, bearing pennants emblazoned with rearing unicorns, while Alison and Billy, carrying flags with black dragon motifs, escorted Sir Jacques de Poitiers.

I was enthralled by the spectacle. The knights' breastplates gleamed, their long hair streamed behind them splendidly, and they rode with swaggering assurance, their striped lances pointed skyward. The four children grinned proudly when they spotted me, but they couldn't wave because their hands were fully occupied.

Although the crowd made it abundantly clear that it favored Sir Peregrine over Sir Jacques, I was fairly certain that the children had been assigned to their respective knights for decorative rather than moral reasons. The twins' gray ponies complemented Sir Peregrine's snowy charger, while their teammates' darker ponies looked better with the Dragon Knight's black steed.

Egged on by wenches planted strategically in their midst, the spectators called out, "Ride on, noble knight!" whenever Sir Peregrine flashed a toothy smile, and jeered each time Sir Jacques sneered. The knights mugged shamelessly, the wenches reacted rambunctiously, and the audience was perfectly happy to play along.

The procession made one complete circuit of the arena before the children lowered their pennants and reentered the marquee. After they'd gone, the knights rode side by side to face the royal gallery, dipped their lances in a salute to the king, then raced to opposite ends of the arena. While the two men acknowledged their liege lord, a bevy of bearded foot soldiers emerged from the marquee and fanned out to the arena's boundaries, to stand to attention before wooden racks that held a variety of weapons.

"For His Majesty's pleasure . . ."

Lilian and I flinched as Lord Belvedere's voice boomed from the speakers, which had evidently been fixed.

". . . and the pleasure of all assembled here today, Sir Peregrine and Sir Jacques will now demonstrate their skill at arms."

"Oh, good," said Lilian. "They're going to give us a full show."

"A full show?" I queried.

"They're not going straight to the joust," she explained. "They'll compete in a few smaller contests first."

The knights exchanged their long, thick lances for skinnier ones plucked from the wooden racks and handed up to them by bearded soldiers. At the same time, the two young squires took up positions in the center of the arena. Each held a small red hoop at arm's length.

"It's called ring jousting," Lilian narrated excitedly. "The knights will try to spear the rings with their lances."

"No way," I said, shaking my head. "The kids holding the rings will lose their arms."

"They're professionals," said Lilian. "I'm sure they've practiced sufficiently to avoid injury."

I tried to share her optimism, but when Sir Peregrine lowered his skinny lance and spurred his steed into a smooth canter, I sucked in a nervous breath. I didn't release it until the knight had successfully speared a ring without detaching the squire's arm from his body.

"Impressive, isn't it?" said Lilian.

"Uh-huh," I said, but as I moistened my dry mouth with a sip of lemonade, I vowed silently that my noble sons would *never* become squires.

Both knights proceeded to make three successive passes at increasingly smaller rings. Amazingly, they never missed. The knights taunted each other mercilessly after each successful snatch. The taunts were echoed by the wenches who cunningly brought a portion of the crowd over to Sir Jacques' side by teaching them the novel chant: "Cheat to win!" When I heard a white-haired grandmother join in, I laughed so hard that I nearly missed the Dragon Knight's final pass. By then I was enjoying myself thoroughly. As Lilian had pointed out, the men involved were professionals. Their well-honed skills laid my fears to rest.

The knights gallantly presented their rings to the dainty damsels who sat on either side of the king, then exchanged their skinny lances for six-foot-long wooden spears topped with lethal-looking steel spearheads.

"Those are throwing spears," Lilian explained. "Sir Peregrine and Sir Jacques will hurl them at the hay bales at the end of the arena."

"While galloping, I presume," I said.

"They'll probably canter," said Lilian, "but I wouldn't put it past Sir Jacques to gallop. He's a fine horseman."

Since there was nothing behind the bales but empty pasture, and since the knights seemed to aim remarkably well, I ignored the dangerous spearheads and focused solely on the contest. In three attempts, each knight hit his hay bale as easily as he'd speared the rings.

The crowd went wild, but instead of shouting with one voice, it seesawed back and forth between Sir Peregrine's "Ride on, noble knight!" and Sir Jacques' "Cheat to win!" Under the wenches' direction, each faction tried to outshout the other, but they fell into a rapt silence when their heroes took up full-sized lances and prepared to demonstrate yet another skill at arms.

"The knights are still tied," said Lilian. "But a true test of their prowess is coming up. I do believe the quintain will be next."

"The what?" I said.

"The quintain." She pointed to a strange device that stood to one side of the arena, a few yards away from the royal gallery. "It's a post with a revolving crosspiece. As you can see, the crosspiece has a wooden dummy attached to one end and a sandbag dangling from the other. The knight has to hit the dummy with his lance, then gallop off as fast as he possibly can, to avoid being hit by the sandbag as it swings round behind him. The quintain is a test of speed as well as accuracy."

"Piece of cake," I said, and as Sir Jacques rode into position, I added my voice to those cheering lustily for Sir Peregrine.

Sir Jacques hefted his lance, took aim, and jabbed his spurs into his steed. The crowd held its breath and the ground seemed to vibrate as the horse raced toward the quintain. The Dragon Knight's lance struck the dummy, the crosspiece spun, the rope holding the sandbag snapped, and the sandbag flew directly at King Wilfred.

Nine

$\mathcal{I}$f King Wilfred hadn't ducked, his skull would have been crushed like a grape. If his throne hadn't been built so sturdily, the courtier seated behind him would have suffered grievous bodily harm. As it was, the errant sandbag smacked into the throne instead of the king, the throne withstood the impact, and the sandbag slid harmlessly onto King Wilfred's back.

A hush fell over the arena. The tension among the spectators was palpable. Those who weren't already standing got to their feet and peered fearfully at the gallery. Sir Peregrine stared in confusion at the spinning quintain while Sir Jacques brought his horse up short, tossed his lance to a gaping foot soldier, and sped back to the gallery, presumably to ascertain the state of his sovereign's health.

Lord Belvedere seized the sandbag and flung it into the arena, then knelt before the king and peered at him anxiously. The courtiers and the damsels left their chairs and clustered around the gray-haired steward, wringing their hands. The soldiers remained at their posts, exchanging worried glances.

King Wilfred slowly straightened, replaced the crown that had fallen from his head, waved Lord Belvedere aside, and rose to address his subjects. Spreading his arms wide, he grinned merrily and shouted, *"Missed!"*

A few people chuckled hesitantly, but when several

more joined in, the hillside erupted with laughter and heartfelt applause. The audience clearly appreciated the king's courage under fire.

King Wilfred accepted the tribute graciously, then resumed his throne and signaled for his attendants to return to their chairs. When they'd done so, he nodded regally to Lord Belvedere, whose amplified voice burst once again from the speakers.

"My lords, ladies, and gentlemen," he said. "Our valiant monarch calls for the joust to commence. What say you?"

A chorus of enthusiastic shouts affirmed the king's decision to overlook the sandbag incident and proceed with the entertainment. The spectators who'd stood sat down again and an expectant murmur rippled across the hillside as the knights prepared themselves for battle.

I stared at the scrap of rope dangling from the quintain and sank onto the ground beside Lilian, feeling slightly queasy.

"Did you see that?" I asked.

"I certainly did," she replied. "The fair seems to be having a few teething problems."

"Teething problems?" I turned to stare at her. "King Wilfred nearly dies twice in one day and you call it teething problems?"

"Of course I do," she said. "What else could it be? A coup d'état?" She chuckled lightheartedly, as if her suggestion were arrant nonsense. "What you must remember, Lori, is that King Wilfred's Faire is a form of theater. Mishaps are commonplace in the theater. Actors nick one another with swords, props break, scenery collapses. There were bound to be a few wrinkles on opening day. I'm sure they'll iron them out by tomorrow."

"But Calvin was nearly *killed*," I pointed out. "*Twice.*"

"He dealt with it beautifully both times, don't you think?" said Lilian. "He displayed the dignity and good humor one would expect from a merry monarch. I'm quite impressed by his aplomb. Hush, now. The joust is about to begin."

I clamped my mouth shut and turned resolutely to face the arena. There was no point in arguing with Lilian because I couldn't prove that she was wrong. Accidents did happen in the theater. Actors were injured from time to time. I might suspect Edmond Deland of sabotaging the quintain's rope *and* the gatehouse's parapet, but I hadn't seen him do it. I'd merely imagined it, and I knew better than to trust my imagination.

While Lilian and I had been chatting, the knights had donned their plumed helmets, taken up their shields, and retrieved their heavy lances from the foot soldiers. Now armed and armored, they faced each other across the length of the arena. A fair-haired damsel in the gallery rose from her chair to dangle a long, silken kerchief over the front railing. Sir Jacques' horse pawed the ground and Sir Peregrine's tossed its head impatiently. The knights adjusted their shields and lifted their lances. The damsel dropped the kerchief.

The knights sprang into action, spurring their steeds forward on thundering hooves. They drew closer, they met, and Sir Peregrine's lance crashed into the dragon shield. The lance shattered, bits of wood whirled into the air, and Sir Jacques flew from his saddle to land, hard, on his back. The Dragon Knight staggered to his feet, looking dazed and winded, but when Sir Peregrine rode back to accept his surrender, he jumped up, seized the unicorn shield with one hand, and pulled Sir Peregrine to the ground.

The crowd roared with delight as the knights threw aside their helmets and drew their swords. As if on cue, the foot soldiers grabbed weapons from racks and began to attack each other. The young squires scurried forward to lead the horses to safety as a sort of combat ballet commenced.

"A melee!" Lilian shouted gleefully above the din.

The knights' swords clanged viciously in the center of the arena, while the soldiers wielded pikes, maces, morning stars, staffs, and axes. There was so much jumping, dodging, ducking, weaving, twirling, and sidestepping that I was sure the sport of ear-lopping would soon make its debut, but the combatants seemed to know what they were doing. As Lilian had foretold, the moves were dramatic rather than deadly and King Wilfred's Faire was not spoiled by bloodshed.

When the dust settled, Sir Peregrine stood with his foot on Sir Jacques' breastplate and the tip of his sword at Sir Jacques' neck. The soldiers froze in place, awaiting the conqueror's decision.

"Cry mercy," bellowed Sir Peregrine, "or die."

"Mercy!" Sir Jacques grunted.

Fully half of the spectators groaned with disappointment when Sir Peregrine released his vanquished foe and turned to bow to the king, but their spirits revived when the Dragon Knight sprang to his feet, clouted Sir Peregrine over the head with the hilt of his sword, and snatched the silken kerchief from the ground to claim the final victory.

"Cheat to win!" shouted the wenches, and everyone joined in, with gales of good-natured laughter.

Sir Jacques and his soldiers left the arena in triumph,

accompanied by mingled cheers and catcalls. The defeated Sir Peregrine declared that he would return to fight another day and led his band of warriors into the marquee. The squires pulled the tent flaps back into place, the king and his entourage departed the royal gallery, and the joust was over.

"Well," said Lilian, "I must say that Calvin was quite correct when he told us that we wouldn't demand a refund. The joust alone was worth every penny of my admission fee."

"Where will you go next?" I asked.

"I'm going home," she replied, "where I will continue to do my utmost to convince Teddy to don his costume."

"I admire your persistence," I said. "I've given up on Bill."

"Never say die," Lilian advised. "Where there's a will there's a way. I could go on, but I'm sure you get the gist. Are you staying?"

"For a little while." I nodded at the marquee. "I want to look in on the twins before I leave."

"Naturally." Lilian gathered up the litter left over from her lunch and stood. "I hope to see you in church tomorrow."

"I'll be there," I said. "I can't promise that Bill and the boys will come with me, but I'll be there."

"In that case, there will be at least two of us present to hear Teddy's sermon. After tasting the delights of King Wilfred's Faire, I'll count it a small miracle if anyone joins us." Lilian nodded pleasantly and joined the stream of satisfied joust fans pouring down Pudding Lane.

I deposited my own trash in a nearby bin, then strolled casually down the hill and along the arena's fence until I reached the royal gallery. I loitered in its shadows until the picnic area was deserted and the arena was empty, apart from a pair of teenaged girls, who seemed to be paying more attention to the marquee than to me. I watched them for a time, to make sure they weren't glancing my way, then climbed through the two-bar fence and walked to a spot below the gallery's front railing.

The sandbag lay on the ground where Lord Belvedere had flung it, half buried in the dirt kicked up by the battling knights. I knew I wouldn't be able to reach the scrap of rope dangling from the quintain, but my diminutive height wouldn't prevent me from examining the remnant of rope still attached to the sandbag.

I squatted beside the sandbag and plucked the rope from the dirt. Its tightly twisted strands of hemp were nearly as thick as my wrist and they didn't look old or worn. I wasn't surprised. It stood to reason that the quintain would be fitted with a new, heavy-gauge rope before the fair opened. The contraption was supposed to be strong enough to withstand a puissant warrior's blows.

I slid the rope through my hands until I held the broken end between my fingers. If it had frayed naturally, I would have expected to see hemp fibers protruding unevenly along the entire edge. Instead, only part of the edge was uneven. The rest of it was as straight as the edge of a paintbrush. It looked as if someone had deliberately sliced halfway through the rope, hoping that it would break completely when a skinny lance struck the wooden dummy.

"I *knew* it," I whispered. "Sabotage."

My hands trembled as the enormity of my discovery hit home. I wasn't conjuring a murder plot out of thin air.

The plot was chillingly real. *Someone was trying to kill King Wilfred.*

My first impulse was to run to the king and tell him that his life was in danger, but the memory of Lilian Bunting's lighthearted chuckle stopped me cold. She'd made it clear that she found the notion of a coup d'état preposterous and I had little doubt that others would agree with her. The king himself had laughed off both attempts on his life, and his cronies appeared to be quite willing to ignore them. If I went to Calvin Malvern with a tale about a love triangle, a handsaw, and a severed rope, he'd either dismiss me as delusional or hire me as a storyteller. Until I could support my claims with solid proof, it would be useless to present them to anyone.

I gazed at the rope pensively. If I'd had a knife with me, I would have cut off the severed end and preserved it as evidence. Unfortunately, my shoulder bag contained nothing sharper than a nail file. I was contemplating the difficulties of laying my hands on Sir Peregrine's sword when a voice intruded.

"My lady?"

I dropped the rope and looked up guiltily. A man was peering at me from the far side of the fence. The sun was behind him, so I couldn't see his face properly, but his silhouette was nothing short of breathtaking. A white shirt with billowing sleeves fell loosely from his broad shoulders, and his dark tights clung seductively to a pair of legs that could have won the Tour de France.

"Uh," I said, straightening. "Hello."

"Good morrow." The man vaulted the fence and strode toward me. "Dost thou not know me, my fair one?"

"No, I don't know thee, and I'm not your fair——" I

gasped as the man drew close enough for me to make out his extremely familiar features. *"Bill?"*

"'Tis I, my sweet," said Bill, with a flowery bow. "I thought you might come to the marquee after the joust. I didn't expect to find you playing in the dirt."

"Bill?" I repeated, gaping at him.

When I'd last seen my husband, he'd been dressed in a polo shirt, khaki shorts, a baseball cap, and sneakers, but his image had undergone a radical transformation since then. Bill no longer looked like a suburban dad. He looked like the hero of a saucy romance novel. He'd laced the deep V of his shirt with a leather thong, buckled a wide leather belt around his hips, donned a pair of knee-high leather boots, and perched a floppy velvet cap at a rakish angle on his head. The white ostrich feather curled around the cap quivered delicately when he spoke.

"C'est moi, chérie," he said. "Why *are* you playing in the dirt?"

"I'm not . . . I'm just . . ." I stuttered to a halt, then began again. "Never mind what I'm doing. What are *you* doing dressed like *that?*"

"Do you like it?" He pointed a toe to show off a shapely leg.

"Do I *like* it?" I glared at him. "You lying *hound*. What happened to 'definitely and irrevocably no'? What happened to 'it's never going to happen'?"

"I changed my mind," said Bill. "Calvin Malvern had some extra costumes lying around and he suggested that I—"

"Oh, I *see*." I folded my arms and regarded him haughtily. "*Calvin Malvern's* word carries more weight than your *wife's.* If you didn't look so outrageously studly, I'd clobber you."

"Do I look outrageously studly?" he inquired coyly.

"You know you do," I retorted. "But if you think it's going to have the slightest effect on me, you're very much—"

Bill silenced me by sweeping me into his arms and giving me a kiss that made me forget what I was saying. When he put me on my feet again, my knees were so wobbly I had to lean against him for support.

"That's cheating," I complained, though not very strenuously.

"All's fair at the fair," he quipped.

I pushed myself away from him in order to take a good look at his costume. "What are you supposed to be, anyway?"

"A cool medieval dude," he replied, hooking his thumbs in his belt. "Now, tell me, Lori. What are you doing in the arena?"

I couldn't bring myself to spoil the moment by telling my husband that I was trying to pin the attempted murder of Good King Wilfred on a lovelorn, poop-scooping handyman, so I told him that I was looking for souvenirs.

"What kind of souvenirs?" Bill asked bemusedly. "Broken teeth? I imagine you might find a few if you sifted the dirt thoroughly, but why would you want to? Come with me, my darling nutcase. I'll find better souvenirs for you."

"I'd like a knife," I said promptly.

Bill's eyebrows rose. "A knife?"

"Yes." I nodded. "All of the wenches wear knives on their belts. My costume will be incomplete without one."

"I think we can find one for you easily enough," said Bill. "Calvin has an entire armory at his disposal. Wait till you see it. . . ."

Bill went on talking as we walked toward the marquee, but I wasn't listening. I was envisioning myself back in the arena, retrieving the only piece of hard evidence I'd unearthed. My new knife would have to be as sharp as a razor to slice through the thick rope, I reasoned, and if I wanted to slice through it in private, I'd have to invent an excuse to leave the marquee without Bill and the twins accompanying me.

"I have to confess that I'm a little surprised at you, Lori."

The sound of my name penetrated the dense thicket of my thoughts, and I roused myself to respond.

"Why are you surprised?" I asked.

"You haven't mentioned the quintain once," he said.

I glanced up at him uncomfortably, wondering if he'd read my mind, then said, much too rapidly, "The quintain? Why would I mention the quintain? What's so interesting about the quintain?"

We'd reached the entrance to the marquee, but Bill didn't reach out to open the tent flap. Instead he smiled down at me and put a hand on my shoulder.

"I know what you were doing in the arena," he said gently.

"You do?" I said, eyeing him uncertainly.

"The accident scared you," said Bill, "so you decided to find out why the rope broke."

"Right," I said. "Yes. That's what I was doing." In a way, I was telling the truth.

"Calvin told me that it was a freak accident." Bill gave

my shoulder a reassuring squeeze. "Cal has seen hundreds of jousts and he's never seen a sandbag come loose like that before. The rope-maker can't understand how it happened. He makes the rope by hand, in Bristol, and he inspects every inch of it before he sends it on. He believes it was damaged during shipping. The replacement rope will be carefully inspected on site before it's attached to the quintain. The chances of such a thing happening again are virtually nil."

"Okay," I said.

"I'm proud of you for keeping your cool," Bill went on. "I expected you to tear across the arena to make sure that the boys were all right."

"Will and Rob were out of harm's way," I said. "And they were with you. Why would I worry about them?"

"There was a time when you did nothing *but* worry about them," said Bill. "If I recall correctly, you thought a vampire was stalking them last October."

"There's no need to bring up the vampire fiasco," I muttered, blushing.

"I'm simply trying to make a point, Lori," said Bill. "And my point is that you've come a long way since then. I'm proud of you." He bent to kiss me lightly on the forehead, then pulled the tent flap aside.

The stench that wafted from the marquee put an end to all rational thought. The miasma was so dense, so appallingly multilayered, and so remorselessly ripe that I fell back a step and retched.

"Ye gods!" I exclaimed, choking. "Has someone *died* in there?"

"What do you mean?" asked Bill.

"It *stinks*." I cupped a hand over my abused nose. "It

smells like a year's worth of dirty socks left to rot on a manure pile."

"Oh, *that*." Bill scratched his chin. "I guess I've gotten used to it."

"Your olfactory nerves have shut down in self-defense," I stated firmly, "and I can't say that I blame them."

"It's a combination of sweat, horses, and leftovers from lunch," Bill explained. "Some of the men had oysters."

"Haven't they heard of air fresheners?" I asked. "Or deodorant?"

"It wouldn't help," said Bill. "The guys who play the soldiers wear padded shirts beneath their jerkins, and since they're all avid reenactors, they've been using those shirts for years. They perspire heavily when they fight, the perspiration soaks into the padding, and the aroma lingers."

"Lingers?" I said, grimacing. "It's strong enough to melt lead. Have they tried soaking the padded shirts in bleach?"

"I doubt it," said Bill. "Our noble warriors have a fairly medieval view of personal hygiene."

"A bar of soap is the devil's plaything?" I suggested.

Bill nodded. "Something like that."

"Why don't they leave the flaps open, to air the place out?" I asked.

"I don't think they realize that the place needs to be aired out," Bill explained patiently. "Besides, they wouldn't want the equipment to get wet or blown about if a storm came through."

"I can't believe they ate lunch in there," I said, fanning the noxious fumes away from my face. "Is there a way to see Will and Rob without going inside?"

"Of course there is," said Bill. "We can go around the

marquee instead of through it. I'll find a knife for you later and bring it home with me after we've finished up here."

"Hold on," I said hastily. I'd forgotten about the knife. "Maybe I'm being too prissy. This is a medieval fair, after all. It's supposed to be . . . atmospheric." I squared my shoulders. "Let's go."

"Are you sure?" Bill asked.

"If you can get used to it, so can I," I said, and marched determinedly into the marquee.

It would take more than a smelly tent to keep me from catching the king's foe.

Ten

y first glimpse of the tent's cavernous interior made me feel as if I weren't simply stepping backstage, but back in time. There was no power hookup and therefore no background hum to spoil the peace and quiet. The only light was that which filtered through the tent's white fabric, and the only sound was the gentle creak of the impressive supporting timbers. The hard-packed dirt floor had been strewn with rushes, and the wide central aisle was six inches deep in authentically soiled straw.

The floor space was divided into sections by ropes strung between barley-twist iron stanchions that looked as though they'd been forged by a burly blacksmith back in the fourteenth century. The weapons and armor had been arranged in an orderly fashion on freestanding wooden shelves and racks that stood along the left-hand wall. The soldiers' padded shirts and leather jerkins lay in neat piles to the right, beneath a wooden rack supporting the furled pennons and banners the children had carried into the arena.

The horses' brightly colored caparisons and plumed bridles hung from ropes strung above a row of saddletrees that held the ponies' simple saddles as well as the knights' larger and more elaborate ones. The back wall, Bill pointed out, could be rolled up to the ceiling, to admit the horses for their grand procession through the marquee and into the arena.

The dressing area near the front of the marquee was furnished with wooden benches, a handful of three-legged stools, an ancient, speckled, full-length mirror, and a covered water butt with a wooden dipper. A pewter platter piled high with oyster shells sat on one of the benches, but the men who'd devoured the oysters were nowhere to be seen.

"Where is everyone?" I asked.

"The Anscombe Manor contingent is out back with the ponies," Bill replied. "The squires are there, too, looking after Angelus and Lucifer, but the rest of the jousting crew has gone back to camp."

"Don't tell me," I said. "Angelus is the white horse and Lucifer is the black one?"

"Predictable, but true," Bill said, nodding. "Angelus belongs to Perry, of course, and Lucifer is Jack's."

"Who are Perry and Jack?" I asked, feeling a bit lost.

"Sir Peregrine the Pure and Sir Jacques de Poitiers," he answered. "When they're off duty, they call themselves Perry and Jack. The soldiers call them Pretty Perry and Randy Jack, but not to their faces." Bill glanced furtively toward the back wall, then leaned forward to add in a confidential murmur, "Apparently, Perry spends more time than he should primping in front of the mirror, and Jack thinks he has a way with the ladies, although the soldiers tell me that the ladies would debate the point."

The curious change in Bill's posture and tone of voice suggested strongly that he'd finally succumbed to an illness endemic to Finch. I'd caught it shortly after we'd moved into the cottage, but Bill had somehow managed to avoid it—until now.

"You're gossiping!" I said triumphantly.

"Guilty as charged," Bill acknowledged sheepishly. "It's easy to get caught up in it. Everyone's always talking about everyone else."

"Are they?" I tried not to show it, but Bill's words filled me with hope. While I'd spent the day observing the fair's public face, he'd seen its private side. He'd had ample opportunities to learn all sorts of useful things about King Wilfred, Edmond Deland, and little Mirabel. "Have you heard anyone badmouth King Wilfred?"

"No," he replied. "Everyone seems to like Calvin."

"Is he popular with the ladies?" I asked.

"Not a clue," said Bill. "Why? Are you going to volunteer to play his queen?"

"I already have my king," I said, smiling up at him. "Have many women volunteered to play the queen?"

"I don't know. I don't even know if the position exists. Calvin's budget may not include a queen." Bill swept his arm in a wide arc to indicate the whole of our surroundings. "Would you like a tour?"

"As long as we keep our distance from the padded shirts," I said warily.

As we moved through the marquee, I told myself to be patient. Bill's apparent lack of interest in King Wilfred's love life was disappointing, but not surprising. My husband was new to the gossip game. He'd need a lot more practice before he could live up to my high standards.

Bill showed me Sir Peregrine's shattered lance, explained the heraldic symbols painted on Lucifer's saddle, and pointed out the fine workmanship that had gone into

creating the chain mail. We were examining Sir Jacques'
dented shield when the bottom edge of the tent's back wall
rolled upward a few feet and a young, red-haired squire
entered the marquee, carrying a bucket filled with curry
combs, hoof picks, and other grooming tools.

"Harold," Bill called. "Come and meet my lady wife.
Harold le Rouge is Sir Peregrine's squire," he explained
to me, adding in an undertone, "His real name is Tommy
Grout."

"No wonder he changed it," I murmured back.

Harold stowed his bucket carefully beneath Sir Peregrine's saddletree, then strode over to meet me. After
we'd been properly introduced, and after he'd finished
doffing his cap and bowing, Bill asked him if I might borrow a knife from the king's armory.

"Your good lady is welcome to mine," Harold said
instantly.

"I can't take your knife," I exclaimed, embarrassed.

"I have many others, my lady," said Harold. "You would
do me a great honor if you would accept a small trifle from
me." He removed the sheathed knife from his belt and presented both knife and sheath to me on bended knee.

I accepted them gratefully and saw at once that
they were no mere trifles. The leather sheath had been
hand-sewn with fine backstitching, and the knife's black
horn handle was bound in brass. More important, the
gleaming blade was nearly six inches long and honed to a
razor-sharp edge. It would serve my immediate purpose
perfectly.

"Thank you, Harold," I said. "You have the makings of a
most chivalrous knight."

"I hope one day to be worthy of the honor," he said,

rising. "I fear I must beg leave of you, friends. My master awaits me at the encampment."

"We'll come with you," said Bill. "Our sons await us."

"I'm glad I didn't ask him for a pair of tights," I whispered to Bill as I dropped the knife into my shoulder bag.

"So is Harold," he said softly.

We stifled our snickers and followed the young squire under the back wall and into a small stabling area equipped with a row of hitching posts, two watering tanks, and an assortment of buckets, ropes, rakes, and shovels. The Anscombe Manor horse trailers were parked ten yards away, near the end of a rough track that led, presumably, to the Oxford Road, and the horses had been turned out to graze in a nearby pasture.

Harold took his leave of us—after more bowing and cap-doffing—and headed toward a row of poplar trees beyond the horse trailers. Will, Rob, Alison, and Billy sat atop the fence surrounding the pasture, watching their ponies, while Lawrence McLaughlin, Emma, and the stable hands stood at the fence, chatting. They were all dressed in period attire, though Emma had covered her leaf-green gown with a voluminous apron. She spotted me and spoke to the boys, who hopped down from the fence and came running.

"Mummy, did you see us?" Will asked.

"Did you see us in the procession?" asked Rob.

"You know I did," I said, hugging both of them, "because *you* saw *me*."

"We heard you, too," Rob informed me.

"You were *loud*," Will said.

"I must have been," I said, "if you could hear me above the crowd."

"We could," Bill asserted, with feeling.

"Perry says we ride better than Jack," Rob announced.

"And Jack says we ride better than Perry," Will declared.

"What does Emma say?" I asked.

"She says we need more practice," said Rob.

"She *always* says that," Will explained.

"And she's always right," said Emma, coming up behind them. "You both did well, for a first try, but we're going to run drills with the pennons next week. We need to keep our hands steadier and our trot smoother."

"We'll skewer the varlets!" Rob cried.

"A pox upon the knaves!" Will added.

The boys galloped off to conduct a mock joust on foot while I cast a wondering look at Bill.

"They've been hanging around soldiers all day," he said. "They were bound to pick up some new phrases. It's making history come alive for them."

"'A pox upon the knaves'? Their teachers are going to love hearing *that* on the playground." I shook my head, then turned to give Emma a measuring look. "I never thought I'd live to see the day when you'd doll yourself up like Maid Marian. I nearly fell over when I saw you in the procession."

"I know," she said, with a self-satisfied smile. "It's fun to surprise people once in a while. The expression on your face was priceless."

"Compared to you and Bill, I feel woefully underdressed," I said. "But I'll make up for it tomorrow." I nodded toward the pasture. "Why haven't you loaded the ponies?"

"They're going to spend the night here," she said. "We'll bring them back to the manor tomorrow, after the show. Less stress for all concerned."

"Emma," Rob said, returning from his joust. "Did you tell Mummy and Daddy about the feast?"

"King Wilfred's feast," Will clarified, pulling up beside Rob.

"Thanks for the reminder, my lords." Emma ruffled Rob's hair, then turned to me and Bill. "King Wilfred has invited all of us to stay on for the evening feast. I've accepted, and so has the rest of our party, but I didn't want to speak for you."

Bill looked at me. "Shall we?"

"You and the boys shall," I said.

Will and Rob whooped joyfully and galloped off to share the good news with Alison and Billy. I contented myself with an inner whoop and silently blessed King Wilfred for giving me the excuse I'd needed to return to the arena alone.

"Aren't you going to join us, Lori?" Bill asked. "I'm sure our noble monarch will make room for one more at his banquet table."

"Maybe next time," I said, and went on to tell him the truth without equivocation. "I shouldn't have worn sandals today. My feet are killing me. I can't wait to soak them in a hot bath."

"You just want to wash away the manly scent of the marquee," Bill teased.

"That, too," I agreed. "I don't think you and the boys will have any trouble enjoying yourselves without me. Where will the evening feast be held?"

"In the encampment." Bill pointed to the row of poplars. "Beyond those trees. I haven't seen it yet, but I'm told it's quite impressive."

"You can tell me about it tonight," I said. "In the meantime, I'd like to say hello to everyone."

Bill, Emma, and I strolled over to the fence to join the others. I praised the children, visited with the adults, and bade them all bon appetit when it was time for them to leave. As they moved in the direction of the poplar trees, I turned on my heel and, with extremely bated breath, scurried back inside the marquee. I raced down the central aisle, peeked through the gap in the tent flaps to make sure the coast was clear, and saw to my dismay that the broken rope was no longer dangling from the quintain.

A surge of apprehension propelled me forward, but by the time I reached the gallery's lengthening shadow I was angry enough to spit tacks. The sandbag had been dragged over to lean lopsidedly against a fence post, but the rope that had trailed from it was gone. While I'd been touring the marquee and socializing, someone had removed all traces of the murder attempt from the arena.

I was certain that Edmond Deland was the culprit. Everyone expected him to tidy up the arena, just as he'd tidied up Broad Street after the horses had passed. No one would have objected to his actions or questioned his intentions as he tossed the two useless bits of rope into his wheelbarrow and trundled them away. He could remove and destroy vital evidence with impunity because no one knew that it *was* vital evidence.

I scanned the area for Edmond, but I didn't expect to see him. If he had two brain cells to rub together, I told myself, he'd be standing in front of a bonfire by now, watching my precious evidence go up in smoke.

I heaved a discouraged sigh, realized that a whiff of medieval soldier sweat still clung to my dress, and decided to call it a day. King Wilfred would have to survive the night without my help. I needed to go home and regroup. Most of all, I needed to speak with Aunt Dimity.

I thought I would beat the rush by leaving the fair an hour before it closed. Unfortunately, hundreds of other fairgoers had the same idea. A trip that should have taken ten minutes turned into a forty-minute stop-and-go nightmare that wouldn't have looked out of place on a Los Angeles freeway.

As Lilian Bunting had foretold, my little lane was clogged by drivers who'd apparently made the mistake of believing that a scenic route could also be a shortcut. I'd discovered long ago that scenic routes in England were almost guaranteed to lengthen any journey. As I inched along, listening to the blaring music, heated arguments, and incessant whining coming from the cars ahead of and behind me, I hoped my fellow travelers would learn from their experience and avoid my lane in the future.

Stanley greeted me with a piteous mewl when I finally entered the cottage, so I cuddled him, fed him, and changed his water before running upstairs to deposit my dress in the laundry hamper and climb into a bath filled with gardenia-scented bubbles. I stayed there until my feet stopped throbbing, by which time the manly scent of the marquee was but a distant memory.

Refreshed, I dressed in clean shorts and a long-sleeved T-shirt, then returned to the kitchen to throw together a salad for dinner. It had been a long while since I'd eaten my last honey cake and I didn't want a rumbling stomach to interrupt my conversation with Aunt Dimity. While I assembled the salad, I also put my thoughts in order. If I couldn't present them in a calm, coherent manner, Aunt Dimity would be hard-pressed to take me seriously.

I was washing a handful of radishes I'd harvested from my vegetable patch when the sound of jingling bells floated to me from the back garden. I cocked an ear toward the open window, recalled Jinks's sly hints about backstage intrigue, and abandoned the radishes to race outside. I was eager to hear everything he could tell me about King Wilfred.

I found Jinks waiting for me atop the stile, still clad in his jester's garb.

"Come down and I'll feed you dinner," I coaxed.

He bowed to acknowledge the invitation, but stayed where he was. "I'm afraid I can't join you this evening, Lori. My lord and master requires my presence at the feast, but I didn't want you to think I'd forgotten you."

"Can you come back after the feast?" I asked.

"I could," Jinks allowed, "but you'll be in bed and asleep by then. The king and his court will be quaffing until the wee hours."

"Surely not," I said, frowning doubtfully. "Tomorrow's Sunday. The fair will be open. If they spend all night quaffing, they'll be too groggy to work in the morning."

"Quaffing *is* their work," said Jinks. "Happily, they recover from drink almost as quickly as they put it away."

"Can we meet at the fair tomorrow?" I suggested. "You must have some time off during the day."

A puzzled smile curled Jinks's crooked mouth. "I can't remember the last time a beautiful woman craved my company. I'd like to think that you're drawn to my rugged good looks, but since I don't have any, you must be drawn to me for another reason. What is it?" His eyebrow arched inquisitively. "You're not still fretting about the broken parapet, are you?"

If I'd had the severed rope in my possession, I might have shared my suspicions with him, but since I stood there empty-handed, I chose instead to gloss over my concerns.

"I'm not fretting about anything," I said blithely. "I'm just fascinated by the fair. I feel as if I've discovered a whole new world. I was hoping to talk about it with someone who knows it as well as you do."

"Your disappointment cuts me to the quick." Jinks rubbed his pointed chin and pondered in silence for a moment. "I'll have a lunch break during the joust tomorrow. Meet me at two of the clock behind the Shire Stage. I'll provide the viands and we'll have a good old-fashioned chin-wag while we dine."

"I'll be there," I told him.

"Until tomorrow, then." He kissed his fingertips to me. "Adieu, fair one."

"Ciao, cheeky one," I said, laughing.

He disappeared over the stile and I returned to the kitchen to finish washing the radishes. I was so hungry by then that I could have eaten them whole, but I cut them up, added them to the salad, and sat down to enjoy my long-awaited meal. A forkful of leafy greens was halfway to my watering mouth when the front door opened.

"Lori?" Bill called. "We're back!"

I whimpered, but put my fork down. A glance at the wall clock told me that I'd left Bill and the boys at the fair less than two hours ago. I couldn't imagine what had brought them home so early, but after a last, longing look at my salad, I went to the front hall to find out.

It was almost worth missing a meal to see my romance hero removing the twins' riding boots. The boys, resplendent in their velvet tunics, sat on the floor with their legs in the air while Bill bent over them, his ostrich feather fluttering. His position gave me a fresh appreciation of men in tights.

"What are you doing here?" I asked. "Why aren't you at the evening feast?"

"Let's just say that it's not a G-rated event," Bill answered. "I'll tell you about it later. Right now their lordships and I are going to take much-needed baths. I hope there's a chance of having an evening feast at home, because we're starving."

"Kill the fatted calf!" Will bellowed, thrusting a small fist into the air.

"Beer! Beer! Beer!" chanted Rob, pounding the floor with both fists.

"Oh, dear lord," I said weakly.

"While we're having our baths," Bill announced, "the boys and I are going to have a little talk about good manners."

"An excellent idea." I jutted my chin toward the kitchen. "I'll prepare the feast."

Since I'd forgotten to stock up on fatted calf, we had salmon patties and a delicious green salad for dinner. Will and Rob didn't complain, nor did they demand beer instead of milk. They spoke in relatively subdued voices and although they chatted enthusiastically about their day at the fair, they didn't issue a single threat against a varlet or a knave. Their return to civilized behavior made it clear that Bill's little talk had not fallen on deaf ears.

"I don't think we'll be attending future feasts," Bill informed me.

He and I were curled up on the living room sofa. The boys were in bed, a load of laundry was in the washing machine, and Bill's unwashable hat was on the front seat of the Range Rover. I had no intention of allowing the cottage to be tainted by eau de marquee.

"Why not?" I asked. "I thought you'd have a great time at the king's banquet table."

"So did I," said Bill. "But the encampment is . . . not a place for children. Not *my* children, anyway."

"What do you mean?" I pressed.

Bill pursed his lips. "Do you remember 'free love'?"

"Vaguely," I said.

"It's still very much in vogue in the encampment," said Bill. "And it's not confined to the privacy of tents or motor homes. It's right out in the open, where everyone can see. I only hope I got the boys away in time. I don't even want to think about the pictures they might draw when they're back in school."

"Did the rest of the Anscombe Manor group leave early, too?" I asked.

"Definitely," said Bill. "We performed a simultaneous about-face as soon as the first naked bottom came into view. We must have looked like a marching band." He threw back his head and laughed, but the laugh quickly turned into a yawn. "I know it's only nine o'clock, love, but I'm beat. Coming to bed?"

"In a little while," I said. "I have to hang your costumes up to dry, and I want to tell Dimity about the fair."

Bill nodded. He was one of the handful of people who knew about Aunt Dimity's ongoing presence in the cottage, and he understood better than anyone how much she meant to me.

"Don't forget to tell Dimity about the naked bottom," he said.

"I won't," I promised.

Bill was half joking, but I wasn't joking at all. He couldn't have known it, but he'd provided me with a clue that might prove vital to the puzzle I was assembling. I had every intention of mentioning it to Aunt Dimity.

We parted at the study's door. Bill went up to the master bedroom and I made a beeline for the blue journal. I'd had plenty of time to gather my thoughts. If I kept them to myself much longer, I was fairly sure that my head would explode.

Eleven

tripped over the ottoman in my haste to reach the blue journal, so I changed direction and headed for the mantelshelf lamps instead. Once I could see properly, I lit a fire in the hearth and stood quietly for a moment, allowing the study's familiar stillness to seep into me.

"I have to be cool, calm, and collected when I present my case to Dimity," I explained to Reginald. "Otherwise, she'll think I've embarked on another vampire hunt. I'd say that I have to be like Emma, but after seeing her at the fair today, I'm no longer sure that she's a good role model for me. She seems to have a more active imagination than I gave her credit for."

My pink bunny regarded me sympathetically. The encouraging gleam in his black button eyes let me know that, whatever happened, he was on my side. His unswerving loyalty was like a tonic for my agitated soul. I reached for the blue journal with a steady hand.

I sat in the tall leather armchair before the hearth, put my tender feet on the ottoman, and rested the journal in my lap. After taking a slow breath, I opened the journal and said, "Dimity? I'm back from the fair."

Welcome home, my dear. The looping lines of royal-blue ink curled across the page as fluidly as quicksilver. *Was it as interesting as you hoped it would be?*

"Oh, yes," I said. "It was interesting."

I'm so glad. Tell me everything.

"It's like another world. . . ." I began.

I went on to describe the fair in great detail, leaving out nothing but the events that concerned me most. I created a comprehensive picture of the fair's physical appearance—the gatehouse, the winding lanes, the stalls, the open-air stages, the joust arena—as well as an impression of its festive atmosphere. I told her about the opening ceremony and the cannon blast, the water-balloon juggler and the belly dancers, the walking tree and the madrigal singers. I marveled over the variety of items for sale in the stalls and remarked on the evocative patois spoken by the vendors.

I took her up Pudding Lane and down Broad Street, pausing to praise the twins' mostly dignified performance in the king's procession and to convey my reaction to seeing Emma ride past in her finery. I brought her to the hillside picnic area, to eat honey cakes with me and Lilian while Rob and Will circled the arena, their unicorn pennons flying. I let her hear the crowd roar when the knights demonstrated their skill at arms, and I helped her to feel the ground tremble as the horses pounded toward each other in the joust. Finally, I introduced her to my ultra-studly husband, took her through the marquee, and entered the stabling area, where my narrative came to a temporary halt.

My word. The fair has certainly provided you with the change of pace you desired, Lori. It's more stimulating than the dog show, the bring-and-buy sale, and the flower show combined, unless you include the year when Patricia Shuttleworth's flea-bitten old pug won the dog show—what a kerfuffle!—but that was before your time. The fair sounds as if it fulfilled all of your wishes and then some. You must be exhausted, my dear.

"I won't be swimming the English Channel tomorrow," I told her, "but I'll get by."

I must confess that I'm not as surprised by Emma's transformation as you were. She is a gardener, after all, and gardeners are dreamers at heart. How else would they be able to look at a handful of seeds and envision a perennial border in all its glory?

"I've never thought of it that way," I conceded.

Bill's conversion, on the other hand, was wholly surprising, though I suppose we should have suspected him of protesting a bit too much. Most men would be peacocks if they were allowed to display their feathers, but I'm afraid they're discouraged from doing so in this day and age. I'm sure he's enjoying his "cool medieval dude" attire more than he ever thought he would.

"I'm enjoying it quite a bit myself," I said, recalling the pleasant scene in the front hall.

Of course you are. You're blessed with an extremely attractive husband. It would have been a waste to swaddle him in a friar's robe. Thank you for giving me such a vivid account of your day, Lori. I feel as if I've experienced every facet of King Wilfred's marvelous fair. But now you must toddle off to bed. If you're going to attend the fair again tomorrow, you'll need your rest.

I cleared my throat. "I haven't finished telling you about my day, Dimity."

I'm sorry. I didn't mean to cut you off. Please, go on.

"A couple of unusual things happened at the fair," I said.

More unusual than a walking tree?

"Yes, because the walking tree was just a guy on stilts," I replied. "The things I'm about to describe are real." I glanced at Reginald for courage, then hunkered down in my chair and tried to sound like a jaded newspaper reporter. "I have a story to tell you. It's all about love. If it's true, which I think it is, then King Wilfred's Faire is going to need a new handyman. Or possibly a new king. It depends on what happens first."

An excellent introduction, Lori. My interest is thoroughly piqued.

"My story involves a handsaw, a broken parapet, a flying sandbag, and a severed rope." I paused. "And a love triangle."

Oh, hurrah! I knew you wouldn't fail me, my dear. Please, proceed with your thrilling tale. I'm on tenterhooks!

Aunt Dimity's response contained more than a hint of sarcasm, but I didn't let it faze me. I'd sailed over the edge of reason so often that it would have been foolishly optimistic of me to expect a more sober reaction. Her playful tone made me more determined than ever to prove to her that I wasn't imagining things.

"Early this morning, before the fair opened, I heard the sound of a single handsaw coming from the direction of Bishop's Wood," I said. "If I'd heard a lot of saws, I wouldn't have thought twice about it, but the sound of one saw indicated that one person was working on one specific project."

It also indicates that someone was working in the early hours, when the fair's grounds were deserted.

"That's right." Mildly encouraged by Aunt Dimity's offering, I continued, "During the opening ceremonies, a section of the gatehouse's parapet broke away from the walkway wall. The parapet broke away when King Wilfred leaned on it. If Lord Belvedere hadn't grabbed the king's surcoat and hauled him back onto the walkway, the king would have fallen twenty feet to the ground."

Good gracious. How very distressing.

"It becomes more distressing," I said, "when one assumes that the king rehearses the opening ceremony, and that he goes through the same routine every morning. In other words, he leans on the same parapet in every performance."

A fairly safe assumption, I would say. Are you asking me to make a connection between the solitary handsaw and the broken parapet?

"Not yet," I said, refusing to be rushed. "I didn't connect the two until a young man named Edmond Deland arrived on the scene to clear away the debris. Edmond is the fair's maintenance man, but he doesn't dress in period attire. In fact, he seems to be the only employee who wears normal clothing to work."

Does his attire suggest a failure to enter wholeheartedly into the spirit of the fair?

"I believe it does," I said. "Furthermore, his reaction to the parapet incident struck me as . . . odd. When he spotted the debris, he looked sullen. When he peered up at the gap in the wall, he appeared to be angry and disappointed. And I couldn't help noticing that he had a handsaw in his wheelbarrow."

Ah, I see! You believe that Edmond Deland used his handsaw to damage the parapet early in the morning, in hopes of disrupting the opening ceremonies. When the ceremonies went on as planned, he was angry and disappointed, because his scheme had failed. Am I on the right track?

"Almost," I said. "I'm now going to skip ahead a bit. Do you remember the madrigal singers I mentioned?"

How could I forget little Mirabel, the pretty girl with hazel eyes and the voice of an angel?

"While I was listening to the madrigal singers," I said, "I saw Edmond Deland again, half hidden in the shadows between two stalls. He stood as still as a statue and gazed only at Mirabel, as if he worshipped the ground she walked on. I promise you, Dimity, his longing for her was almost palpable. She seemed to be unaware of him, and he didn't draw attention to himself."

Any sensible observer would conclude that Edmond Deland is hopelessly in love with little Mirabel. Et voilà—we have two sides of our love triangle! Who completes it, I wonder?

"I'm getting to that," I said patiently. "As I told you earlier, the sound of trumpets announced the start of the king's procession. Mirabel got very excited when she heard the trumpets, and the group promptly moved from their quiet alleyway to Broad Street. It seemed to me as if they moved in order to allow Mirabel to watch the procession."

How did Edmond react to their departure?

"When he heard the trumpets, he looked absolutely furious," I said. "He didn't say a word, but he stomped off in a huff. I followed Mirabel."

Naturally.

"She could hardly keep still during the early parts of the procession," I said. "She was all aflutter, as if she were waiting for the man of her dreams to come into view. When she saw King Wilfred, she gasped, and when he blew a kiss to her, she blushed like the setting sun and dropped a curtsy to him. If the other singers hadn't dragged her away, I think she might have followed the king up Broad Street."

The king, therefore, is the third person in our love triangle.

"Which makes him Edmond's rival," I pointed out.

So it does. Does the king realize that he's the rival of an angry young man with a handsaw?

"I don't know," I said. "But I can tell you what happened next."

I quickly related the quintain incident, underscoring Bill's assertion that it was an exceptionally rare occurrence. I went on to describe my discovery of the partially severed rope as well as my failed attempt to retrieve it, then sat back and waited for Aunt Dimity to draw her own conclusions. She didn't take long.

Correct me if I'm wrong, Lori, but you seem to be suggesting that Edmond's goal isn't merely to disrupt the fair, but to murder his chief rival.

"I realize that it sounds far-fetched," I said calmly. "And I may be jumping to a few thousand conclusions, but yes, I believe that Edmond Deland is trying to kill King Wilfred."

It's a very serious accusation.

"I know it is, but think about it, Dimity," I said. "Edmond is an ideal suspect. He has access to every square inch of the fair, night and day. He has the tools he'd need to sabotage the parapet as well as the quintain. He can also get rid of the evidence easily, because it's his job to keep the grounds clean."

I don't doubt that Edmond has the means and the opportunity to carry out the deeds you've ascribed to him. I do, however, question his motivation.

"He's insane with jealousy," I said.

He'd have to be insane, to be jealous of Calvin Malvern. The Calvin I knew was an affable, pudgy daydreamer. I find it difficult to think of him as the answer to a maiden's prayers.

"Ren fests are all about role-playing," I explained. "At the fair, Tommy Grout, ordinary teenager, becomes Harold le Rouge, squire to the noble Sir Peregrine. Similarly, Calvin Malvern, pudgy daydreamer, becomes King Wilfred, lecherous swain."

Why must he be lecherous?

"Oh, sorry," I said, sitting up straighter. "I forgot to tell you about Bill's naked bottom."

I'm not entirely certain that I want to hear about Bill's naked bottom.

"I'm not talking about his personal bottom," I said hastily. "I'm talking about the naked bottom he saw when he and the twins were crossing the performers' encampment on their way to the king's evening feast."

I'm at once baffled and intrigued. Are the performers nudists?

"Not exactly." I cleared my throat again, then asked hesitantly, "Have you ever heard of free love?"

For goodness' sake, Lori, free love wasn't invented yesterday, as so many of you children seem to think. I believe the term was coined in the 1860s, though it didn't have quite the same meaning then. Nevertheless, I'm well acquainted with its modern meaning. What part does free love play in your story?

"According to Bill, free love is, if you'll forgive the expression, rampant in the encampment," I replied. "Edmond is so conservative that he won't even wear a costume while he's at work. I can't imagine that he would approve of the behavior Bill witnessed in the camp. Calvin, on the other hand, is in love with Ren fests. He probably includes hanky-panky in his job description." Another idea darted into my head and I ran with it. "It would explain why Calvin is spending the summer in a luxurious motor home instead of in his uncle's farmhouse. Horace Malvern wouldn't allow things like that to happen under his roof."

I take your point. Calvin Malvern might not indulge in naughty shenanigans, but King Wilfred wouldn't hesitate to take advantage of an impressionable young madrigal singer.

"I'm just guessing," I said cautiously, "but I think Edmond is a romantic. I think he wants to rescue his innocent angel from the king's lewd clutches, and at the same time punish the king for trifling with her."

Murder is a rather extreme form of punishment.

"Love has been known to push people to extremes," I said wisely.

There was a long pause before the graceful handwriting continued.

Well, well, well. . . . You did leave a few interesting details out of your initial account, Lori. What a very busy day you've had.

"I know what you're going to tell me, Dimity," I said. "You're going to tell me that I've gone off half-cocked again, that I'm reading too much into the situation, and that my conclusions are based on too few facts. Before you do, though, ask yourself one question: What are the odds against King Wilfred having two bizarre, near-fatal accidents in one day?"

I'm not sure they're as high as you seem to think they are. As Lilian Bunting pointed out to you, King Wilfred's Faire is a complex form of theater. Things are bound to go wrong from time to time in any theatrical venture.

"But would you expect spectacularly bad things to happen to the same person twice in one day?" I pressed.

Perhaps not. But I wouldn't expect someone like Edmond to engineer spectacularly bad things. If your observations are correct, his murder attempts haven't taken place in dark corners, but in full view of large audiences. Would a conservative young man have such a flair for drama?

"It's not about drama," I countered. "Edmond is being pragmatic. Sabotage allows him to be somewhere else when the so-called accidents happen. He's cleverly distancing himself from the crime scenes."

But would a romantic young man use sabotage as a means of achieving his goals? Wouldn't he simply snatch up a sword and fight for his angel's honor? Heaven knows, there are enough swords lying about for him to use.

"If Edmond attacked the king openly, he'd be carted off to jail," I said. "Edmond can't defend Mirabel's honor if he's behind bars."

True.

I pursed my lips and sighed wearily. "I don't have all of the answers, Dimity. But my gut tells me that something funny is going on at the fair."

Something funny . . . and potentially deadly. Perhaps it isn't good to be king.

I read her words twice before asking tentatively, "Do you think I may be on to something?"

I wouldn't go so far as to accuse anyone of attempted murder just yet. We may be dealing with a case of malicious mischief. Someone may wish to frighten people away from the fair by making it seem unsafe.

"Why would someone do that?" I asked.

I can think of a dozen reasons—spite, envy, jealousy, greed, vengeance. Your task will be to discover the correct one.

"Will it?" I said, my spirits rising.

Indeed, it will. I believe that the situation merits further investigation.

"You do?" I said, blinking at the journal in happy disbelief.

I most certainly do. I'm glad that you're attending the fair again tomorrow. It will give you the opportunity to gather more information. I, for one, would like to know who was wielding the solitary handsaw this morning and what he or she was doing with it. If someone was seen making unnecessary alterations to the parapet, we may have our culprit.

"I'll ask around," I said.

I'd also like to know more about the quintain. Do the knights practice their skills before displaying them to the public? If so, the saboteur must have tampered with the rope after the practice session, but before the fair opened.

"If he damaged the rope before the practice session, it would have broken too soon," I said, nodding eagerly. "And if he damaged it while the fair was in progress, he would have run too great a risk of being seen. The fair was crawling with people almost as soon as the gates opened, and most of them were just wandering around, taking in the sights."

Our culprit may have been seen by one of the performers. Try to find a witness who can place him in the arena within the proper time frame, preferably with a sharp knife in his hand.

"I'll do my best," I assured her.

I would also urge you to wear your costume tomorrow.

"After seeing Bill and Emma, I don't need urging," I said. "I felt like a party pooper today."

I want you to feel like a performer tomorrow. Find out if anyone involved in the fair has a grudge against King Wilfred. People will confide in you more readily if they think you're a cast member. Let your costume be your disguise. It may even gain you access to the encampment.

"I'll outwench the wenches," I promised. "But I'll keep my clothes on in the encampment."

I'm relieved to hear it. I need hardly tell you to keep an ear open for general gossip.

"I'm going to have lunch with Jinks the jester tomorrow," I said. "He's promised to clue me in on the scuttlebutt."

You speak the gossip's language fluently, Lori. Finch has taught you well.

"I'll give Bill a crash course on the way to church tomorrow morning," I said. "It'll be useful to have an extra set of eyes and ears working for us behind the scenes."

Will you share your suspicions with him?

I gave the matter careful consideration, then shook my head. "I won't put Bill into the picture until I've collected more facts. If I jump the gun, he'll just laugh at me."

Your husband is a dear man, but he can be sarcastic at times.

"Yes, he can," I agreed fervently. "Especially when it comes to my suspicions."

If you could discover tangible proof to support your claims, Bill would be more willing to give credence to them. It's a pity about the rope, but perhaps something else will turn up. If it does, please try not to lose it.

"Thanks for the tip, Dimity," I said, rolling my eyes.

Sarcasm runs in the family, I see. Never mind. I've been known to indulge in it myself on occasion. Back to business. It's up to you, my dear, to find out who the saboteur is and—if you can do so without compromising your own safety—to stop him before he harms the king. It may quite literally be a matter of life and death.

"Leave it to me, Dimity." I peered grimly at the journal as I paraphrased Lilian Bunting's words. "I don't want King Wilfred's Faire spoiled by bloodshed."

No indeed. On a lighter note: I wonder what impact the performers' free-and-easy lifestyle will have on the village.

"I don't think it'll have any impact on the village," I said. "Most of the performers are staying in the encampment. If they go anywhere, it'll be to Oxford or some other big town. Finch isn't exactly the excitement capital of the universe."

You may be right. It's getting late, Lori. You should go to bed. You'll need your wits about you if you're to catch our saboteur tomorrow.

A warm rush of gratitude welled up in me as I read the last sentence. I'd entered the study expecting to be doubted, teased, even ridiculed for inventing yet another improbable scenario. Instead, Aunt Dimity had believed my story, with reasonable reservations, and suggested several lines of inquiry for me to pursue. Her confidence in me had never been more apparent.

Smiling, I traced the fine copperplate with a fingertip. "Thanks for hearing me out, Dimity. I wasn't sure you'd ever listen to me again, after the vampire fiasco."

Was it a fiasco? I thought it was a highly successful and rewarding enterprise. Now run along, my dear. We'll speak again tomorrow.

I waited until the curling lines of royal-blue ink had faded from the page, then closed the journal and hugged it to my chest. I was still smiling as I tidied the study, bade Reginald good night, and went to the laundry room, but as I removed the costumes from the washing machine and hung them up to dry, my mind traveled back to the fair.

Where was Edmond Deland? I wondered. And what would he do next?

Twelve

There was no need to load the twins' ponies into trailers and transport them to Bishop's Wood the following morning, but Bill and the boys rose at the crack of dawn anyway, and I rose with them. They were champing at the bit to get back to the fair. For very different reasons, so was I.

I intended to change into my garb after I returned from church. Will and Rob wanted to jump right into theirs, but I insisted that they put them aside until they were at the fair. I didn't want porridge stains on their clean tunics. Bill clinched the decision by zipping their costumes and his into the garment bag and stowing it in the Range Rover with his hat.

After some discussion, the overloaded day pack was left at home. Bill argued successfully that they could find anything they might need at the fair, including rain ponchos, bottled water, and sunblock. If the temperature took an unexpected dip, he reasoned, they could borrow leather capes from the foot soldiers.

I began my fact-finding mission as soon as we sat down for breakfast. I doubted that Bill would be able to tell me much about the solitary handsaw, because he and the twins had arrived at the fair long after the telltale sound had drifted to me in the back garden, but he would almost certainly be able to describe the early morning activities in the arena.

"Bill," I said, passing the honey pot to him, "did the knights rehearse their show yesterday morning?"

"They were hard at it when we arrived," he said. "Perry and Jack may be entertainers, but their skills are real. They take practice sessions seriously."

"So they went through the whole routine," I said. "The spear-throwing, the ring-jousting, the quintain . . ."

"The whole nine yards," Bill confirmed.

"How long did they practice?" I asked.

"Two solid hours," he said, spreading a dollop of honey on his toast. "Perry told me that they practice from seven until nine every morning. It's better to work the horses in the cool morning air, and it gives them plenty of time to rest before the afternoon performance."

"Were the soldiers and the squires there as well?" I asked.

"The squires were." Bill leaned forward on his elbows, as if he found the subject interesting. "The knights can't don their armor without help, and they certainly wouldn't be able to practice ring jousting without a trained squire to hold the rings for them. If Harold and Drogo hadn't been there—"

"Drogo?" I interrupted.

"Sir Jacques' squire." Bill smiled wryly. "His real name is Kevin McGee, but he prefers to be known as Drogo Dragonfire."

"Who wouldn't?" I said.

"At any rate," Bill continued, "if Harold and Drogo hadn't been there, the knights would have had to dismount every time they wanted to change weapons. It's not easy to get on and off a horse while you're wearing armor and carrying a lance."

"I can imagine," I said. "Why didn't the soldiers hand them their weapons?"

"The soldiers didn't attend yesterday's practice session." Bill gave the twins a sidelong glance before adding in a meaningful undertone, "I think they'd enjoyed themselves a bit too much the night before."

"They were drunk as lords," Will said conversationally, between spoonfuls of porridge.

"Sloshed," Rob clarified.

"Pie-eyed," Will remarked.

"Legless," Rob offered, in case I hadn't understood.

"I . . . I beg your pardon?" I said, flabbergasted.

"It's what soldiers do," Rob explained matter-of-factly. "Drogo said the soldiers had sore heads because they can't say no to a pint of the hard stuff."

"They were quaffing," Will added helpfully. "And ravishing wenches."

"What's ravishing wenches, Daddy?" asked Rob, turning a pair of innocent brown eyes on his father.

My mouth fell open and Bill choked on a snort of laughter. I shot him a piercing look and he sobered immediately, but his voice trembled with suppressed mirth as he answered Rob's question.

"It's a game for grown-ups," he said, and went on briskly, "I think we've seen enough of the arena for the time being, boys. What do you say to exploring the rest of the fair today?"

Rob and Will were amenable and I was relieved. It seemed to me that they'd already spent far too much time at the arena. I wanted my sons to learn about spinning and weaving, not quaffing and ravishing. I was so rattled by their unexpected contributions to our breakfast conversation that it took me a moment to regain my focus.

"What did the knights and the squires do after practice?" I asked. "Did they hang around the marquee, polishing armor?"

"Harold and Drogo went out back to look after the horses," said Bill. "But Perry and Jack cleaned themselves up and went to Gatehouse Square, to be on hand for the opening ceremonies. King Wilfred and his court assemble in Gatehouse Square at nine-thirty on the dot, and the ceremonies commence at nine thirty-five precisely. Calvin may seem like an easygoing guy, but he runs a tight ship."

"It must be challenging to run a tight ship with so many free spirits onboard." I sipped my tea. "Have there been any mutinies?"

"Not that I've noticed," said Bill. "I told you yesterday, everyone likes Cal. I think they respect his management skills. A strong king makes for a happy kingdom, apparently."

I didn't want Bill to catch on to the fact that I was pumping him for information, so I dug into my cheese omelet and let Bill work on his. After he'd eaten a few bites, I began again.

"The grounds must be pretty quiet before the gates open," I commented. "Apart from the arena area, of course."

"The place is like a ghost town," Bill agreed. "Things don't get going until nine o'clock, when the food vendors show up. I could smell the steak-and-kidney pies baking while Will and Rob were grooming Thunder and Storm. I almost drooled all over my dude shirt."

"It's called a poet's shirt," I told him. "I saw a whole rack full of them in one of the stalls."

"We've finished," Will and Rob announced.

"In that case, you'd better run upstairs," I said. "I want your teeth brushed, your hands washed, and your hair combed before we go to church."

The twins' faces registered surprise, as did their father's.

"Are we going to church?" Bill inquired.

"Of course we are," I said. "We don't want the vicar to think we've forgotten him, do we? And it seems to me that a certain pair of young men will benefit greatly from a period of quiet reflection."

Bill took the hint and nodded to the boys. "Off you go, guys. Teeth, hands, and hair."

I let Bill finish his omelet in peace, but resumed my interrogation while he and I loaded the dishwasher.

"When do the rest of the vendors set up?" I asked.

"Most of them come wandering in around half past nine," he replied.

"Do the vendors live in the encampment?" I asked.

"Most do," said Bill. "Some live at home during the week and spend weekends at the fair. They're called weekenders."

"Fascinating." I closed the dishwasher, then asked another question out of sheer curiosity. "What do the non-weekenders do during the week?"

"I imagine the knights practice jousting. As for the others . . ." Bill shrugged. "I guess we'll find out."

As Bill and I went upstairs to tend to our own teeth, hands, and hair, I analyzed the timetable he had constructed for me. If my calculations were correct, the arena would have been virtually deserted for a full thirty minutes after the rehearsal had ended. Once the squires had taken the horses to the stabling area and the knights had departed for Gatehouse Square, the saboteur would have had more than enough time to damage the quintain's rope, unobserved by any members of the jousting crew.

The food vendors, on the other hand, could have seen him. They'd gone to work an hour before the fair had opened, and their stalls were so close to the arena that Bill had been able to identify the savory aroma wafting from their ovens. I made a mental note to visit Pudding Lane as soon as I reached the fair. As an afterthought, I decided that my first stop would be the honey cake stall. I saw nothing wrong with mixing business with pleasure.

The early service at St. George's Church was the only one my menfolk would consider attending, because it was the only one that would allow them to arrive at the fair before ten o'clock. My last-minute decision to bring them with me meant that we got a late start, but when we left the cottage we still had a modest chance of reaching a pew before the vicar offered up the first prayer.

Thankfully, we left early enough to avoid the stream of vehicles I'd encountered the previous morning. I savored the sensation of having our lane to ourselves, though I was distressed to see the glint of beer bottles in a ditch and a few discarded chewing gum wrappers clinging to the hedgerows. Under normal circumstances, we would have stopped immediately to pick up the trash, but since we were running late, I decided to wait until after church to begin our cleanup campaign.

While I ruminated darkly on litter and litterbugs, Bill, Will, and Rob performed the raucous family rituals that made a trip to Finch complete. They cheered for the ponies when we passed Anscombe Manor's curving drive, and even though the Pym sisters were away at the seaside, the boys saluted their redbrick house when we passed it. All three hooted like hyenas when we reached the top of the humpbacked bridge. Bill encouraged me to join in the hooting, but we were all shocked into silence by the sight that met our eyes when we came down the bridge and saw the village stretched out before us.

It was as if a tornado had swept through Finch, leaving a trail of destruction in its wake. Candy wrappers, potato chip bags, grocery sacks, empty beer bottles, and odd bits of clothing carpeted the village green. Crumpled soda cans lay in drifts along the pavement and an abandoned fashion magazine fluttered forlornly on the bench near the war memorial. The pub's sign hung at a crazy angle, a leg was missing from one of the bins in front of the greengrocer's shop, and a splintered web of cracks covered the Emporium's big display window. It looked as though someone had been sick on the tea-room's doorstep.

Bill and I were too stunned to speak, but the twins didn't hesitate to share their take on the situation.

"Pirates," Will said decisively.

"Marauding pirates," agreed Rob.

"We're too far from the sea for pirates," said Bill, finding his voice.

"We're not too far from the fair," I said tersely.

"No one from the fair would do this," said Bill. "They may be free spirits, but they're not fools. It's in their interest to get along with locals."

"Who, then?" I demanded.

"Tourists," Bill answered succinctly. "I think we can lay the blame for this mess on marauding *tourists*."

I was almost too angry to speak. "If they've touched St. George's, I'll hunt them down and——"

"Let's find out, shall we?" Bill interrupted, to keep me from spoiling the Sabbath day with strong speech. Peering somberly through the windshield, he put his foot on the accelerator and drove forward slowly, almost at a snail's pace, as if we were inspecting the site of a natural disaster.

Someone had smeared mustard on the schoolhouse doors and trampled the flowers Emma had planted around the war memorial, but the rest of the village had escaped obvious damage. Wysteria Lodge, where Bill had his office, appeared to be unharmed, as did Crabtree Cottage, Briar Cottage, the old schoolmaster's house, the vicarage, and Mr. Barlow's house.

The church seemed to be fine as well. The lych-gate hung solidly from its hinges and none of the headstones in the cemetery had been knocked over or defaced. Relieved, we parked on the verge, released the boys from their booster seats, and hurried inside. Our slow progress through the village had delayed our arrival considerably.

It was impossible to enter the church quietly. The weighty oak door creaked when Bill opened it and boomed when it swung shut behind us, and we could do nothing to keep our footsteps from echoing hollowly as we made our way across the flagstone floor.

A pale-faced congregation turned to watch us as we shuffled contritely into a back pew, and the vicar, who looked shattered, waited courteously until we were settled to continue the service. When he mounted the pulpit, I expected him to read the first lesson, but he'd apparently been inspired by recent events to give a sermon instead.

"Matthew 24:6." Theodore Bunting's pleasantly sonorous voice was cracked with fatigue and his long, dolorous face was haggard. "'Ye shall hear of wars and rumors of wars: see that ye be not troubled: for all these things must come to pass, but the end is not yet.'"

"Is he talking about the end of the world?" I whispered to Bill.

"Must have been a rough night," Bill whispered back.

Thirteen

The vicar's doom-laden sermon was mercifully short, and he brought the service to a close as swiftly as decency would allow. Afterward, he didn't stand at the church door to exchange pleasantries with his departing flock, but staggered off to the vicarage, as if he needed to conserve his strength in order to make it through the next service.

The rest of the villagers milled around the churchyard, twittering excitedly as they exchanged views on the catastrophe that had befallen Finch. A surprisingly large number of my neighbors had shown up for the early service. I wondered how many of them had come in order to get a jump start on the fair and how many had needed spiritual aid to sustain them after seeing the village green.

While the twins ran off to play hide-and-seek among the headstones, Bill and I gravitated toward a circle that included Emma and Derek Harris, Lilian Bunting, Mr. Barlow, Grant Tavistock, Charles Bellingham, Christine Peacock, and Sally Pyne. Sally was venting her spleen when we joined the group.

"What is the world coming to when full-grown adults behave like rampaging water buffalo?" she demanded "What kind of example are they setting for their children? They should be ashamed of themselves, every last one of them. If

I'd been here, I would have given them a few choice words *and* the back of my hand."

"If I'd been here, I'd've broken a few heads," growled Mr. Barlow.

"George Wetherhead won't come out of his house," said Christine Peacock. "He's a nervous wreck."

"Teddy's terribly shaken, too," Lilian said, looking anxiously at the vicarage. "He thought he'd left hooliganism behind when we left London."

"What happened?" I asked. "Who's responsible for the mess?"

"Yahoos," said Mr. Barlow.

"Savages," said Sally Pyne.

"Barbarians," said Grant Tavistock.

"Fairgoers," said Lilian. "A flood of them swept through the village on their way to and from the fair. They stormed the shops, wrought havoc on the village green, and vanished, like a plague of locusts."

"Locusts are a force of nature," Emma pointed out. "Our disaster was definitely man-made."

"Did it go on all night?" I asked, surveying their wan faces.

"No," said Lilian, "but most of us were too worn out after our day at the fair to deal with the situation when we returned home."

"I was up till all hours finishing Peggy's new bodice," Sally put in. "I'm going to make her pay dearly for robbing me of a good night's sleep."

"Why did you have to make it overnight?" Emma asked.

Sally's eyes twinkled. "She heard about the wenches and the belly dancers. I have a feeling that Jasper will be left in charge of the Emporium from now on, while Peggy takes over the stall at the fair."

"If she goes at all," Lilian added portentously. "I'm afraid that yesterday's events have revived her antipathy toward the fair."

"I'm not too keen on it myself, at the moment," said Derek. "People threw rubbish out of their car windows as they drove through Finch. We're lucky no one was hurt."

"Very lucky," said Grant. "A beer bottle came within inches of striking Charles on the head."

We all turned to Charles, to express our sympathy and to make sure that he was all right.

"No harm done," he said airily. "I must say that when Grant and I purchased Crabtree Cottage, we didn't expect to find ourselves in the middle of a war zone. We were afraid to stand on our own doorstep yesterday."

"Finch isn't normally a war zone," Lilian assured him.

"It's normally the most peaceful little village in the world," I added earnestly.

"It wasn't yesterday," said Christine Peacock. "Dick had to use the soda siphon on some idiot who was swinging on the pub sign. After that, he put two of the Sciaparelli boys on the door, to keep drunks away from the pub. Half of the people who drove through the village were squiffy before they got here."

"The sober ones were just as bad," said Sally Pyne. "I left my niece in charge of the tearoom while I was at the fair. A riot nearly broke out when she ran out of scones. When she ran out of fairy cakes, she was so terrified that she locked the front door and hid in the kitchen until I got back."

"Teddy attempted to remonstrate with the invaders,"

said Lilian, "but he was outnumbered and ignored. Peggy Taxman was so busy minding the till at the Emporium that she didn't have time to assert her authority, and everyone else who might have helped Teddy was at the fair." She bowed her head remorsefully. "I can't tell you how guilty I feel. While I was off watching magicians and knights, my poor husband was under siege."

"If you're guilty, we're all guilty," said Bill, putting a comforting hand on her shoulder. "We underestimated the destructive power of irresponsible day-trippers."

As he withdrew his hand, I saw him glance at his watch, then look toward the boys, who were using willow wands to conduct an action-packed sword fight among the headstones.

"Go," I told him. "You can leave the Rover here with me. Emma and Derek can take you and the boys to the fair."

"Shouldn't we stay here to help with the cleanup?" he asked.

"No, you shouldn't," I said. "We'll have plenty of opportunities to teach our sons civic responsibility. Right now they have a responsibility to their friends. If they stay here, they'll let Alison and Billy down."

"What do you think, Emma?" Bill asked.

"I think Lori has a point," Emma replied. "The show must go on."

"I agree," Lilian said firmly. "Rob and Will have earned their moment in the sun. We mustn't allow the inconsiderate actions of a few bad apples to rob them of it."

"Hear, hear," I said.

"Emma can drop me off at home on the way to the fair," said Derek. "I'll round up a crew of riding students and stable hands and bring them back with me in the van. We'll manage the cleanup without you, Bill."

"Well," Bill said reluctantly, "if you're sure. . . ."

"The motion is carried," said Emma. "We'd better get going. It's already half past nine. I want to make sure that the ponies have been looked after properly, and I'd like the children to practice carrying the pennons before they ride in the king's procession this afternoon."

"I'll round up the twins," I said.

"I'll fetch our garb," said Bill.

I felt a twinge of regret as I saw them off, but it was a very small one. Although I regretted putting my investigation on hold, my priorities were clear. My village needed me. I wouldn't have been able to look my neighbors in the face if I'd gone to the fair while they floundered beneath a mountain of trash.

"What happened to the window in the Emporium?" I asked, after I'd rejoined my friends.

"It was struck by a flying mango," Charles answered. "Five or six little darlings had a food fight in front of the Emporium with whatever they could nick from the greengrocer's bins."

"Their parents paid for the produce and the damage to Peggy's window," Mr. Barlow told me, "but they didn't stay behind to clear up the mess."

"I'm afraid that task has been left to us," said Lilian.

"Ladies and gentlemen, if I may have your attention?"

Peggy Taxman's voice was loud enough to wake the dead, but they stayed put, while every living soul in the cemetery swung around to face her. She stood on the church steps, her hands on her hips, her massive bosom heaving with righteous indignation. The morning sun glinting on her rhinestone-studded glasses made it seem as though sparks were flying from her eyes.

"I told you a month ago that it would be a mistake to let Calvin Malvern impose his will on our community," she thundered. "I told you that nothing good would come of it. I predicted chaos and calamity . . ."

"And profits for the Emporium," Sally interpolated under her breath.

". . . and ruin for our village, but would you listen? No, you would not. Some of you have been so foolish as to welcome these undesirables into your homes."

"Don't you dare criticize my wizard!" Sally shouted, stamping her foot angrily. "Magus Silveroak is a perfect gentleman." In an aside to our circle, she explained, "The name on his credit card is Gary Pelham, but he likes to be called by his wizard name. It helps him to stay in character."

"It's the same with Merlot," Christine commented. "The name on *his* credit card is Albert Moysey, but he won't answer to anything but Merlot. And I won't have a word said against our magician *or* our jugglers," she went on in a much louder voice. "They had nothing to do with what happened yesterday."

Newcomers to the village invariably kept their opinions to themselves in Peggy's presence, but Grant Tavistock set a new precedent by speaking up in defense of the guest he and Charles had welcomed to Crabtree Cottage.

"You can leave our mime out of it, too," he called. "Simon was devastated when he returned from the fair last night and saw the state of the village." He read the question in our eyes and added quietly, "His name is Simon Maris, but since he's a mime, he doesn't really answer to anything."

We nodded, our curiosity satisfied, and turned our attention to Peggy Taxman, who was looking daggers at our circle of dissidents.

"You're missing the point," she bellowed. "The fair itself brought this blight upon our village. If it weren't for the fair, Finch would still be a haven of peace and tranquillity. Because of the fair, many of us have lost whatever chance we might have had to win the tidy cottage competition."

The startled gasp that traveled through the churchyard indicated that I wasn't the only one who'd forgotten about the tidy cottage competition.

"The judging was to take place this afternoon," Lilian murmured.

"It'll have to be canceled," said Sally. "You can't see half of the cottages for the rubbish."

"We'll never shift it all by this afternoon," Mr. Barlow said gloomily.

"A time-honored village tradition has been disrupted because of the fair," Peggy continued. "Our lives have been blighted by the fair. If we'd shown some backbone at the May meeting, we could have prevented—" She broke off suddenly and peered toward the village green.

Every head capable of movement in the churchyard swiveled to look in the same direction.

"Do you hear . . . music?" I asked hesitantly.

"It sounds like drums and . . . bagpipes," Mr. Barlow said, cocking an ear toward the village green.

"Definitely bagpipes," said Lilian.

"Come on," I said, starting for the lych-gate. "Let's find out what's going on."

"You can't leave!" Peggy roared, as her audience followed me into the lane. "You haven't heard my plans yet!"

"I don't know what she's worried about," Sally muttered. "If she stays here, we'll still be able to hear her on the green."

Lilian and I stifled uncharitable chuckles and kept walking. By the time we reached the green, we'd been joined by nearly every villager who hadn't attended the early service at St. George's. A few who were trudging along in bathrobes and bedroom slippers grumbled that they wouldn't have bothered to set their alarm clocks if they'd known the Scots were going to invade.

Miranda Morrow never went to church, but she was on her knees nonetheless, replanting the trampled flower beds around the war memorial. She waved a muddy trowel at us when we arrived.

"We have visitors!" she announced cheerfully.

Her words weren't entirely necessary, because we couldn't have missed the visitors if we'd tried. Forty men from the fair were arrayed in ranks at the bottom of the humpbacked bridge. The first row was made up of foot soldiers in leather jerkins, the second, of courtiers in fine velvets and silks. The last two contained a mixed bag of pirates, Vikings, monks, beggars, and bards.

Most of them looked bleary-eyed, as if they'd stayed up late the night before, quaffing. I couldn't imagine how they'd managed the long slog from Bishop's Wood to the village until I saw two of Horace Malvern's farm trucks parked in front of the tearoom and realized that they'd used modern transport.

Six drummers stood before the assembled men, beating a stirring rhythm on hip-slung marching drums.

"They're called tabors," Lilian informed me.

"What are?" I asked.

"The drums," she replied.

The drummers were flanked by a pair of pipers wearing kilts in muted shades of brown and gray. Their bagpipes were smaller and simpler than the pipes I'd seen in Scotland, and the sound they produced wasn't quite as deafening.

A short, round-bellied man stood before the drummers, facing us. Like the soldiers, he was wearing a leather jerkin, but his black cape and the black ostrich plume in his cap suggested that he might be their leader. He waited until our group had come to a somewhat befuddled halt in front of the war memorial, then raised his hand to stop the music and strode across the green to meet us.

"I am Sir James le Victorieux, Knight of the Southern Cross, and the king's field marshal," he announced. "I come to parley with your ruler."

The villagers parted automatically to let Peggy Taxman through. She stepped forward and faced the field marshal unflinchingly.

"My lady." Sir James doffed his feathered cap and revealed a balding pate. "I am commissioned by His Royal Highness, King Wilfred the Good, to offer our services to you. My liege lord has commanded us to restore your charming hamlet to its original, untrammeled condition. I await your permission to proceed."

Peggy surveyed him from head to foot, then snapped, "Well, don't stand there like a booby. Get to work!"

The corners of Sir James's mouth twitched, as if he found Peggy comical rather than intimidating, but he wisely chose to contain his merriment as he acknowledged her order. He turned to face his men, raised his right arm, and brought it down in a chopping motion.

Those of us gathered around the war memorial watched in stunned amazement as the performers responded to the field marshal's signal. They broke ranks to form squads, retrieved garbage bags and cleaning paraphernalia from Mr. Malvern's farm trucks, and began to move through the heart of the village, clearing debris as they went.

It was as though a bearded, hungover, and sweaty maid service had arrived to clean and polish Finch until it shone. One squad did nothing but gather soda cans. Another picked up beer bottles. Yet another collected paper trash, and the pirates removed everything else. A bard armed with a bucket and a mop cleaned the tearoom's doorstep while a Viking scrubbed the schoolhouse doors. A pair of beggars measured the Emporium's broken display window.

"I'll brew some coffee," Christine Peacock said quietly. "They look as if they could use it."

"A cup of tea never goes amiss," Sally Pyne observed. "And I think they'll welcome a bite to eat when they're done."

In less than ten minutes, Lilian Bunting, Peggy Taxman, and I were the only villagers remaining on the green. The rest—even the ones in bathrobes—had gone off to prepare a buffet-style meal for the hardworking squads and set it up in the schoolhouse.

"Oh, my," I said softly. "I don't know who I love more at this moment—King Wilfred's men or my neighbors."

Peggy Taxman snorted derisively. "What's so wonderful about the king's men? They're only doing what they ought. As for our neighbors . . . hasn't it dawned on anyone that we'll have to go through the whole process over and over again every weekend from now until the fair closes?"

A truck's door opened and Horace Malvern climbed down from the cab, a cell phone pressed to his ear. He shoved the phone into his pocket as he hastened toward us.

"Lori, Lilian, Peggy," he said, nodding to each of us in turn. His brow was furrowed and his ruddy face was even redder than usual. "I'm sorry about all of this. I should have seen it coming."

"*I* saw it coming," Peggy reminded him.

"That you did." Mr. Malvern paused to glance at his watch, then looked toward Fivefold Farm, frowning.

"Is something wrong, Mr. Malvern?" I asked, suddenly alert.

"It's gone five past ten," he said. "We should have heard the cannon by now."

"I didn't realize that it could be heard from here," said Lilian.

"I heard it yesterday," Peggy told her. "And I was at the counter inside the Emporium."

I felt a flutter of unease as I followed Mr. Malvern's gaze, but quickly realized that I was being overly suspicious. I had no reason to worry about a silent weapon. If someone had tried to use the cannon to kill King Wilfred, it would have gone off with a big bang.

"I've called in a few favors," Mr. Malvern said, shrugging off the distraction, "and I've made some arrangements that should keep the village from being overrun from now on."

"What sort of arrangements?" Peggy asked coldly.

"Police officers will set up two drink-driving checkpoints," he replied, "one at the fair's car park and one here, in the village. They'll administer breath tests to anyone who appears to be over the limit. As well, the county is going to put a road crew to work repairing your lane, Lori."

"My lane doesn't need to be repaired," I said.

"I know it doesn't," Mr. Malvern said patiently, "but the roadwork signs will discourage most drivers from using it as a throughway."

"Brilliant!" I said, beaming at him.

Mr. Malvern scratched the back of his neck and sighed. "You'll still have some extra traffic. We won't be able to keep all of the fair's patrons out of Finch——"

"Nor would we want to," Peggy interrupted. "The decent ones are good for business."

"——but we'll keep out most of the yobbos," Mr. Malvern concluded. "There's nothing like the sight of a few coppers to keep folk on the straight and narrow."

"If Finch awarded medals for problem-solving," Lilian declared, "you'd receive one, Horace. I'm going straight home to put Teddy's mind at ease. He'll want to offer up prayers of thanksgiving for our industrious helpers and our kind and thoughtful friend." She patted Mr. Malvern's shoulder and turned toward the vicarage.

"If you'll excuse me, I have other business to attend to," Peggy said loftily. "I won't congratulate you, Horace, until we see if your plans work."

"I wouldn't expect her to," said Mr. Malvern after she'd disappeared into the Emporium. "Nor would I expect her to thank Magus Silveroak for ringing my nephew from the tearoom last night to tell him that the village had been trashed. And I certainly wouldn't expect her to thank my nephew for sending his men to lend a hand with the cleanup."

"This was Calvin's idea?" I said, gesturing to the work crews.

"He put it to the fellows and they agreed to help," said Mr. Malvern.

"No coercion?" I said.

Mr. Malvern gave me a sidelong, disbelieving look. "Coercion doesn't work on chaps like these, Lori. If they don't want to do something, they don't do it. If you push them, they move on. No, Cal just talked to them, got them to see things from his point of view. He grew up here, remember. Finch means a lot to him. And he wants to stay on Peggy's good side. If she went to the press to complain, it could spell trouble for the fair."

"He's looking out for Finch's interests as well as his own," I said.

"Aye," said Mr. Malvern. "He's got a good heart, does Cal."

"So do you," I said. "In my book, you're a knight in shining armor."

"I'm a burgher," he corrected. "Whatever that is. Will we see you today at the fair, or are you going to boycott it?"

"You'll see me there," I said. "I'm going to change into my costume as soon as I get home."

"I'll stay here until the men finish," he said. "But I'll see you later."

"See you later," I said, and headed for the Range Rover.

After speaking with Mr. Malvern, I was convinced that the saboteur was trying to kill or injure Calvin Malvern for personal rather than professional reasons. Calvin might run a tight ship, but he ran it by using persuasion rather than coercion, because he had no other choice. Harsh tactics didn't work with Ren fest people. If they disliked an employer, they simply moved on to another gig.

The saboteur, therefore, wasn't a disgruntled employee. He was someone who had a private quarrel with the king. Edmond Deland, a young man seething with jealousy, resentment, and the heartache of unrequited love, fit the profile. He wouldn't rest until he'd destroyed his rival.

And I wouldn't rest until I'd stopped him. Nodding grimly, I climbed into the Rover and started for home. I couldn't wait to get to the fair and start interrogating the food vendors. Thanks to Sir James le Victorieux and his motley band of heroes, I could pursue my investigation with a clear conscience.

Fourteen

I changed into my wench attire—my disguise, as I now thought of it—in less than fifteen minutes, but it took me another twenty to work up the courage to wear it outside of the cottage. The soft leather flats were a great improvement over the sandals I'd worn the day before, the muffin cap was adorable, and the flowing skirts allowed for ample freedom of movement, but the low-cut, body-shaping bodice gave me pause. Every time I took a breath, I wished I had a shawl.

I reminded myself forcibly that there was enough cleavage on display at the fair for mine to go unnoticed, and that Bill had forfeited any right he'd ever had to object to my garb. If my cool medieval dude of a husband opened his mouth to complain about wifely overexposure, I'd simply point to his clinging tights and remind him of what the pot called the kettle.

Fortified, I hung Harold le Rouge's splendid knife on my leather belt, slipped a few small necessities into the belt pouch Sally Pyne had provided, and stepped out into the sunshine. The weather was so lovely, and I was so wary of being caught in another traffic jam, that I decided on the spot to leave the Mini at home and walk to the fair. It would take me less than an hour to reach Bishop's Wood on foot, via Mr. Malvern's pastures, and if I needed a lift home later on, I could always catch a ride with one of my neighbors. I was certain that most of them would return to the fair, if for no other reason than to show their gratitude to King Wilfred for helping Finch in its hour of need.

I closed the cottage's front door, went around to the back garden, hitched up my skirts, and climbed over the stile. Had it been earlier in the morning, I would have been worried about disturbing Jinks or intruding on his privacy, but I'd gotten such a late start that I didn't expect to find him at home. By midmorning, the royal jester would no doubt be at work, entertaining fairgoers with his wit and his amazing tumbling runs.

I'd refrained from poking my nose over the stile ever since Jinks had moved into Mr. Malvern's cow pasture. Once I'd climbed down from the stile, however, it seemed only natural to look around. Jinks's camper-van was very small and rather rusty, but the bright yellow curtains in the windows and the lawn chair sitting beside it gave it a homey look. I would have found it trying to spend a whole summer in such cramped quarters, but I imagined that Jinks was used to it by now. If he didn't love the vagabond life, I reasoned, he would have found another line of work long ago.

Mr. Malvern's dairy herd had worn a smooth path along the hedgerow dividing my property from his. I followed the track, clambering over a few gates along the way, until I reached the edge of the fair's extremely crowded parking lot.

The parking lot was a sign of things to come. I had to wait in one long line to buy my ticket and a second to pass through the gatehouse. The delay would have been frustrating if I hadn't put the time to good use, studying the section of wall that had nearly brought about the king's downfall. The parapet had been seamlessly repaired and it showed no signs of more "accidental" breakage, so I assumed that the opening ceremonies had taken place without incident. I hadn't expected it to be otherwise. The saboteur would have aroused serious suspicion if he'd pulled the same stunt twice.

When I finally passed through the main entrance, I found myself adrift in a sea of people. Gatehouse Square was bursting at the seams with chattering fairgoers, and the winding lanes leading off of it appeared to be more congested than they had been the day before. If, as Aunt Dimity had suggested, the saboteur was trying to scare people away from King Wilfred's Faire, he was failing miserably.

By the time I reached Pudding Lane, the food vendors were too busy catering to the needs of their customers to spend time gossiping with me. I consoled myself with a honey cake, resolved to return for another try later in the day, and went in search of the quiet lane in which I'd first seen the madrigal singers.

I hoped the lane would still be quiet, because I wanted to renew my brief acquaintance with the crystal-ball vendor. She'd seemed like a friendly, talkative soul when she'd answered my questions about little Mirabel. If her booth wasn't swamped by aspiring fortune-tellers, I was certain that she'd be willing to continue our conversation.

I thought it would be easy to retrace my steps to the crystal-ball stall, but it wasn't. The noise, the bustle, and the fair's infinite distractions made it challenging to plot a steady course though the labyrinth of crisscrossing lanes. A program book with its handy map would have helped, but I'd left Saturday's edition at home and refused Sunday's because it was too big to fit into my belt pouch.

My progress was impeded by the crowds, but it was brought to a complete halt by a Cyrano de Bergerac clone, who waylaid me at the junction of Harmony Lane and Broad Street. After presenting me with a long-stemmed red rose, the flamboyant dandy went down on one knee to recite a poem in praise of my eyes, while fixing his gaze firmly on my chest. His utterly shameless flirtation attracted a small gathering of amused spectators who seemed to think I was in on the act. By the time he pressed his lips—and his oversized nose—to my hand, I was convinced that my disguise was working. With a little luck, and a little medieval attitude, I'd be able to infiltrate any part of the fair I chose.

I was still searching for the crystal-ball stall when Peggy Taxman's unmistakable roar smote my ears.

"Water! Water! Ice-cold water! Get thy water here!"

Her stentorian cry stopped me in my tracks. I shot a furtive look over my shoulder and saw Peggy standing before a small stall not twenty feet away from me. My disguise must have fooled her, because her eyes swept over me without betraying a flicker of recognition. Relieved, I scurried to hide behind a tree, then peeked cautiously around the trunk to watch her hawk her wares.

"Precious ointment for thy skin!" she bellowed, holding up a tube of sunblock. "Protect thine epidermis from the orb's baleful rays!"

Peggy's stall was possibly the most popular one at the fair, in large part because she'd stocked it with items that were useful rather than decorative. Sun visors, sunblock, lip balm, disposable cameras, bug spray, packets of tissue, and bottles of hand sanitizer seemed to fly off the shelves, and she could hardly keep up with the demand for bottled water.

In addition to meeting her public's material needs, Peggy gave them a memorable show. Whether she meant to be or not, she was a superb performer, a sort of iron-lunged medieval carnival barker. People lingered after making their purchases, as if they found the sheer volume of her cries entertaining, though they may have been impressed by her appearance as well. Peggy filled her yellow-and-blue-striped bodice to its furthest extent, but instead of looking ridiculous, she looked majestic. Her statuesque figure, commanding presence, and practical products attracted a steady stream of buyers to her stall.

"Don't know how long those laces will hold," said a quiet voice behind me.

I turned to find Sally Pyne peering past me at Peggy.

"They're made of nylon, but even nylon has its limits," she went on. She took a step back and regarded me critically, while making sure we were still hidden by the tree. "You fill out your top nicely, Lori—not too much, not too little."

"Sally," I protested, folding my arms across my chest.

"Don't tell me you haven't noticed," she chided. "I saw that chap with the fake nose giving you the business."

In hopes of diverting her attention from my more conspicuous charms, I surveyed her cotton blouse, baggy shorts, and sneakers, and asked, "Why aren't you wearing a costume?"

"I've been too busy making clothes for other people to make anything for myself," she replied. "Besides, I'm comfy as I am." She stuck her hands in her pockets and rocked back on her heels. "Have you heard about King Wilfred's crown?"

My jaw dropped as an earthshaking insight exploded in my brain. It was so glaringly obvious that I felt like a complete dunderhead for not seeing it sooner. The good people of Finch were veritable bloodhounds when it came to sniffing out juicy gobbets of information. They were observant, attentive, relentless, and always eager to pass along what they'd learned. I didn't need to interrogate strangers in order to find out what was going on at the fair. All I had to do was chat with my neighbors.

"No," I said, leaning toward Sally. "I haven't heard about King Wilfred's crown."

Sally leaned toward me and lowered her voice. "He's wearing a different one today. Word has it that the pointy one he wore yesterday has gone missing."

"Missing?" I repeated suggestively.

"Stolen," she confirmed. "Worth a tidy sum, they say."

"You're kidding," I said. "It looked like a piece of costume jewelry to me."

"Most of the stones are paste," Sally conceded. "But the sapphire and the diamonds are real. He took 'em from his mother's engagement ring and put 'em in the crown, in memory of her. So they say."

"Poor Calvin," I said, shaking my head sadly. "Has he notified the police?"

"No," said Sally. "Calvin doesn't want the police nosing around the camp. They might not like some of the things they find there." She winked. "Unconventional tobacco, that sort of thing."

Mr. Barlow appeared at Sally's elbow. He seemed to materialize out of nowhere, but he, too, was careful to put the tree between himself and Peggy Taxman. Like Sally, Mr. Barlow was dressed in everyday summer clothing, but apparently neither of them needed to disguise themselves in order to garner gossip.

"I expect you've told Lori about the crown," he said to Sally.

"I was just telling her," she said.

"It's appalling," I said. "Absolutely appalling."

"Wait till you hear about the cannon," said Mr. Barlow.

"I was getting to that," Sally said, frowning irritably.

"What happened to the cannon?" I asked.

"Someone tampered with it," said Mr. Barlow. "That's why it didn't go off this morning."

"So they say," Sally put in.

"Good grief," I said. "How was it tampered with?"

"Someone fiddled with the barrel," said Mr. Barlow. "If it had gone off, it would have blown the cannoneers to kingdom come."

"That's not what I heard," Sally objected. "I heard that someone filled the barrel with cannonballs and aimed it at the gatehouse."

"Whatever the case," said Mr. Barlow, frowning skeptically at Sally, "Horace Malvern was fit to be tied. Says he won't have the dratted thing used again. Wants it off his property before someone gets hurt."

"Where is it now?" I asked.

"Seems they dragged it off to that camp of theirs," said Mr. Barlow, nodding vaguely in the direction of the encampment.

"Shouldn't have brought it here in the first place," Sally opined. "Dangerous things, cannon."

"They're not dangerous if they're handled properly," said Mr. Barlow.

"They are if they're tampered with," retorted Sally.

"If they've been tampered with, they haven't been handled properly," Mr. Barlow explained.

I sensed a Finch-style tug-of-war argument coming on and quickly excused myself.

"Sorry," I said, handing the long-stemmed rose to Sally. "I have to run. I told Bill and the boys I'd meet them at the petting zoo."

"Good to see you, Lori," said Mr. Barlow.

"Though we're not used to seeing quite so much of you," Sally said archly.

Their sniggers followed me as I fled, red-faced, up the next lane. Sally's saucy comment had reminded me that there were drawbacks to speaking with neighbors, but my mortification was forgotten when I lifted my gaze from the ground and saw in the distance the glitter of a vagrant sunbeam striking a crystal ball. I hurried forward, spotted the stall filled with bronze dragons, and knew that I'd found the quiet lane at last.

The crystal-ball vendor was holding an animated discussion with a young woman wearing a turban, a spangled bolero, and a pair of genie pants. I assumed that the young woman was a customer and hung back, waiting for her to finish, but my attention was quickly drawn to a flurry of whispers coming from the gap between two stalls on my left.

My busybody instincts kicked into gear. Without hesitation, I sidled over to the gap to eavesdrop on the whisperers. In less than a second, I knew that I'd struck gold. Edmond and Mirabel were engaged in a hushed but spirited argument, and they weren't bothering to use medieval patois.

"I don't care if you ever look at me again," Edmond was saying. "I just don't want you to be hurt."

"I'm not going to be hurt," said Mirabel.

"You don't know what you're getting yourself into," said Edmond. "He has a reputation——"

"A man like him can't help having a reputation," Mirabel interrupted. "I simply refuse to believe most of the stories I've heard about him."

"They're all true," Edmond insisted. "I've seen him use other girls the same way. He always picks the youngest and most inexperienced cast member."

"I'm twenty years old, Edmond," Mirabel said heatedly. "I'm not a child."

"I know," said Edmond, "but you're new to this sort of thing. It's easy to get caught up in the fantasy."

"I think I can tell the difference between reality and fantasy, thank you very much,' Mirabel snapped.

"If you could, you'd realize that he's toying with you," said Edmond. "It's a game to him. It's not real. He's playing a role, and part of his role is to sweep girls off their feet."

"I rather enjoy being swept off my feet," Mirabel said airily.

"You won't when you land on your face," Edmond warned sternly. "He'll use you, then he'll toss you aside."

"You're talking about his past," said Mirabel. "I happen to know that he's changed."

"Is that what he told you?" Edmond gave a strangled groan of exasperation. "It's the oldest line in the world."

"He means it this time," said Mirabel.

"You're deluding yourself," said Edmond. "Please, Janet——"

"I'm not Janet," she scolded. "I'm Mirabel."

"You're Janet Watkins," Edmond stated doggedly. "You were born and raised in Nottingham and you'll go back there when the summer's over because it's your home, it's where you belong. Mirabel is a role you play."

"Do you know what your problem is, Edmond?" Mirabel said, her voice rising. "You're *boring*. Here we are, in the most romantic place in the world, and you act as though it's just another job. Look at you, in your jeans and your boring shirt. You're *ordinary*. You have no imagination. You don't have an ounce of poetry in your soul. You'd never throw me over your shoulder and carry me off to your castle. You'd ask me to sit in your *wheelbarrow* and trundle me off to your *bungalow*. Now, will you please get on with your work and stop following me around like a pathetic puppy? I can look after myself."

I heard the swish of Mirabel's skirts and swung around to face the nearest stall. While I pretended to examine a display of grotesque gargoyles, Mirabel stormed past me to join the other madrigal singers, who'd assembled in front of the bronze dragons. Some of the girls appeared to commiserate with her, but the tallest one quickly called them to order. A moment later, the lane was filled with their exquisite harmony.

I was about to peek between the stalls, to see if Edmond had lingered, when he emerged from the shadows to cast a hopeless look in Mirabel's direction. She missed a note, glared at him, and went on singing with a furious gusto that made the tallest girl put a hand on her shoulder, as if to calm her down. Edmond bowed his head and clenched his jaw as if he were in pain, then turned on his heel and slipped silently back through the gap.

I followed him. If he'd been desperate enough to steal the king's crown and tamper with the cannon before his confrontation with Mirabel, there was no telling what he'd do after it. He might retreat to a private hideaway to lick his wounds, or he might behave like a cornered animal and lash out. Whatever he did, I wanted to be on hand to witness it.

Aunt Dimity had cautioned me against putting myself in harm's way, and I had every intention of heeding her warning. Edmond was a strapping young man and I was handicapped by long skirts and a bodice that might burst under stress, so I wouldn't hurl myself in front of him if he decided to attack the king outright, nor would I wrestle him to the ground to keep him from committing a fresh act of sabotage. I would, however, shout a word of warning to foil a physical assault, if necessary, and I would do my best to prevent any act of sabotage from succeeding.

Edmond seemed to be too absorbed in his own misery to notice the strange woman flitting from stall to stall behind him. It was hardly surprising. Mirabel hadn't simply rejected him, she'd slammed his good intentions to the ground and stomped on them. Her final riposte had been crushing enough to send anyone into a tailspin. If Edmond hadn't already won my vote for Most Likely to Murder, my heart would have gone out to him.

The dark-haired young handyman walked with his head down, but he appeared to have a definite destination in mind because he never paused to double-check his location or stand irresolute at a crossroads. He cut between stalls several times, and though many vendors and performers called out friendly greetings to him as he passed, he didn't respond to any of them.

I had no idea where we were going until we reached the small field between the archery range and the Farthing Stage. When I saw dancers, acrobats, foot soldiers, and courtiers forming up behind the king's heralds, I realized with a tingle of foreboding that Edmond had marched directly from his shattering quarrel with Mirabel to the staging area for the king's procession.

My heart raced as he approached King Wilfred, and my bosom heaved as I prepared myself to let out a bellow worthy of Peggy Taxman, but I never issued the lifesaving shout. Instead of lunging forward to thrust a dagger into the king's lecherous, treacherous heart, Edmond turned aside before he reached the king and headed for a shed behind the stage. While the heralds sounded their trumpets and led the procession from the field onto Broad Street, Edmond pulled his wheelbarrow from the shed, put a shovel and a large sack of sawdust into it, and waited.

The sense of anticlimax that swept over me was so acute that I had to lean against a tree until it passed. Edmond hadn't gone to the field in order to assassinate his hated rival. He'd gone there in order to retrieve the tools he'd need to clean up after the horses in the procession. I didn't wish King Wilfred ill, but I'd expected such high drama that I was almost disappointed when it fizzled.

Deflated, I made my way to Broad Street to wave to Will, Rob, Alison, Billy, and Emma as they rode by. I stuck around long enough to make sure that Edmond was doing exactly what he was supposed to be doing, then started the long cross-fair trek to the Shire Stage.

I didn't want to be late for my meeting with Jinks. I planned to grill the king's jester about the parapet, the quintain, the cannon, the missing crown, and much more besides, but I was also in sore need of a laugh.

Fifteen

"Avaunt ye, thou gorbellied, milk-livered measle!"

"Callest thou me a measle, ye mammering, boil-brained foot-licker?"

"Yea, verily, I do. For so art thou known by all honorable men, ye lean-witted, onion-eyed, sheep-biting maggot-pie!"

"Malt-worm!"

"Pigeon-egg!"

The audience roared with laughter as a pair of extravagantly overdressed Elizabethan courtiers conducted an insult contest on the Shire Stage. The courtiers' colorful palette of expressions brought home to me how pale the English language had become in the past six hundred years. It would never have occurred to me to call anyone a measle or a maggot-pie. I hoped it wouldn't occur to Will or Rob.

The courtiers stopped their verbal volleys long enough to call for volunteers to join them onstage. During the lull that ensued, I heard the faint jingle of bells. I threw my shoulders back and affected the carefree flounce of an authentic wench as I skirted the jam-packed wooden benches and slipped into the backstage area, where a ventriloquist with a skeletal dummy sat, awaiting his turn to perform. My ruse seemed to work, because neither the ventriloquist nor the dummy questioned my right to be there.

Jinks stood a few yards behind the stage, near the privacy fence that enclosed the fairground, his arms wrapped around a large cloth-covered picnic basket. He smiled when he saw me and spoke softly, so as not to disturb the ongoing performance.

"Well met, my lady," he said, inclining his head over the basket. "Pray follow me."

We walked behind a row of stalls to a small, almost invisible gate in the privacy fence. I regarded the gate doubtfully. I hadn't anticipated leaving the grounds.

"Where are we going?" I asked.

"Away from the noise of the general populace and the smell of the goats, lambs, and calves," he replied. "Do not mistake me, fair one. I revel in bucolic settings. My taste buds, alas, rebel at the thought of consuming delectable victuals so near the petting zoo."

We could have avoided the animals' intrusive aromas by moving to the picnic area, but I allowed Jinks to open the gate for me and stepped willingly into the woods beyond. I thought I understood his need to get away from the fair. His job was so people-intensive that, had I been in his shoes, I would have spent all of my lunch breaks in quiet seclusion. I would also have eaten as many meals as possible in the open air rather than in his cramped camper-van.

The woods were familiar to me, but I let Jinks take the lead. After a dozen steps, he removed his jester's cap, tucked it under the basket's handle, and dropped back to walk beside me. I didn't miss the incessant jingling, nor, I expect, did he. As we ambled along side by side, we chatted about King Wilfred's cleanup squads, Horace Malvern's sobriety checkpoints, and the surge in the fair's attendance. Finally, Jinks brought the conversation around to our ill-fated meeting the previous evening.

"I want to apologize again for standing you up last night," he said.

"There's no need." I shrugged. "A jester's gotta do what a jester's gotta do."

"A jester's gotta do what his king commands him to do," he said, laughing. "I don't usually mind, but I did last night. Much as I enjoy quaffing with the lads, I would rather have spent time with you, Lori."

"Lori?" I said, feigning dismay. "What happened to 'my lady'?"

"She's here, beside me." He gave me a brief, sidelong glance, then continued, "I tend to give Ren-speak a rest when I'm off duty, but I'll go on using it if you want me to."

"You don't have to stay in character for me," I assured him. "I'd go crazy if I had to entertain people twenty-four hours a day. Would you like me to call you Rowan instead of Jinks?"

"Better not," he said. "It brings back too many painful memories of my school days." He winced slightly as we stepped over a log.

"Painful memories?" I teased.

"Painful knees," he replied, pausing to rub his left leg. "I misjudged a landing during the procession. My joints aren't what they used to be."

"Whose are?" I said as we walked on. "Lucky for you, it's Sunday. You'll have the rest of the week to recuperate."

"I seem to spend more and more time recuperating," he said, with a wry smile.

"In that case," I said, "why don't you let me set up an

appointment for you with my neighbor, Miranda Morrow? She's an excellent massage therapist and a certified homeopathic healer. She'll have you feeling right as rain before you know it."

"Thank you, from the bottom of my knees," he said. "Unfortunately, they'll be far away from Finch during the coming week. They're traveling with me to Cheltenham, to stay at a friend's flat. I'll be spending weekdays there throughout the summer."

"I'm glad," I said.

"Are you?" he asked. "Why?"

"I saw your camper," I told him. "It's okay for weekend stays, but I wouldn't want to spend an entire summer in it."

"Nor would I, which is why I've made other arrangements." Jinks came to a sudden halt. "Well? What do you think? Will it do for our picnic?"

We stood near the edge of a sparkling brook that ran through a sylvan glade. Sunlight streamed through leaves that hadn't yet lost their springtime suppleness and water gurgled and splashed over smooth, mossy stones, providing a natural music that was far easier on the ears—and the nerves—than the fair's constant din. Wildflowers grew among the long grasses, filling the air with sweet, subtle fragrances, and small birds twittered in the trees.

"It's lovely," I said. "Is this your secret place?"

"It's our secret, now," he said.

"If Bishop's Wood were farther away from Finch," I said, "I'd agree with you. But most of my neighbors have probably picnicked in this very spot at one time or another. I know for a fact that Miranda Morrow collects herbs in these woods."

"We'll just have to pretend, then," said Jinks. "We'll make believe we're the first humans to set foot here. We'll be the Adam and Eve of Bishop's Wood."

"If I see a snake, I'm leaving," I declared.

When Jinks placed the picnic basket on the ground, he groaned and grabbed his back, so I ordered him to sit on a fallen tree and let me take care of the heavy work. While he dug his knuckles into his twinging muscles, I spread the cloth on the ground and set out the food and drink he'd brought from the encampment—cold chicken, ripe strawberries, dried figs, honey cakes, a round loaf of bread, a generous wedge of Cheddar, and a bottle of Riesling.

"The wine's from my own cellar," he announced, lowering himself gingerly onto the cloth. "Trust me, it's possible to grow tired of quaffing ale." He opened the bottle with a corkscrew, filled two plastic cups with wine, and handed one to me. "A toast, my lady?"

"To King Wilfred," I said, raising my glass. "Long may he reign."

"To the king," said Jinks. He touched his glass to mine, then set it aside and reached for a chicken breast. As he chewed his first bite, he let his green eyes travel well south of my chin. "I've been meaning to compliment you on your garb. It's most becoming."

"Thanks," I said, without a trace of self-consciousness. Jinks had been working at Ren fests for so long that he had to be used to seeing dresses like mine. "I wanted to be a noblewoman, but my seamstress didn't have enough time to make a fancy dress, so I ended up as a wench."

"Noblewomen are tedious," he said dismissively. "You're much better off as a wench. Less dignity, perhaps, but more license, and I know which one I prefer. Wench roles usually go to our more buxom cast members, but not always. Wenching, you see, is a state of mind. And, as you demonstrate so admirably, one can achieve marvelous effects with a fitted bodice."

"It's not bad," I said, glancing downward. "Bill hasn't seen my garb yet, but I think he'll like it."

"If he doesn't, he's a bigger fool than I am." Jinks dropped his gaze for a moment, then looked up again to continue his analysis of my appearance. "Technically, you shouldn't wear your hair short—even nuns had long hair in medieval times—but your curls are so adorable that we'll let it pass. Also, you've used the old Rennie trick of—"

"Rennie?" I broke in.

"A hard-core Ren fest participant," he translated, "one who travels from fair to fair throughout the year, who sees it as a way of life rather than a hobby. You are a mundane—an outsider, a member of the public—though no one could tell by looking at you. You've used the classic Rennie trick of disguising your short hair with a cap, which is exactly the right thing to do."

"The credit should go to my seamstress," I said. "She made the costume."

"But you give it its lovely shape," he said.

"Enough," I said, shaking a chicken leg at him. "I'm happy to know that you approve of my costume, and I realize that flattery is part of your act, but you've exceeded the quota of compliments you're allowed to give to a married woman."

"Is there a quota?" he asked innocently.

"There certainly is, and you've sailed right over it," I said. "Let's move on to another subject, shall we? Is it true that someone stole Calvin's crown?"

Jinks choked on a sip of Riesling, wiped his mouth with the back of his hand, and gazed at me incredulously. "You've heard about the crown? My word. News does travel fast at a Ren fest."

"Sounds like Finch," I said. "Is it true, then? Was the crown stolen?"

"It's missing," Jinks allowed. "Whether it was stolen or merely misplaced remains to be seen. No one burgled Cal's motor home, so my money is on misplacement."

"How could Calvin misplace his crown?" I asked. "It's set with his mother's jewels."

"By my troth," Jinks said, his eyes widening with delight. "You *are* in the know, aren't you?"

"I keep my ears open," I acknowledged modestly. "And I'm still waiting to hear your answer. How could Calvin misplace something that means so much to him?"

"After an evening of quaffing, one can easily misplace anything that isn't actually attached to one's body." Jinks stretched out on his side, propped his head on his hand, and began nibbling a fig. "We searched the camp this morning, before the fair opened, but we didn't find it."

"You don't seem too worried about it," I said.

"I'm not," he admitted, popping the rest of the fig into his mouth. "Pranks and practical jokes are a staple of camp life, Lori. I fully expect the crown to turn up next weekend, on one of the ponies."

"Do you think the quintain incident started out as a practical joke?" I asked.

"No, I don't," he replied more seriously. "Our cast members may share a rather sophomoric sense of humor, but they know better than to muck about with the equipment in the arena. It's too dangerous. A defective rope is to blame for the quintain accident."

"Are you sure about that?" I asked. "Did someone examine the rope after the accident?"

"Yes, of course," said Jinks. "Edmond brought it back to camp—"

"*Edmond* brought the rope to camp?" I interrupted.

"Of course. He's the general dogsbody. It's his job to straighten the arena after the show. When he'd finished, he brought the broken rope to the encampment, where we all had a look at it." Jinks's eyes narrowed and he peered up at me inquisitively. "Why are you taking such a great interest in the rope, Lori?"

"I'm not sure," I said, ducking my head to avoid his penetrating gaze. "It just seems as if Calvin's been having an unusual run of bad luck since the fair opened."

"And you suspect . . . what?" Jinks asked.

I slipped Harold le Rouge's knife from its sheath and busied myself with cutting up the generous wedge of cheese.

"Lori," Jinks said, his voice laden with disbelief, "you're not suggesting that someone is trying to bump off our beloved monarch, are you?"

I could feel the entire top half of my body blush.

"You witnessed a series of accidents and deduced that a . . . a pretender to the throne is attempting . . . regicide?" Jinks rolled onto his back and began howling with laughter. "Ring the alarm bells! Call out the watch! Raise the hue and cry! The king's life is imperiled by felons most foul!" After a few minutes of unrestrained chortling, he caught his breath and heaved an amused sigh. "Oh, Lori, you belong in my world. You have precisely the right sort of imagination."

My head snapped up.

"I'm *not* imagining things," I said through gritted teeth, and then it was off to the races. "I hear someone using a handsaw three hours before the fair opens—*one* person using *one* saw—and the next thing I know, the parapet falls apart. And it just happens to be the parapet Calvin leans on during the opening ceremony. Then he's nearly decapitated by the sandbag and I examine the rope and it just happens to look as if someone sliced into with a knife. Then his crown disappears and someone tampers with the cannon and . . . and . . ." I thumped the ground with my fist. "*I'm not making things up!*"

"No, no, of course you're not." Jinks sat up with a groan and held a placating hand out to me. "But who would want to harm our merry monarch? Cal is the kindest boss in the world. Everyone loves him." His hand fell and his tone softened to a patronizing purr. "Isn't it possible that you may be reading a little too much into things?"

"It's . . . possible," I conceded stiffly.

"The saw, for example," he went on. "Is it really so shocking that you heard it when you did? Builders were up all night putting last-minute touches on various projects. The paint was still wet on the gatehouse when the opening ceremonies began, and the walkway was a long way from finished. All of the parapets were held in place by temporary struts. Calvin should have known better than to put his weight on any of them."

"All of the parapets were weak?" I said, with a doubtful frown. "You told me that the walkway was perfectly safe."

"I didn't want you to spend your first day at the fair worrying about whether or not the gatehouse would collapse," said Jinks. "The truth is, it was still a work in progress."

"But the quintain's a different matter," I argued. "Someone could have sabotaged it after the knights left for the opening ceremonies, when the arena was deserted."

"The arena is never deserted," Jinks pointed out, smiling patiently. "There's always a gaggle of girls hanging around the marquee, hoping for a chance to flirt with the squires or the soldiers or the knights. Deadly weapons are babe magnets, apparently."

"My husband didn't mention a gaggle of girls," I said.

"Wise man," Jinks muttered.

"What's that supposed to mean?" I demanded.

"Wives don't always approve of groupies," he said carefully, peering skyward.

"Oh," I said, thinking of Bill's tights. "I see."

"Be that as it may," Jinks went on hastily, "a quintain would be a highly unreliable murder weapon. It would be too difficult to predict when the rope would break, and it would have to break at exactly the right moment to send the sandbag sailing toward a specific target. I don't see how it could be done."

"Maybe the saboteur was trying to scare the king," I said.

"No one was trying to scare the king," Jinks countered. "When we examined the rope's shipping crate, we discovered several nails that hadn't been hammered into place correctly. The pointy ends were protruding inside the crate. No one cut the rope intentionally, Lori. It was damaged during shipment by the nails in a poorly made crate."

"And the cannon?" I said.

Jinks pursed his crooked lips. "We think it was someone's idea of a joke. A stupid, dangerous joke, but a joke nonetheless."

I frowned. "You just told me that Rennies know better than to pull dangerous stunts."

"We don't think a Rennie is responsible for this one," he said grimly. "Two teenaged boys—fairgoers, not cast members—were seen near the cannon yesterday afternoon. They were asked to leave, but they may have returned later on. We believe they're responsible for the prank." He reached for a honey cake. "It wasn't aimed at the king, by the way. If anyone had been hurt, it would have been the artillery team. Fortunately, they're too conscientious to fire a gun without inspecting it first."

Silence fell between us. While Jinks savored his sweet confection, I turned his explanations over in my mind. I would have found them reassuring if they'd accounted for all of the facts, but it was patently clear that they hadn't. Contrary to popular opinion, King Wilfred wasn't universally beloved. He had at least one mortal enemy. The entire gatehouse may have been a jury-rigged mess, but only one parapet had fallen. Edmond could have sawn through the temporary struts holding it in place, just as he could have altered the appearance of the rope before presenting it for inspection—the clean cut I'd seen had been made by a knife, not a nail.

I glanced at Jinks, then looked at the sparkling water streaming over the mossy rocks. I simply couldn't bring myself to ask him about Edmond and Mirabel. If I added a love triangle to the regicide plot, he'd patronize me again, and I would have to kill him. I took a calming breath and reminded myself firmly that I wanted to *prevent* a murder, not *commit* one.

"Strawberry for your thoughts," Jinks said, holding one out to me.

"You've heard enough of my thoughts for one afternoon," I told him.

"Take it anyway." He placed the strawberry in my hand. "As a peace offering. You're looking very stormy."

"It's just . . ." I shrugged helplessly. "There's a lot to take in, at a Ren fest."

A sweet smile curved Jinks's crooked lips. He stretched out on his back, crossed his legs, cupped his head in his clasped hands, and gazed up at the trees.

"You mentioned earlier that the fair reminded you of Finch," he said. "In many ways, a Ren fest is a small village. Granted, there's a heightened sense of drama among the people in my village, but what would you expect? We're actors. We live by our emotions. We have our petty squabbles and our long-running feuds, but we also have a strong sense of camaraderie and a deep awareness of how lucky we are to be able to practice our crafts in such a congenial setting. If there's a pretender to the throne, he doesn't kill the king. He auditions for the role at another Ren fest. Or he starts his own." Jinks chuckled quietly, then turned his head to look at me. "We take our work seriously, Lori, but we're well aware that it's make-believe."

Jinks seemed to be telling me, in the nicest possible way, that I'd gotten so caught up in the fair that I could no longer tell the difference between fantasy and reality. It was exactly the same thing Edmond had told Mirabel, but my reaction was quite different from hers. I didn't fire cutting phrases into Jinks's well-meaning brain. I decided instead to prove that he was wrong.

"Thanks." I swept a hand through the air. "For all of this. I've really enjoyed your lunch break."

"I hope you're enjoying the fair as well," he said.

"I'd enjoy it more if I could get the recipe for those honey cakes," I said, batting my eyelashes at him.

"Consider it done." He moaned softly as he pushed himself into a sitting position. "You have no idea how much I hate to say it, Lori, but I have to go back to work."

"I should get back, too," I said. "I don't know how I'm going to explain to my sons why I wasn't on hand to watch them in the arena."

"Tell them you were investigating an attempted regicide," he suggested, his eyes twinkling. "They'll be impressed."

"Good idea," I said. After all, I thought, with an inward smile, mothers should always tell their children the truth.

Sixteen

*J*inks and I parted ways at the nearly invisible gate. He went off to the Great Hall, where the king was conferring knighthoods on pretty much anyone who wanted one, including women, children, and small dogs, while I made my way back to the crystal-ball vendor's stall. I had no trouble finding it. I simply followed the sound of Peggy Taxman's voice and darted up the lane next to hers.

The vendor was delighted to see me again, possibly because she had no other customers. Her Rennie name, I discovered, was Mistress Farseeing, and she was every bit as talkative as I'd hoped she'd be. In no time at all I learned that she lived on Feversham Lane in Glastonbury with her husband, Hubert, and their cocker spaniel, Mr. Wink; that she ran a fortune-telling supply business from her home; that her three grown children—Hubert, Jr., Gwen, and Lance—were mortified by her fascination with the occult; and that Edmond Deland's tent was one of the smallest in the encampment.

"No bigger than a peasant's pocket," she said, chuckling merrily, "but neat as Lord Belvedere's beard. You won't find rubbish strewn about dear Edmond's dwelling place."

"You're fond of him, then," I said, recalling the friendly greetings Edmond had received from other vendors as he'd crossed the fairground.

"That I am," she agreed. "Poor lad. His afflictions are grievous, but he bears them nobly."

"Afflictions?" I prompted.

"Matters of the heart." Mistress Farseeing folded her arms and bent her muffin cap close to mine. "His ladylove scorns him and bestows her favor on another. 'Tis a tale as old as time, with a sting is as sharp as an adder's."

I would have pursued the topic further, but Mistress Farseeing transferred her attention to a black-clad young woman sporting an eye-popping array of tattoos and so many body piercings that, by rights, she should have leaked. Since I'd shown no inclination to spend money at the stall, the vendor's defection was understandable and I bade her adieu with a cordial nod.

The time for talk was over anyway. I was ready to take action. Aunt Dimity had urged me to find tangible proof to support my claims, and after speaking with Jinks, I had a good notion of where to look for it. My next stop would be the encampment.

The cannon seemed like a dead end—I wasn't interested in teenagers' pranks—but the missing crown presented definite possibilities. Jinks doubted that the crown had been stolen, believing instead that it had been "borrowed" by a cast member who planned to return it in a humorous manner—on a pony's head, for example.

I thought it far more likely that Edmond had stolen the crown. After his first two assassination attempts had failed, he would have found it enormously satisfying to dethrone his rival symbolically. Since the king's motor home hadn't been burgled, however, I suspected that Edmond had acted on impulse instead of with cool calculation.

It wasn't hard to imagine the scenario. I could picture King Wilfred weaving tipsily from the banquet table to his motor home after a long evening spent quaffing with the lads. He'd bent to adjust a garter, perhaps, and the crown had tumbled from his head. Although the king had been too far gone to notice its absence, the young man who'd been tailing him was cold sober.

Edmond had seized the opportunity to deal the king another blow—not a physical blow this time, but a blow to the mind and the spirit—by retrieving the fallen crown and fading back into the shadows. He'd returned with it to his tent and stashed it among his belongings, where it would remain until a clever person came along and found it.

I would be that clever person. I would make Aunt Dimity proud of me by proving that Edmond had stolen King Wilfred's crown. I would slip into the encampment, locate his tent, and search it from top to bottom. I'd lost the rope, but I was determined to find the crown.

When the town crier informed those within earshot that it was half past three of the clock, I lifted my skirts and quickened my pace. In ninety short minutes, the fair would close and the workers would return to the camp. I had to reach Edmond's tent before he did.

I scurried through the picnic area, past the arena and the royal gallery, which had been taken over by a knot of giggling wenches who were, I assumed, lying in wait for a soldier, a squire, a knight, or any male who looked reasonably attractive in tights. I gave them a withering glance, then jogged around to the far end of the white marquee, where I paused to scan the stabling area and the pasture.

Angelus, Lucifer, Thunder, Storm, Pegasus, and the

McLaughlin ponies were grazing peacefully in the pasture, but their owners were nowhere to be seen. I wondered fleetingly where the Anscombe Manor team had gone, then ran for the row of poplars.

The tall, slender trees stood on a small rise overlooking a vast field that had once held Mr. Malvern's largest herd of cattle. The cows had been moved to the slightly smaller field on the other side of an imposing hedgerow and their old stomping ground had been turned into a veritable metropolis.

My heart sank as I beheld the most complex campground I'd ever seen. It seemed to contain tents of every imaginable size, shape, and color. Most were the freestanding nylon variety used by outdoorsmen the world over, but scattered among them were teepees, yurts, geodesic domes, old-fashioned pup tents, tarpaulins strung between poles, elegant pavilions that looked as though they'd sprung from the pages of *The Arabian Nights,* and cavernous canvas behemoths with vinyl windows and covered patios.

Recreational vehicles sat in an orderly row a short distance away from the tent jungle. The RVs were arranged according to size, from the smallest, which were similar to Jinks's camper-van, to the largest, which was so gargantuan that only a madman would have attempted to drive it down an English country lane. I decided that the last one had to be Calvin's, both because of its regal proportions and because it was the only RV with a cannon parked in front of it.

Since my chances of finding Edmond's tent in less than ninety minutes ranged from slim to nonexistent, I elected to check out the cannon. Although I knew absolutely nothing about field artillery I felt compelled to investigate *something,* and the cannon was the most obvious choice. I was about ten steps away from it when a gruff voice ordered me to stop.

I turned to find myself looking up at the gray-bearded face of a glowering Lord Belvedere. He was about a foot taller than me and his right hand was resting on the hilt of a sword that looked terrifyingly sharp and shiny. For a moment I was afraid he'd either run me through or challenge me to a duel.

He surveyed me with a hawklike gaze, then barked, "Who are you and what are you doing here?"

There was no question of lying to such a fierce-looking authority figure, so I told most of the truth as quickly as I could.

"My name is Lori Shepherd and I live next door to Horace Malvern—well, not next door, exactly, but my property runs alongside his," I babbled in a half-panicked squeak.

"You don't sound English to me," he growled, eyeing me suspiciously.

"That's because I'm not English," I told him. "I'm from the States originally, but I've lived near Finch for years and years. My husband and I are raising our sons in a cottage not far from here. Perhaps you've met them? My husband is Bill Willis—I didn't change my name when we got married—and our sons are Will and Rob. They're riding in the—"

"—procession and in the arena," he finished for me. He seemed to thaw ever so slightly, but he didn't remove his hand from his sword hilt. "What are you doing here, near the cannon?"

I gulped. "I heard that it misfired this morning—"

"It didn't misfire," Lord Belvedere interjected irritably. "It didn't fire at all."

"Why not?" I asked, and when his lordship's scowl darkened, I added hurriedly, "It's just that I've heard all sorts of rumors and I want to be able to tell people what really happened so they won't be afraid to come to the fair next weekend."

"You can tell the rumormongers that the cannon is in perfect working order," said Lord Belvedere. "It wasn't used this morning because some blithering idiot put projectiles in the barrel."

"Aren't there usually projectiles in the barrel?" I asked.

"Certainly not," said Lord Belvedere, looking offended. "This cannon isn't used as an offensive weapon. Its purpose is to create an impressive sound. If the barrel hadn't been cleared, it would in all likelihood have exploded, killing or severely injuring the cannoneers."

"Good lord," I said, casting a nervous glance at the barrel.

"Thankfully, our men are well trained," Lord Belvedere continued. "They follow a strict routine before every firing. The prank was discovered as soon as the men sponged the bore. Once the projectiles were removed, the cannon could have been employed, but Mr. Malvern was so upset by the incident that we decided not to use it."

"It sounds as though the blithering idiot didn't know much about proper artillery procedures and practices," I commented. "If he had, he would have known that his prank would be found out before it ever got off the ground . . . so to speak."

"Very true," said Lord Belvedere.

"What kind of projectiles did he use?" I asked.

"Since the matter is still under investigation, I'd rather not say." Lord Belvedere raised an iron-gray eyebrow. "Have I appeased your curiosity, madam?"

"You have," I said. "And you've done so most graciously." I turned to look at the encampment. "I've never seen anything like this before. Jinks told me—"

"You know Jinks?" said Lord Belvedere.

"I've chatted with him a few times," I said. "His camper-van is parked in the pasture next to my back garden."

"Yes, of course." Lord Belvedere nodded, as if my words had tweaked his memory. "He needed space in which to practice his tumbling."

"He certainly does," I said, venturing a smile. "There's not enough room here to swing a gerbil. I don't think I'd be able to find my own tent in such a mishmash."

"It's not a mishmash," said Lord Belvedere. "It's a highly stratified community." He finally lifted his hand from his sword and gestured for me to walk with him. "Come with me and I'll show you."

Together we retraced my steps to the top of the rise, then turned to look out over the encampment. Slowly and carefully, Lord Belvedere helped me to see patterns in the seeming chaos.

The tents were, in fact, arranged in carefully delineated clusters defined by the roles people played in the fair. Within the general encampment, there was the weekenders' camp, the Rennies' camp, the actors' camp, the vendors' camp, the jousters' camp, and a mixed area known simply as "the other camp." The RV area was called "electric row" because the larger RVs had their own generators.

Hygiene was evidently not a prime concern in the encampment, because the nearest laundromat was ten miles away, in the small market town of Upper Deeping, and the bathroom facilities were limited to four portable showers and two dozen chemical toilets. Lord Belvedere assured me that most of the resident cast members brought their own washing facilities with them, but the thought of spending an entire summer—or even an entire weekend—washing my hair under a perforated plastic bag filled with cold water made my scalp crawl.

"I imagine you must have a few handymen on staff for emergency repairs," I said. "Where do they stay?"

"In the tradesmen's camp," he said, pointing to a small cluster of modest tents to the left of a large multicolored pavilion.

I fastened my gaze on the tradesmen's camp and tried to visualize the most direct route to it.

"I'm afraid I must leave you," said Lord Belvedere. "Closing ceremonies are upon us."

"Already?" I said, and I wasn't feigning disappointment. I'd come too close to turn back. "Would it be all right if I looked around the encampment? I promise not to bother anyone."

"You mustn't touch anything, either," he cautioned. "You might injure yourself, and our insurance costs are high enough already."

"I won't touch a thing," I promised. "May I look around? Please?"

Lord Belvedere stroked his beard reflectively and for the first time allowed his hawklike gaze to slide downward from my face. "Of course, my dear. You are a neighbor, after all. And a very pretty one at that." He bowed gracefully. "Until we meet again."

"Until then," I responded, and as I headed into the encampment, I silently blessed Sally Pyne and her uplifting needlework.

Seventeen

*T*he downside of wearing a fitted bodice became apparent when I took a wrong turn and stumbled into the jousters' camp. If the wind had been blowing in the other direction, I would have been forewarned by the unmistakable manly stink, but with the wind at my back, I didn't notice it until it was too late.

Up to that point, my journey through the encampment had been an eye-opening experience for entirely different reasons. In many ways, the encampment was like any other campground. The spaces between the tents were littered with usual jumble of barbecue grills, lawn chairs, insulated coolers, picnic tables, washtubs, cricket bats, soccer balls, laundry lines, and overflowing trash bins.

In many more ways, however, the encampment was unlike any place I'd ever been. Pennons emblazoned with heraldic devices fluttered from the roof poles of nearly every tent, as if each were a separate country, and the laundry lines were hung with doublets, pantaloons, and muffin caps rather than T-shirts, hiking shorts, and bathing suits.

Some campers had rigged up complicated cast-iron spits over open fires. Others had casks of ale cooling in the shade of small lean-tos. I walked past pyramids of juggling balls, stacks of fire-eaters' batons, scores of antique musical instruments, and enough lethal-looking weaponry to start a second Hundred Years' War. I didn't see any naked bottoms, but I figured they'd show up later, after work had ended and playtime had begun.

I was so engrossed in the details of my surroundings that I didn't know I'd entered the jousters' camp until I looked up to see five grubby foot soldiers lounging in lawn chairs around a bonfire pit, with their backs to the entrance of a huge multicolored pavilion flying the black dragon standard.

It took me less than a nanosecond to conclude that the soldiers gathered there would never be interested in my mind. As I backed away from their much-too-admiring gazes, the bulkiest soldier, who looked as though he hadn't bathed or combed his hair since the Battle of Hastings, called over his shoulder, "Jack! The evening's entertainment has arrived early! She must be eager to get started."

I stopped dead in my tracks, planted my hands on my hips, and said frostily, "I beg your pardon?"

"Oh-ho!" said the bulky soldier, nudging the man next to him. "A feisty one. Jack'll like her."

The rest of the men emitted grunts of agreement accompanied by a low rumble of lascivious laughter. I was calculating how long it would take me to slap the goatish grins off of their faces when Sir Jacques de Poitiers emerged from the pavilion, adjusting his dragon-embossed black leather jerkin. His eyes met mine and a small, puzzled smile played about his lips. He made a flicking motion with his hand and the grinning, grunting soldiers dispersed.

"You must forgive my comrades." He crossed to stand a few feet away from me, as if he feared that I might make a run for it if he came any nearer. His voice was deep, slightly hoarse, and very attractive, and his coal-black eyes were fringed with long, dark lashes. "They're barbarians. They know no better."

"I'll teach them," I offered, clenching both hands.

"I'm afraid your lessons would fall on deaf ears, and your fists on rather thick skulls," he said with a winsome grimace. "Please allow me to apologize on their behalf. They will not trouble you again."

"Apology accepted," I said shortly. "Now, if you'll excuse me—"

"One moment more, I beg of you," he said. "I don't believe we've been introduced." He pointed his toe and sank into a low bow. "Sir Jacques de Poitiers, at your service."

"Madame de Bergere," I said, curtsying politely. I hadn't planned to acquire a Rennie name, but I was glad that a suitable one had popped into my head. "*Bergere*" was the French word for shepherdess, which was as close as I would allow the Dragon Knight—or any of his comrades—to come to my real last name. "Pleased to meet you. Now I really must—"

"Why have we not met before, Mistress?" Sir Jacques interrupted.

I shrugged. "Just lucky, I guess."

"Come, now," the knight chided gently. "You mustn't be cross with me because of my men's unchivalrous behavior. Unlike them, I know how to treat a lady."

He took a step forward and exhaled a cloud of ale fumes potent enough to pickle granite. I coughed, glanced at the symbol embossed on his leather jerkin, and suddenly understood the meaning of the term "dragon breath."

"Mistress," he continued, "you appear to be distressed. Have you perchance lost your way? You have only to command me and I will escort you safely to your destination."

The clock that had been ticking in the back of my brain ever since the town crier had announced the time grew noticeably louder. It struck me that it would be worth spending a few minutes in Randy Jack's company if he could help me to find Edmond's tent before nightfall. I gazed into his dark eyes and began to invent a cover story to go along with my new name.

"I don't need an escort," I told him, "but I could use a good set of directions. The problem is, a customer broke a shelf in my stall. I'd like Edmond Deland to fix it, so I'm trying to find his tent."

Sir Jacques frowned. "Eddie won't return to his quarters until long after closing ceremonies. He never does, and though I'm sorry to say it, all work and no play has made him a very dull boy indeed."

"That's odd," I said, trying to sound both troubled and perplexed. "He told me to meet him there right about now."

"Did he?" The knight's puzzled frown slowly morphed into a knowing grin. "Steady Eddie is skiving off work early in order to meet you in his tent, is he? It'll be a tight fit in that sad little cot of his, but well worth the effort—for him, at least. Having seen you, I can sympathize fully with his sense of urgency, though I confess that I never expected him to act on his . . . *urges*."

Sir Jacques' insinuations were as alarming as they were unsubtle. I attempted to set him straight.

"I think there's been a slight misunderstanding," I began. "Edmond Deland and I aren't—"

"You can have no secrets from me, Mistress," said the knight, waving me to silence. "Your bewitching blushes admit the truth, even if your shapely lips will not. I'm pleased to hear that Eddie has moved on, though I daresay some in camp will be disappointed to learn that he isn't as lily-white as he seems." He took another step toward me. "I hope, for his sake, that you aren't, either."

"Don't be ridiculous," I said impatiently. "I'm old enough to be his—"

"What has age to do with passion?" Sir Jacques interrupted. "If youth fails to quench your thirst, however, I hope you'll remember that an older, more experienced man—a *real* man—is ready and willing to fulfill your wildest fantasies. Come, my petal, don't be shy. Taste the delights that await you."

Before I could react to his preposterous speech, he lunged forward, caught me by the waist, slammed me into his body, and clamped his mouth over mine. I couldn't tell whether it was a good kiss or not because I was too busy trying not to vomit. Randy Jack had clearly never heard of toothpaste, let alone mouthwash, and he was in dire need of both.

I jerked my head away from his and pushed with all my might against his chest, but his workouts in the arena had given him the strength of a gorilla. His arms tightened around me like steel bands.

"She has spirit," he breathed. "She has fire."

I choked on ale fumes and raised my knee until it touched the hem of his jerkin.

"If you want to sit straight in the saddle again," I said, gasping, "you'll unhand me *this instant!*"

Sir Jacques lowered his gaze, took stock of his position, and released me. I backed away from him, trembling with rage.

"Don't *ever* come near me again," I snarled. "And for God's sake, *buy a toothbrush!*"

I spat disgustedly into the bonfire pit, turned on my heel, and took off. I kept walking until I'd put a couple of yurts between me and the Dragon Knight, then ducked into the space between two empty pup tents and stood there, spitting repeatedly and shuddering with revulsion.

While I waited for my blood pressure to drop, it gradually dawned on me that I'd acquired two extremely useful facts during my unexpected encounter with Randy Jack. For one thing, I'd learned that Edmond wouldn't return to his tent for some time yet, and for another, I'd remembered that the tradesmen's camp was a hundred yards to the left of the multicolored black dragon pavilion.

Heartened, I wiped my mouth with the sleeve of my chemise and set out for the tradesmen's camp. I found it without further delay and, bearing Mistress Farseeing's description in mind, went from tent to tent until I found the tidiest one. Apart from a metallic-blue motorbike parked next to it and a huge plastic water jug perched on a small wooden stool near the tent's entrance, the space around it was completely clear and clutter-free. I wasn't certain that I'd reached my goal, however, until I spotted a monogram on the leather tool kit attached to the motorbike's handlebars.

"ED," I whispered, tracing the letters with a fingertip. "Edmond Deland. Eureka, I've found it!"

Edmond's tent wasn't quite as small as the average peasant's pocket, but it wasn't the Taj Mahal, either. With its ropes, stakes, and khaki-colored canvas, it looked like an old army-surplus tent, with straight walls and a peaked roof. It wasn't fancy, but it appeared to have plenty of headroom and enough floor space to accommodate four very close friends. I borrowed a handful of water from the jug and used it to rinse my mouth thoroughly before pulling the tent flap aside and entering Edmond's domain.

It was a humble, almost spartan domain. The tent didn't have a floor, but Edmond had made provisions for rainy days by stacking his meager belongings atop plastic milk crates. The only other furnishings were a narrow camp bed, a card table, and a folding chair. The table was set with a plastic plate, a plastic cup, and plastic utensils, and a camping lantern hung from the roof pole. His shaving kit, a neatly folded towel, and a small square mirror rested on a milk crate at the foot of the bed.

A crate near the head of the bed held one solitary object. The framed photograph of little Mirabel had been turned to face the thin pillow. In it, her long brown hair was pulled back into a ponytail. She wore a pale pink T-shirt, blue jeans, and brown sandals, and stood on the steps of a modest brick bungalow, smiling bashfully at the camera lens, as though she were a bit embarrassed to be immortalized on film.

As I looked down at Mirabel's shy, smiling, and very young face, I wondered if she knew how much Edmond loved her. I doubted it. The Steady Eddies of the world didn't get much credit for having deep emotions, yet Edmond's love for Mirabel was as powerful as it was pure. *I don't care if you ever look at me again,* he'd said. *I just don't want you to be hurt.* His happiness counted for nothing, as long as he knew she was happy, but he could not stand idly by and do nothing if he knew she was at risk of being hurt.

I felt sorry for Edmond, but I thought I understood Mirabel, too. She was too young to value what Edmond had to offer her. Reliability was an admirable trait, but it wasn't exciting. At this stage in her life, Mirabel wanted fireworks, not a steadfast, dependable flame, and I couldn't blame her. Who wouldn't trade the ordinary world for one filled with wizards and dragons and dreams? She hadn't lived long enough to learn that wizards could be evil, that dragons could breathe fire, and that the worst dreams were sometimes the ones that came true.

Mirabel wouldn't appreciate Edmond's true worth until her fantasy world came crashing down around her. I had to keep the young handyman from doing something that would land him in jail for the rest of his life because a noble heart like his was worth saving, and because his ladylove would need him desperately when the king's dalliance with her had run its course.

I turned away from the photograph, surveyed my surroundings, and sighed. I didn't need to search the tent to know that King Wilfred's crown wasn't there. A pointy diadem set with glittering gems would have stood out like an inflatable alligator among Edmond's meager belongings. I examined the dirt floor hopefully, looking for signs of a recently dug hole, but I found nothing to indicate that he'd hidden the crown by burying it.

I could have howled with frustration. I'd gone through an awful lot to reach Edmond's tent. I'd been scared half to death by Lord Belvedere, leered at by grubby foot soldiers, and physically assaulted by Sir Jacques de Poitiers, and it had all been for nothing. Though I refrained from howling, I allowed myself a small, self-pitying moan before

I returned to the entrance. I'd accomplished all I could accomplish in Edmond's tent. I wanted to go home.

My fingers were touching the tent flap when I heard the sound of approaching footsteps.

"Edmond!" a man called. "Hold on a minute, will you? I need to talk to you about the schedule for next weekend."

I snatched my hand away from the flap and jumped back from the entrance, feeling cornered and incredibly stupid. If Edmond caught me inside his tent, I stood a good chance of ending up in prison before he did. I briefly considered staying put and brazening it out, but concluded that such tactics would do me no good in the long run. Once Edmond saw me close-up, he'd remember me, and I'd never again be able to follow him covertly.

I scanned the milk crates, the camp bed, and the card table, but if there was no place to hide a crown, there was certainly no place to hide a full-grown woman. Then my eyes caught the gleam of daylight shining through the gap between the tent's bottom edge and the dirt floor, and I hit upon a daring escape plan.

I darted to the rear of the tent, flung myself to the ground, and dragged myself under the back wall to freedom. The tricky maneuver cost me my muffin cap, but I thrust a groping hand back through the gap, found the cap, and pulled it to safety mere seconds before Edmond said good night to his friend and strode into the tent.

Weak with relief, I jammed the cap on my head and tried to crawl away on all fours. I learned almost instantly that it's not easy to crawl in two ankle-length skirts and an apron. I managed to cover about three feet of ground before I accidentally knelt on the apron and pitched face-first into the dirt. After that, I threw caution to the wind, got to my feet, and ran.

It took me longer than I'd anticipated to return to the fairground, because the encampment was a lot more crowded than it had been when I'd first arrived. Everywhere I looked, people were cooking dinner, playing guitars, practicing yoga, quaffing ale, engaging in naughty shenanigans, and generally finding ways to blow off steam after a hard day's work. The spike in the population seemed to confirm what Edmond's return had already suggested. The fair's opening weekend was over and the fairground was closed to the public.

It meant, of course, that the main entrance doors in the gatehouse would be locked and bolted, but I wasn't worried about spending the night trapped inside the fairground or, worse, in the encampment, because I knew of an alternative exit. As soon as I reached the fairground, I headed for the Shire Stage and the nearly invisible gate Jinks had opened for me on the way to our picnic on the banks of the babbling brook.

I was so dispirited by then that I wouldn't have let out a peep of protest if I'd been arrested for trespassing. A ride in a police car would have spared me the long walk home, but though I kept an eye out for an officious night watchman, the fair's lanes were deserted, the stalls were closed, and the stages were empty. It was sad to see a place that had been so full of life brought to a silent standstill and I felt no regrets as I slipped through the gate and closed it quietly behind me.

I followed the privacy fence to Mr. Malvern's pasture, then followed the cattle track to the stile. Jinks's camper-van was gone when I got there. He'd evidently wasted no time kicking the dust of the fair from his feet and setting out for his friend's flat in Cheltenham.

"No quaffing with the lads tonight," I murmured as I climbed over the stile. Then I recalled his preference for Riesling and hoped for his sake that his Cheltenham friend had a decent wine cellar.

It wasn't until I was standing in my own back garden that I remembered Edmond's shed. The storage unit behind the Farthing Stage would make a perfect hiding place. King Wilfred's crown could be concealed inside a toolbox, covered with an oilcloth, or tucked behind a sack of sawdust, and no one but Edmond would ever know it was there. The realization that I'd thrown away a golden opportunity to search the shed at my leisure while the fairground was deserted was so monumentally demoralizing that I swayed on my feet.

"Stupid, stupid, stupid," I muttered, thumping my forehead with the heel of my hand.

"Lori?" said Bill, stepping out of the solarium. "Are you okay?"

When I'd imagined Bill seeing me in my garb for the first time, I'd imagined him seeing me as Jinks and Lord Belvedere and even foul Sir Jacques had seen me. Instead, I was filthy, sweaty, disheveled, dejected, and beet-red in the face from exertion. The injustice of it all welled up in me and the howl I'd suppressed in Edmond's tent could no longer be contained. I threw myself into Bill's arms and burst into tears.

"I'm f-fine," I managed, sobbing uncontrollably into his shoulder. "It's j-just been a v-very long d-day."

Eighteen

Will and Rob galloped into the garden to find out what all the fuss was about. After studying me judiciously, they deduced that I was upset because I'd gotten my new dress dirty and advised their father to get it off of me and into the washing machine as quickly as possible.

Bill thought a hot bath would help, too, and after he'd followed the boys' advice to the letter, he ran one for me and left me to soak in it while the boys set the table and he put a roast in the oven. Their solicitousness only made me feel worse. By the time Bill came back to check on me, I'd added copious amounts of salt water to my bath.

My poor husband had to sit on the edge of the tub for a solid half hour and assure me that I wasn't a terrible mother or a horrible wife or the most bird-witted twit who'd ever walked the planet before I could stop crying long enough to finish bathing and get dressed. Before we left the bedroom, I leaned into his arms again.

"I'm sorry I missed the joust," I said in a very small voice.

"I know," he said, stroking my back.

"I'm sorry I didn't spend time with you and the boys at the fair today," I said.

"I know," he repeated.

"I've got a lot to tell you," I said.

"I kind of figured you might have," he said dryly. "We'll talk later. After the boys are asleep."

I nuzzled his neck, shook off the last of my tears, and went with him downstairs to the kitchen. Uncontrollable sobbing was a fairly reliable indication that I'd bitten off more than I could chew. Once Will and Rob were in bed, I would bite the bullet as well and tell Bill about my investigation. He might even offer to help me with it—if he ever stopped laughing at me.

I had a momentary setback when Will and Rob sat down at the dining room table and plopped two new stuffed animals beside their plates. I had no problem with stuffed animals joining us for dinner, but the sight of two black dragons peering at me over the boys' baked potatoes had a quelling effect on my appetite. Had the twins named either one of them Jacques, I might have been forced to leave the table. Luckily, the new members of their stuffed animal family were named Flame and Fireball, and they were so adorably goofy-looking that I fell in love with them before I'd finished my first helping of carrots.

The twins had been itching to tell me about their day at the fair, so I didn't have to contribute much to our dinner conversation. I threw in an occasional "Fantastic!" or "Wow!" to let them know I was listening, and they rattled on happily without any aid from their parents.

They had a lot to talk about. In addition to riding in the procession and in the arena, they'd played in the bouncy castle, learned to braid rope, eaten wild boar sausages on sticks, watched a Punch and Judy show, learned to juggle two beanbags, listened to a story about a lost dragon, met a woman who had a unicorn tattooed on her shoulder, learned how to churn butter, snacked on sugared almonds, fudge on sticks, and cotton candy, and visited the petting zoo, where, as I'd predicted, they'd been overjoyed to make the acquaintance of Ajeeta, the six-foot-long python Lilian Bunting and I had seen before Saturday's opening ceremonies.

I was delighted to hear that they'd adopted Flame and Fireball not because they admired a certain unworthy knight, but because they pitied the lost dragon in the story. I nearly lost it, however, when they informed me that they'd turned down King Wilfred's offer of knighthoods because I wasn't there to see the ceremony, and when they asked why I hadn't been at the arena to cheer them on, my guilt glands went into overdrive.

"I was having lunch with Jinks the jester," I explained. "The only time Jinks can eat lunch is during the joust."

The boys' faces lit up as soon as they heard the jester's name.

"We like Jinks," said Rob, with a firm nod.

"He showed us how to do cartwheels," said Will. "Want to see?"

"Let's save the cartwheels for tomorrow," I suggested. "It'll give me something to look forward to."

"Okay," they chorused.

I gazed at my sons fondly. Although they hadn't offered to forgive me, because they saw nothing wrong with skipping the joust in order to have lunch with a likable man who'd taught them a cool new trick, I felt forgiven.

I was about to clear the table and bring in dessert—fresh strawberries with absolutely no added sugar—when the boys announced that they had something for me. After exchanging significant looks with Bill, who promised not to say a word while they were gone, they left the room. They returned a short time later bearing a tiny gold crown, a little red cape, and a minuscule silver scepter.

"They're for Reginald," said Will, laying the scepter and the cape beside my plate.

"King Reginald," Rob corrected, handing the crown to me.

"We found a stall dedicated entirely to costumes for stuffed animals," Bill informed me. "I was tempted to buy a cape for Stanley. You wouldn't believe some of the stuff we saw there."

I would have believed it, since I'd discovered the stall the day before, but I wasn't going to spoil the fun by saying so. I gave the boys big hugs and many kisses, and beamed happily at Bill. The crown they'd presented to me was more precious by far than King Wilfred's would ever be.

We trooped into the study to hold a coronation, and ate our strawberries in the living room, attended by King Reginald and his bodyguards, Flame and Fireball. His powder-pink Majesty's presence inspired a game of Kings and Queens—a card game similar to Go Fish—and then it was off to bed for my little ones.

By nine o'clock, my extremely tired husband and I were stretched out on the couch facing each other, with our heads propped on cushions and our legs entwined. Stanley was curled into a sleepy ball on Bill's favorite armchair. The playing cards had been put away, my wench garb had been hung up to dry, the dishwasher was running, Flame and Fireball were keeping watch over the twins, and King Reginald had returned to his realm in the study. A companionable silence had settled over the living room, broken only by the steady hum of Stanley's purr. All was well in our world.

"So," said Bill. "How was your day?"

I couldn't help smiling. Not many men were as forbearing as Bill. Instead of demanding an immediate explanation from his hysterical wife, he'd waited until the storm had passed, then asked for one indirectly. It was good to be reminded of his finer qualities just then, when I was about to throw myself open to his caustic wit. Dreading the trial-by-sarcasm to come, I took a deep breath and answered his deceptively simple question.

"It sort of started yesterday morning," I began, "after you and the boys left for Anscombe Manor. I was standing in the back garden when I heard a saw. . . ."

I made a clean breast of everything, from the sound of the handsaw to my failure to search Edmond's shed. I told him about the parapet and the quintain, the crown and the cannon, Edmond and Mirabel, and my fruitless quest for the crown. Bill's jaw muscles tightened alarmingly when I described my unfortunate encounter with Randy Jack, but he didn't interrupt. He didn't say a word until I'd finished.

"Are you all right?" he asked, after I'd fallen silent.

I knew what he meant, and nodded.

"I'm fine," I said. "Grossed out, but fine."

"Do you want me to have a word with him?" Bill asked.

"I'd like you to put him on an island filled with strong, fastidious women," I said. "He'd come back a changed man."

"I'm serious," said Bill.

"I know you are, and I love you for it, but a word won't penetrate his cast-iron ego," I said. "If he comes within ten feet of me again, you have my permission to punch his lights out, okay?"

"Okay," said Bill, but his jaw muscles still looked a bit tense.

"What about the rest of my story?" I said, hoping to lighten his mood. "Go ahead, have a good laugh. Tease me about my overactive imagination. Tell me I've been on another vampire hunt. I can take it."

"I'm not going to laugh at you," he said. "You're not on another vampire hunt."

"Sure," I said, rolling my eyes. "I'm on a *dragon* hunt, right? Good punch line, Bill."

"There's no punch line, Lori," said Bill, gazing levelly at me. "You've been right all along. Someone is trying to harm Calvin Malvern."

It was the last thing in the world I'd expected to hear from my husband. I blinked at him in disbelief and said hesitantly, "The assassination plot is . . . *real?*"

"It's real," said Bill. "Horace Malvern told me about it just before the fair closed today. You haven't been imagining things, love. Someone deliberately weakened the struts supporting the parapet. Someone tampered with the cannon early in the morning, long before the teenaged boys stopped to look at it. Horace didn't know about the quintain's rope, but he won't be surprised when I tell him what you saw. And the king's crown was stolen from his motor home."

I frowned. "Jinks told me—"

"Jinks is under strict orders to quash rumors," Bill informed me. "The entire royal court has been ordered to keep mum about the situation. Calvin refuses to listen to his uncle. He won't call in the police or hire bodyguards or move into the farmhouse, where he'd be less vulnerable. I think he's afraid that the fair will be shut down if word gets out that someone is trying to kill him."

"The fair should be shut down," I said earnestly. "What if an innocent bystander gets hurt? What if you or the twins end up in the line of fire?"

"The fair can't be closed without Calvin's cooperation," Bill informed me. "And he's not cooperating. He's written off everything that's happened as an accident or a prank. It's a pity you lost the quintain rope."

"Yeah, I know." I gazed past him at the bow window that overlooked our front garden, and thought of the traffic that had clogged our lane. The fair's popularity meant that Calvin's wasn't the only life in danger. "I hate to say it, Bill, but I think we have a responsibility to go to the newspapers with the story. It's a matter of public safety."

"I agree, but I'd like to hold off for a few days," said Bill. "Horace has hired a private investigator. If the PI can collar the perpetrator before the fair opens next weekend, there'll be no need to shut it down."

"I should tell the investigator what I've learned about Edmond Deland," I said.

"I'll fill him in," said Bill. "Horace wants to limit the number of people who know about the investigation, so keep it to yourself, will you? The PI's job will be ten times harder if his presence on the case becomes common knowledge."

"Mum's the word." I rested my head on the cushion and gazed up at the ceiling. "I hope Mr. Private Investigator is good at his job. Will and Rob will be crushed if the fair closes after its first weekend."

Bill sat up, swung his legs over the side of the couch,

and peered at me intently. "Now that Horace has hired a professional detective, I want you to promise me that you'll stop your investigation, Lori. No more snooping around on your own. No more following Edmond Deland or sneaking into his tent or eavesdropping on his conversations. There's no telling what the perpetrator might do if he felt threatened by you. He might . . ." Bill took a shaky breath before adding steadily, "The boys need their mother. And I need my wife."

"You're going to make me cry again," I said, taking his hands in mine. "I promise to stop sneaking around, but I can't promise to stop listening to people. I'm an unregenerate eavesdropper. It's too late to change the habits of a lifetime."

"All right. I won't expect miracles." Bill managed a smile, but squeezed my hands to drive home his point. "Listen if you must, but don't act on what you hear. Deal?"

"Deal," I said.

"Back to work tomorrow." Bill groaned as he got to his feet, then yawned hugely and stretched. "I'm off to bed. The boys wore me out today. I'll be asleep before my head hits the pillow."

"Any trips on the schedule this week?" I asked.

As an international attorney who specialized in estate planning for the fabulously wealthy, Bill spent a lot of time flying all over Europe to meet with his demanding clients. It was a rare treat to have him at home for more than two weeks in a row.

"None planned," he replied, "but you know how it is. If a client kicks the bucket unexpectedly, I'll be summoned to sort out the paperwork."

"Let's hope everyone stays healthy, then." I rose from

the couch and put my arms around his neck. "I like having you here."

"That's good, because I like being here." He pulled me into a long good-night kiss, then murmured, "Coming to bed?"

"In a little while," I said. "I want to—"

"—report to Aunt Dimity," he finished for me. "Try not to stay up too late." He kissed the tip of my nose. "You've had a very long day."

Nineteen

he satisfaction of knowing that I hadn't imagined the assassination plot vanquished my need for sleep. I strode confidently into the study, curtsied politely to King Reginald, lit a fire in the hearth, and settled into the tall armchair with the blue journal. I was wide-awake and ready to chat until dawn with Aunt Dimity.

"Dimity?" I said, opening the journal. "You're not going to believe what I have to tell you. You're simply not going to believe it!"

I smiled wryly as Aunt Dimity's old-fashioned copperplate curled gracefully across the blank page.

Why shouldn't I believe you, my dear? I've never doubted your veracity before—except on a few occasions when I had reason to believe that you were withholding details about your unfortunate interactions with certain good-looking men.

"There aren't any good-looking men in the picture this time," I assured her. "Except for Bill, of course."

I'm extremely pleased—and relieved and somewhat surprised—to hear it. Well? What is your incredible news? Out with it!

"Hold on," I said, disconcerting myself. "Before I give you the big news, I should tell you what happened after church this morning. It's pretty incredible all by itself."

I'm never bored by news of Finch.

"You definitely won't be bored," I told her. "Today will go down in the annals of Finch as the day of too many tourists. . . ."

I was anxious to move on to Bill's gratifying revelations, so I sped through a description of the havoc wrought on the village by the tourist tornado, gave a thumbnail sketch of the cleanup campaign instigated by Calvin Malvern, and outlined the schemes Horace Malvern had implemented to prevent such a catastrophe from occurring again. Aunt Dimity listened without comment until I'd finished. Then the handwriting began flowing again.

You've left me quite breathless, Lori. As I'm sure the tourists left Finch.

"The villagers were completely overwhelmed by the barbarian invasion," I said. "And when the guys from the fair showed up, they were overwhelmed in a different way. They may erect a statue of King Wilfred on the village green. Without him, we'd still be picking candy wrappers out of George Wetherhead's front garden."

Has Mr. Wetherhead found the courage to emerge from his house yet?

"I don't know," I said. "I guess I'll find out tomorrow. I have to stop by the Emporium to pick up some milk."

While you're in the village, please ask after the vicar as well. It was brave of him to face a horde of blundering louts on his own, but it may take him several days to recover.

"I'll drop in at the vicarage to make sure he's okay," I promised.

I'll also be interested to hear if Peggy Taxman's display window has been replaced.

"Knowing Peggy, I'm sure it has," I said, then added

wryly, "Knowing Peggy, I'm sure it's been replaced with a *better* window."

She certainly wouldn't hesitate to demand one. I do hope that Miranda Morrow has been thanked properly for replanting the flower beds around the war memorial. And you must find out if the pub sign has been repaired. You should be able to tell whether or not Horace's police officers have done their job as soon as you enter the village.

"True," I said. "If the village looks like a shipwreck, a couple of constables are going to find themselves in hot water with Horace." I shifted restlessly in the chair. "Do you mind if we leave the village for a little while and return to the fair?"

Not at all. I assume your incredible news has something to do with the fair and I'm eager to hear it.

I gazed down at the page with an air of quiet triumph and announced, "I was right about the assassination attempts, Dimity. I was right from start to finish. I wasn't imagining things or reading too much into situations or jumping to conclusions. My instincts told me that something was out of kilter at King Wilfred's Faire, and they were spot on."

Your instincts have always been quite sound, Lori. It's your imagination that has led you astray from time to time.

"It hasn't led me astray this time," I said. "Someone really is trying to kill King Wilfred."

I understand the reason for your elation, but I'm afraid I can't share it. In truth, I wish with all my heart that you were wrong. Has the saboteur been arrested?

"Not yet," I said. "I don't know if he'll ever be arrested. But I'm sure he'll be caught soon. Let me explain. . . ."

I gave Aunt Dimity a lengthy and detailed recapitulation of my conversation with Bill, including everything I'd told him about my day as well as everything Horace Malvern had told him about the behind-the-scenes drama at the fair. After Aunt Dimity's unnecessary comment about my unfortunate interactions with good-looking men, I was tempted to skip over the part about Randy Jack, but since I'd been an incredibly unwilling recipient of his amorous attentions, I decided that it would be safe to leave it in.

Predictably, Aunt Dimity zeroed in on the Randy Jack episode as soon as I'd finished my account, but her take on it seemed to come out of left field.

I'm glad you were able to repel Sir Jacques' attack, but I wish you'd been equally firm with the jester.

"What do you mean?" I asked, bewildered.

He took you to an isolated location, poured wine for you, paid you too many compliments . . . Need I go on?

"No, but for the first time in living memory, I think *you're* the one who's reading too much into a situation," I said, laughing. "Let me make a few things clear, Dimity. First, Jinks is a highly recognizable performer. People expect him to be funny all the time. If he tried to eat lunch inside the fairground, he'd be constantly harassed by fans. Second, he made no attempt to get me drunk. He poured one small glass of wine for me, and he didn't try to refill it when I wasn't looking. Third, I was grateful to him for critiquing my garb. Fourth, I didn't take his compliments seriously. They're part of his job. He dispenses them automatically, and when I asked him to stop, he stopped. End of story."

But will it be the end of the story? Handsome men aren't your only weakness, Lori. You're also attracted to men who make you laugh.

"Well, I'm not attracted to Jinks," I said firmly. "After seeing my husband in his medieval dude garb, I doubt that I'll ever look twice at another man."

Hope springs eternal.

"You seem to be missing the big picture, Dimity," I said. "It isn't about me. It's about Calvin and Edmond and little Mirabel."

I must confess that I feel sorry for each of them. It goes without saying that Edmond must be stopped, but he can hardly be blamed for wanting to protect a girl as foolish and naive as Mirabel. As for Mirabel . . . I agree with you, Lori. She's blinded by the stars in her eyes. I fear that she's in for a very rude awakening.

"And Calvin?" I said.

He should have his face roundly slapped for toying with Mirabel's affections, but he doesn't deserve a death sentence.

"I don't think he realizes that he's doing anything wrong," I said thoughtfully. "According to Edmond, he has a reputation for taking advantage of new cast members. I'm willing to bet that, in his mind, he's just following his usual routine and enjoying a bit of slap and tickle with the new girl in town."

In that case, Mirabel isn't the only one in for a rude awakening.

"He'll find it hard to believe that someone on his payroll hates him enough to want him dead," I said, nodding. "Calvin sees himself as a merry monarch. He thinks everyone loves him."

He appears to be as delusional as Sir Jacques.

"No one is as delusional as Sir Jacques," I countered vehemently. "Randy Jack honestly believed that, once I'd tasted his 'delights,' I'd come running back for more." I shuddered hard enough to make the journal shake. "Ick, ick, ick, and yuck."

Men who consider themselves irresistible seldom are.

I stared into the fire, pushing away the memory of Sir Jacques' breath, but remembering the strength of his arms.

"I wish I hadn't told Bill about Sir Jacques," I said worriedly. "I'm afraid he'll do something heroic, like give Randy Jack a black eye."

Would that be such a bad thing?

"Bill is a fine figure of a man," I allowed, "but he's a lawyer. He wields words, not swords. Randy Jack is built like a tank, and he practices armed combat every day. Bill's heart would be in the right place, but I'm fairly certain that Randy Jack would knock his head into the next county."

Would it matter? Without warning, Aunt Dimity departed from her usual format and wrote a passage from a poem on the page.

> *How can man die better*
> *Than facing fearful odds*
> *For the ashes of his fathers,*
> *And the temples of his gods?*

Macauley's immortal words aren't entirely applicable to Bill's circumstance—I don't want Sir Jacques to kill him, for example, and ashes and temples don't really come into it—but the sentiment holds true. Bill's willingness to risk almost certain injury lends nobility to his effort, whatever the outcome. There's nothing noble about entering a fight one knows one can win. Knights must sometimes pit themselves against dragons, regardless of the fearful odds. I'm not advising you to encourage him, Lori, but if Bill decides to defend your honor, I'd suggest you stand back and let him get on with it. You never know. He might surprise you. Knights have been known to slay dragons.

I rested my elbow on the arm of the chair, propped my chin in my hand, and sighed mournfully. Though I disliked Aunt Dimity's advice, it made a certain kind of sense. I'd jokingly given Bill my permission to punch Randy Jack's lights out, but he didn't need my permission. He was my husband, and he was also a man. There was a clause in our marriage contract that gave him the right to protect his wife, and there was a cog in his brain that gave him a burning need to fight for his woman. I cringed to think of the awful things that could happen to him in such an unequal match, but if he wanted to engage in a physical altercation with the man who'd assaulted me, I wouldn't get in his way.

"I'll put an ice pack in the freezer before I go to bed tonight," I said. "And I'll put Miranda Morrow on alert when I go into Finch tomorrow, in case we need some of her herbal poultices. They work really well on bruises and sprains."

Very wise.

I looked down at the journal with a faint smile. "It'll be strange to go back to the village, after spending so much time at the fair. Everything and everyone will seem so . . . normal." I fell silent for a moment, absorbing the thought, then caught my breath as another one flashed in my brain. "Oh, my gosh, I wonder who won the tidy cottage competition."

You'll find out tomorrow, while you find out about Mr. Wetherhead and the vicar and Peggy Taxman's window and the pub's sign and the thank-you owed to Miranda Morrow. I'm looking forward to hearing your description of the new flower beds. Her taste in plants is so original.

"If I'm going to spend a whole day catching up on village gossip," I said, "I'd better head for bed."

I was about to make a similar suggestion. As you know, gossip-gathering can be quite taxing. Sleep well, my dear. And congratulations. You may have failed to catch a vampire, but if you're lucky, you'll be on hand to watch your knight in shining armor slay a dragon.

"If *Bill's* lucky, you mean," I murmured. After the lines of royal-blue ink had faded from the page, I looked up at King Reginald and groaned softly. It wasn't easy, being a damsel in distress.

Twenty

S ince Bill hadn't so much as looked at his ever-present pile of paperwork over the weekend, he left for the office earlier than usual on Monday morning. The twins and I had breakfast on our own, then climbed into the Range Rover and headed for Anscombe Manor. I dropped them off at the stables for their riding lessons with Kit Smith and was pulling the car around to drive back toward the lane when Emma Harris dashed out of the manor house, carrying a cardboard box and calling for me to wait. I hit the brakes and lowered my window.

She paused at the window to catch her breath before asking, "If you're going to Finch, do you mind if I ride with you? I haven't unhooked the horse trailer yet, and I don't want to drive into Finch with it still attached to the truck."

"Hop in," I told her.

She walked around the Rover and hauled herself into the passenger seat. I waited until she'd shifted the cardboard box in her lap and fastened her seat belt, then rolled slowly down the long, curving drive that led to our quiet lane.

"What's in the box?" I inquired.

"Blackberry jam," she replied.

My best friend was one of those profoundly depressing people who are not only good at everything they do, but who find the time to do everything they're good at. Like me, Emma was an American living in England, but unlike me, Emma designed computer programs, ran a stable, tended an enormous garden, helped her husband run his architectural restoration business, and bottled her own fruit, among many other things.

"To whom are you bearing gifts?" I asked.

"Miranda Morrow," she answered. "I want to thank her for refurbishing the flower beds the tourists destroyed on Saturday. I can't wait to see what she's planted. I don't know if any of the new plants will be legal, but I'm sure they'll be pretty."

Emma didn't need to explain herself. Everyone in Finch knew that a wide variety of interesting herbs lurked in the junglelike gardens surrounding Miranda Morrow's cottage. No one minded, because there wasn't a villager alive who hadn't benefited at one time or another from her herbal teas, poultices, massage oils, and tisanes. I knew that Aunt Dimity, for one, would appreciate Emma's neighborly gesture.

"What a coincidence," I said. "I'm going to Briar Cottage, too. I may need a few of Miranda's poultices before the week is out." I told Emma about my wrestling match with Sir Jacques, and about my fears for Bill's health and welfare should he choose to retaliate.

"If Bill takes a swing at Randy Jack, I'll be there to cheer him on," Emma said firmly. "Jack made a pass at me, too. He thought my riding crop was alluring until I smacked him across the face with it."

"Good grief," I said. "Is any woman safe from him?"

"If I were Horace Malvern," said Emma, "I'd hide the cows."

We laughed until we reached the Pym sisters' house and I asked Emma if she knew when they'd be back from their seaside jaunt.

"Next week," she replied. "I think Ruth and Louise will like King Wilfred's Faire."

"They'll love it," I agreed. "Can't you just see them, dripping in velvet and gold?"

We paused to savor the mental image of the two ancient, genteel, and utterly identical twin sisters wearing the finest, most elegant medieval garb Sally Pyne could create for them.

"Calvin is bound to ask them to be part of his court," I said. "Ruth and Louise are natural aristocrats."

"Queens to the core," Emma agreed.

When we drove over the humpbacked bridge, my first reaction was one of relief to see that the Emporium's broken window had been replaced, and that the village in general looked as neat as a pin. My second reaction was a bit more complicated.

"What on earth . . . ?" I muttered.

A lone figure stood in the center of the village green. He was quite tall and so lean that every tendon, ligament, and muscle in his body seemed to stand out individually, as if he were a walking anatomy lesson. His grizzled hair fell past his shoulders and his gray beard hung to his collarbones. He wore a silver chain with a half-moon pendant suspended around his neck.

"I believe," Emma said hesitantly, "it's a wizard . . . doing tai chi."

"I believe you're right," I said, nodding slowly. "The pointy purple hat is a dead giveaway."

"I guess he finds clothes restrictive," Emma observed. "Or maybe an evil wizard made them disappear."

"It would explain why he's out there in his underpants," I said equably.

"And his hat," Emma put in helpfully. "Don't forget the hat."

"He's lodging in Sally Pyne's spare room," I said.

"How exciting for Sally," said Emma.

We didn't even try to hide our giggles as we drove past. Anyone who practiced tai chi in his underpants on a village green was asking to be giggled at. Beyond the wizard, closer to the war memorial, two jugglers were keeping an apple, two bananas, and three honeydew melons flying rhythmically between them. Beyond the jugglers, yet another solitary figure was behaving very strangely indeed.

"Is he having a seizure?" I asked.

"No," said Emma. "He's a mime."

"Ah," I said, as understanding blossomed. "He's staying with Grant and Charles. What do you suppose he's doing?"

"He's walking an imaginary dog, of course," Emma said.

"It must be a big dog," I commented. "It almost pulled him over just then."

Grog, the Peacocks' basset hound, was watching the proceedings from his usual spot near the pub's front door. He seemed fascinated by the mime's jerky and irregular movements, but unthreatened by the imaginary dog. After ten seconds or so, he put his head on his paws and dozed off. The pub's sign, I noted approvingly, was hanging evenly from new chains, and no one was swinging from it.

George Wetherhead and Mr. Barlow sat on the bench near the war memorial, sharing a bag of crisps and observing the jugglers. Buster, Mr. Barlow's cairn terrier, was helping the performers to hone their concentration skills by bouncing between them and occasionally nipping at their toes. We waved to our neighbors as we drove by and they waved back.

"I'm glad to see that Mr. Wetherhead is out and about," I said.

"It took Lilian Bunting an hour to convince him that it was safe for him to come to evensong yesterday," said Emma. "She had to walk with him from his house to St. George's, then walk home with him afterward."

"Bench therapy seems to be helping his recovery," I observed. "There's nothing like fresh air and a shared bag of chips to calm the nerves."

I parked the Rover on the verge near Briar Cottage. Miranda Morrow greeted us at her front door, received Emma's thank-you gift with evident pleasure, and assured me that she would be able to whip up a supply of poultices at a moment's notice.

"They work best when they're fresh," she advised me. "But I can bring them to you anytime, night or day. Ring me, and I'll be there."

"I don't think a midnight delivery will be necessary," I assured her.

"Anytime, day or night," Miranda reiterated. "If Bill breaks Randy Jack's nose, I'll give him a lifetime supply of poultices, gratis."

"I take it you're not a Randy Jack fan," I said.

"With good reason, I'm sure," said Emma.

"What happened?" I asked.

"He has bad karma," said Miranda, "and he tried to share it with me."

"Welcome to the club," said Emma.

Miranda tossed her strawberry-blond hair. "If Bill breaks Randy Jack's jaw, I'll throw in a year's worth of therapeutic massages for you as well as him."

"Bill will need a year's worth of therapeutic massages if he goes up against Randy Jack," I said. "My husband's a lover, not a fighter."

"Lovers make the best fighters," said Miranda. "Haven't you noticed?"

Emma shook her head wonderingly as we retreated through Briar Cottage's tangled front garden.

"You'd never know that Miranda is a pacifist," she said.

"Randy Jack can turn any woman into a rabid ax murderer," I said blithely. "It's a gift."

We strolled over to the war memorial to examine the replanted flower beds. To our surprise, they looked much as they had before the rampaging tourists had ruined them. Instead of adding her own creative touches—and unusual herbs—to the display, Miranda had followed Emma's original plan and planted a patriotic mix of red geraniums, blue petunias, and white lobelia.

"Maybe she's playing it safe out of deference to Mr. Malvern's weekend police patrol," I speculated.

"Let's hope they don't decide to take a garden tour," said Emma.

The jugglers had stretched out on the grass to take a break, so Mr. Barlow and Mr. Wetherhead rose from their bench and joined us at the war memorial. Buster sniffed the new flowers while the two men informed us that Sunday's tourist invasion had been kept in check by an alert and imposing police constable.

"Six-foot-six, if he's an inch, and built like a bull," said Mr. Barlow. "When Constable Huntzicker directed folk to take their rubbish home with them or put it in the bins, he didn't even have to raise his voice."

"The Sciaparelli boys were back on the door at the pub," said Mr. Wetherhead, smoothing the few strands of hair that covered his otherwise bald head. "But they didn't have much to do. Constable Huntzicker kept everyone in good order."

"You missed a fine time at the pub last night," Mr. Barlow informed us. "It was fair bursting with fair folk. Dick and Chris could hardly keep up with the dinner rush. Good business for them, but bad business for the fair folk."

"What do you mean?" I asked.

"Food poisoning at the banquet table," said Mr. Wetherhead importantly. "King Wilfred was taken off to hospital."

I gasped and swung around to face him squarely. "Is he all right?"

"He's fine and dandy," said Mr. Barlow at my shoulder. "Pumped him clean and sent him back to his motor home this morning."

"Did anyone else get sick?" I asked sharply.

"Three courtiers and Sir James le Victorieux had rummy tummies after the banquet," Mr. Wetherhead replied, "but they weren't as sick as poor Calvin."

"The rest of the king's court played it safe by eating at the pub last night," said Mr. Barlow. "It was quite a scene. They sang and danced and told funny stories until closing time. Knew songs I'd never heard before—old ones, from

Queen Bess's time. I reckon it would be a fine thing if they came back again tonight."

I glanced uneasily in the direction of Bishop's Wood. It seemed obvious to me that the alleged food poisoning incident had in reality been yet another attempt on Calvin's life. While my neighbors continued to discuss the lively scene at the pub, I considered offering my findings directly to Horace Malvern's private investigator. It was entirely possible that, when Bill had relayed my story to Mr. Malvern, he'd accidentally left out a crucial detail that would crack the case wide open. Without my firsthand account to aid him, the investigator might not be able to keep King Wilfred alive long enough to reign over the fair's second weekend.

I was still pondering my decision when Lilian and Theodore Bunting walked over from the vicarage to find out what was happening at the war memorial. The vicar had evidently bounced back from Saturday's ordeal. He looked as though the end of the world was the furthest thing from his mind.

"Good morning, all," he said. "I hope the jugglers haven't finished practicing. I was rather looking forward to watching them."

"Teddy's as fond of jugglers as I am of magicians," Lilian told us.

"Does anyone know who won the tidy cottage competition?" Emma inquired.

"Ta-da!" Grant Tavistock called. He and Goya, his golden Pomeranian, scurried from Crabtree Cottage to the war memorial. "Charles and I won! As new residents, we didn't think we'd be in the running, but apparently our begonias put us over the top."

"Are you still bragging about our begonias?" scolded Charles, trotting across the lane with Matisse, his friendly little Maltese.

"Still?" said Grant, taken aback. "We won the prize *yesterday,* Charles. If you'd read the fine print you'd know that we're entitled to one week's worth of bragging rights."

"I always forget to read the fine print," Charles said apologetically. "Brag on!"

He and Grant released their dogs to play with Buster. Grog, sensing a party, padded over from the pub to frisk with his friends. Sally Pyne, no doubt sensing the same thing, emerged from the tearoom and hastened toward the war memorial. A moment later, Christine and Dick Peacock followed Grog's example and left the pub to join our merry band.

"Have you heard?" Charles said excitedly after the late-comers had arrived. "King Wilfred has offered to hold the village dog show at the fair."

"Everyone's heard," said Sally. "Which is why I now have a dozen orders for medieval *dog* garb."

The dog owners in the group flushed simultaneously and avoided one another's eyes. I turned to Emma, who owned an elderly black Labrador retriever, and raised my eyebrows.

"Don't look at me," she said. "Hamlet's too mature for beauty contests."

"I wish Peggy would get off her high horse and accept Calvin's offer," Sally grumbled. "If we don't hold village events at the fair this summer, there won't be any village events. She's already canceled the bring-and-buy sale."

"Why?" asked Emma.

"Lack of interest," said Lilian. "On Peggy's part, that is."

"That's right," said Sally. "She can't run the bring-and-buy if she's at the fair, and she's not about to close that stall of hers. It's a gold mine."

"Thankfully," said Lilian, "Calvin's generous donation to the church roof fund will more than offset the lack of proceeds from the bring-and-buy. Sir Peregrine delivered the first check last night. He called it a tithe."

Information was flying so thick and fast that an inexperienced gossipmonger would have needed a tape recorder to remember it all. Distracted as I was by thoughts of Calvin's threatened demise, I had to focus hard in order to keep up.

"I was pleasantly surprised to see so many of you in church yesterday," said the vicar. "Attendance was down at the morning service, but the early service and evensong were, as they say, sold out. I hope the trend will continue throughout the summer."

"Our jugglers will be there next Sunday," Christine Peacock piped up. "They told me they like costume drama."

"How very . . . ecumenical of them," the vicar faltered.

"I wouldn't count on seeing our magician," said Dick.

"I do envy you your magician," said Lilian, turning shining eyes on the publican. "Merlot the Magnificent pulled scarves from my ears on Saturday. I have no idea how the trick was done, but it was such fun. Is it true that he's going to give an impromptu performance on the green this afternoon?"

"If he's awake by then," Christine muttered.

She gave the reclining jugglers a wary, sidelong glance,

and our group closed ranks. The well-practiced maneuver came into play whenever a speaker needed to lower his or her voice in order to impart sensitive news.

"They don't call him Merlot for nothing," Christine informed us quietly. "He knows how to make wine disappear."

An appreciative "Ooh" went through the group.

"I found twelve empty bottles in his room when I cleaned it yesterday afternoon," said Christine. "Twelve empty bottles! He'd only been there for two nights!"

"Poor man," Lilian said sadly. "He did seem a bit fragile on Sunday. He winced whenever the town crier announced the time."

"It's a miracle he didn't fall off the stage," said Christine, folding her arms. "And those jugglers—the noises coming from their room all night long . . ." She clucked her tongue.

The closed ranks suddenly closed further. I could almost see my neighbors' ears prick up.

"What sort of . . . noises?" Sally asked carefully.

"Thuds, bumps, bangs . . ." Christine shook her head. "It sounds as though they spend half the night chucking things round their room."

"Practice makes perfect," the vicar pointed out.

"It also makes for broken lamps," Dick retorted, "as well as a good deal of annoying racket. They can take their dratted practice outside from now on."

Christine turned to Charles and Grant. "How are things working out with your mime? You must not even know he's there."

Our newest neighbors exchanged dismayed glances.

"That's the problem," said Grant in a slightly desperate

undertone. "We never know *where* he is. I nearly tripped over him in the parlor last night. He was miming a dying swan. I think. It may have been a cat coughing up a hair ball."

"He mimes *everything*," Charles went on. "It took me twenty minutes to figure out that he wanted Bovril for his toast. How in God's name was I supposed to decipher his artistic visual interpretation of *beef extract*? I finally had to make him write it down."

"I dread to think of what he'll do when he needs more loo paper," said Grant, shuddering.

Snorts of laughter escaped most of us, but they were quickly suppressed. Grant and Charles appeared to be genuinely distressed, and no one wanted to hurt their feelings.

"It sounds as though I've struck lucky this time," Sally said complacently. "Magus Silveroak is a charming houseguest."

The rest of us turned as one to gaze at the underdressed wizard. I wasn't sure about the others, but my mind was reeling with wild surmises.

"He has lovely manners," Sally continued. "And he keeps his room ever so tidy. I haven't had to pick up so much as a sock."

I longed to ask her if he owned a sock, but I kept my mouth shut. Something told me that Sally would react badly to any jokes made about her wizard.

"Well," said Mr. Barlow, breaking the very thoughtful silence that had descended on everyone but Sally. "Must run. The Pyms' garden won't water itself."

"Mr. Barlow," Emma said. "As long as you're going out that way, would you mind giving me a lift home?" She turned to me. "You don't mind if I leave you to your shopping, do you? I'd like to get back to the stables."

"It's fine with me," I said.

"And with me," said Mr. Barlow.

Mr. Wetherhead and the Buntings moved to the bench to watch the jugglers, who had recommenced flinging fruit at each other. Sally Pyne bustled off to open the tearoom, Charles and Grant returned to Crabtree Cottage with Goya and Matisse, and Grog led the Peacocks back to the pub.

Mr. Barlow called Buster to his side and squatted down to scratch the terrier's ears.

"Between the three of us," he said, looking up at me and Emma, "I know how the Peacocks could solve their magician's drinking problem."

"How?" I asked.

"Leave a bottle of Dick's homemade wine in his room," Mr. Barlow replied. "One sip will make him a teetotaler for life."

He gave a bark of laughter as he straightened, which was echoed by a bark from Buster, then he and his dog escorted Emma to his car. After they'd gone, I headed for Wysteria Lodge to have a word with Bill.

I found him sitting at his paper-strewn desk, peering intently at one of his three computer screens. Behind its quaint and charming facade, Wysteria Lodge was brimming with cutting-edge technology.

"Did you hear—" I began.

"About the food poisoning?" he interrupted. "I just got off the phone with Horace. The private investigator is looking into it."

"Good," I said, and turned to leave.

"Lori?" Bill said. "Remember our deal?"

"I'm going to the Emporium to buy milk," I told him indignantly. "I'm not going anywhere near Bishop's Wood or Fivefold Farm or the fairground or the encampment."

"Just checking," Bill said serenely, and returned his attention to his computer.

I left the office weighing the pros and cons of having a husband who could read my mind.

Twenty-one

I spent the next two days doggedly following my
normal routine. I cooked, cleaned, did laundry,
ran errands, visited friends, gossiped with neighbors, put in a few hours of volunteer work in Oxford,
and remained preternaturally alert for the tiniest morsel
of news concerning Calvin Malvern.

By all accounts, he'd made a speedy recovery from the
so-called food poisoning incident and nothing untoward
or unexpected had happened to him since. I was happy to
hear that Calvin had made it through two whole days without becoming deathly ill or having a near-fatal accident,
but I would have been happier to hear that an arrest had
been made.

On Wednesday evening, after Will and Rob were in
bed, Bill announced that he and I had been invited to witness a special dress rehearsal in the joust arena. The knights
and the foot soldiers, Bill informed me, had been working hard to perfect a new act. They wanted to perform it
before a small audience before presenting it to the public
at large. The rehearsal would take place at two o'clock the
following afternoon, he said, and we were not required to
wear costumes.

Since the twins hadn't been invited to the event, we
elected not to tell them about it, but we wouldn't have
taken them with us in any case. With a potential killer on

the loose, the fairground wasn't a safe place for our sons. Bill wanted to attend the rehearsal because he thought it would be good fun. I wanted to attend it because I thought he was lying through his teeth.

I believed that a rehearsal would take place, and that we'd been invited to see it, but I didn't for one moment believe the reason Bill gave for wanting to attend it. My husband was a confirmed workaholic. He left for work early, came home late, and spent more than half the year flying hither and yon, catering to the special needs of his clients. I had to twist his arm to get him to leave the office on a weekday, and he usually spent quite a few weekend hours there as well. He simply didn't have it in him to play hooky. Therefore, when he told me that he wanted to attend a Thursday afternoon event because it would be "good fun," I knew that something fishy was going on.

I was certain that Bill regarded the rehearsal as an opportunity to prove himself to me. I was convinced that my heroic fool of a husband was going to hurl himself into the joust arena on Thursday afternoon and attempt to flatten Sir Jacques de Poitiers. I was so sure of it that I put an extra ice pack in the freezer and programmed Miranda's number into my cell phone. I wouldn't try to stop him, I promised myself solemnly, but I would be there to catch him when he fell.

A ticket wench was on hand to let us in when Bill and I arrived at the gatehouse the following day. The fairground seemed to be deserted as we made our way through Gatehouse Square and across Broad Street, but when we reached the end of Pudding Lane, a cacophony of human sounds—singing, shouting, laughing, and non-stop talking—smote our ears.

A large number of people had gathered in and around the arena, and they all appeared to be Rennies. A quick scan confirmed that Bill and I were the only members of the audience wearing modern clothing instead of much-used and finely detailed period costumes. I felt strangely self-conscious in my twenty-first-century summer garb, but the Rennies didn't seem to be bothered by it. They were too involved with each other to notice the mundanes in their midst.

Foot soldiers and pretty wenches chatted flirtatiously over the arena's two-bar fence, vendors congregated around the picnic tables, and performers sang, danced, and played guitars, drums, tambourines, and fiddles on the hillside where Lilian Bunting and I had eaten our honey cakes.

Neither the knights nor their squires were present in the arena, but the king's court had filled the seats in the royal gallery. Courtiers, noblewomen, and silk-clad damsels lounged comfortably beneath the striped canopy, and King Wilfred stood beside his high-backed throne, talking animatedly with round, balding Sir James le Victorieux, the gallant field marshal who'd led his troops into battle against the trash that had blanketed Finch.

"Where's Lord Belvedere?" I asked, frowning. "Has Sir James taken his place?"

"Possibly," said Bill. "Perhaps a shared attack of food poisoning created a special bond between Calvin and Sir James. Come on. Let's find a good place to watch the rehearsal."

I wanted to sit as far away from the arena as possible—in

our back garden, for example, or in my father-in-law's living room in Boston——but Bill insisted that we stand at the fence, between the royal gallery and the marquee. It was the spot I would have chosen had I intended to vault over the fence and challenge the Dragon Knight to a duel.

My sense of foreboding became one of certain doom when King Wilfred descended the steps of the royal gallery, entered the arena, and called for Sir Peregrine and Sir Jacques to join him. I gripped the fence's top rail tightly and braced myself for carnage when the knights emerged from the marquee, but Bill didn't move a muscle. He seemed to be more interested in King Wilfred than Randy Jack, but he didn't fool me. I knew he was just biding his time.

"This must be the new twist in the show," he said. "King Wilfred is interacting with the knights at ground level."

King Wilfred held a laurel wreath, which he apparently planned to present to the victorious knight at the end of the revamped show. He practiced several different poses with the knights and asked them to comment on his stance and his placement in the arena. Sir Peregrine gave his opinions freely, but Sir Jacques' attention wandered. He looked like a juvenile delinquent in a candy shop as his coal-black eyes slid from wench to noblewoman to damsel.

I ducked my head quickly when his gaze moved toward me, but when I raised it again, he was staring at me with a faintly puzzled expression on his face. I must have seemed vaguely familiar to him, but since he'd never seen me in mundane garb, he couldn't quite remember where we'd met. His curiosity finally got the better of him and he began to walk toward me. Bill stiffened suddenly, his nostrils flared, and his jaw muscles tightened ominously, but before Sir Jacques had taken more than five steps in our direction, angry shouts rang out from the marquee.

Sir Jacques stopped midstride and swung around to stare at the tent flaps. The king and Sir Peregrine fell silent. The royal retinue sat bolt upright, the soldiers and wenches stopped flirting, and the music and dancing on the hillside came to an abrupt halt. Every pair of eyes in and around the arena was focused on the marquee's front entrance.

"Stop treating me like a child!" Mirabel bellowed.

"Stop behaving like one!" Edmond thundered.

The madrigal singer and the handyman came storming out of the marquee, bickering ferociously and at the tops of their lungs. They charged directly to the center of the arena, then stopped to continue their shouting match face-to-face. They seemed wholly unaware of anyone but each other.

"You can't tell me what to do," Mirabel hollered.

"*Someone* has to," Edmond roared.

The foot soldiers and the wenches withdrew discreetly to the picnic area, and Sir Peregrine and King Wilfred retreated with them. As performers, they knew when to surrender center stage.

"We were engaged for a year," Edmond shouted, "and you changed your mind in less than a week. We were supposed to have a romantic summer working the fair together, but you threw it all away the minute he looked at you. Don't you understand? You're not yourself. You've let him scramble your brains!"

"There's nothing wrong with my brain," Mirabel said fiercely.

"If you think he's ever going to take you seriously, your brain has stopped working," Edmond retorted. "Haven't you heard about him? Don't you know what people call him behind his back? *Randy Jack! That's* what they call him!"

My brain twitched. Randy Jack? I thought blankly. What happened to King Wilfred?

"You should talk!" Mirabel hurled back. "You act as though you're Sir Edmond the Pure, but I've heard all about your woman."

"My . . . my *what?*" Edmond faltered, looking mystified.

"Your *woman,*" Mirabel raged. "Alex and Leslie and Jim and Diane saw her sneaking away from your tent! Did you think you could keep your new girlfriend secret by making her crawl under the back wall?"

I blinked, gasped, clapped a hand over my mouth, and stared, thunderstruck, at Mirabel.

"I don't know what you're talking about," Edmond said staunchly.

Sir Jacques strolled casually toward the couple. "No use denying it, Eddie. I ran into your bit of fluff when she was on her way to meet you. She's a tasty morsel. I should know." He licked his lips. "I had a taste."

Mirabel looked at him sharply, but said nothing.

"You're lying," growled Edmond. "I've never even *looked* at another woman."

"Keep your eyes closed, do you? I prefer to keep mine open." Sir Jacques gave Mirabel a slimy, sidelong glance. "I like to see what I'm getting."

Edmond uttered an inarticulate roar and launched himself at Sir Jacques. It was a mistake. Edmond was a strapping young man, but he wasn't a trained fighter. Sir Jacques parried his blows easily, then knocked him flat with one mighty punch and kicked him viciously in the ribs. Mirabel stood frozen, her eyes like saucers, but King Wilfred strode forward.

"I say," he cried. "That's enough. Leave him alone, Jack."

"Keep out of it, Calvin," snarled Sir Jacques. "Eddie's had it coming for some time."

"You heard the king." Bill vaulted over the fence and strode toward the Dragon Knight. "Back off."

Sir Jacques favored him with a measuring look, then snorted derisively. "Stay on your side of the fence, old man, and you won't get hurt."

He flexed his muscles and reared back for a second kick, but Bill was on him before his foot left the ground. I'm not sure what happened next because I closed my eyes and cringed, but when I opened them again, Randy Jack was sprawled on the ground. Blood was pouring from his nose, his lip was split, his right eye was beginning to swell, and he was sucking air as though the wind had been knocked out of him. My husband stood over him, looking slightly flushed and a bit rumpled, but otherwise fine.

"It's not sporting to kick a man when he's down," Bill said loftily, straightening his polo shirt.

Edmond pushed himself to his knees, holding his ribs and wincing, but Mirabel flung herself to the ground beside Sir Jacques, looking horrified by the sight of so much blood. King Wilfred walked to Bill's side and gazed sadly at the tableau. Bill dusted his palms together and turned to face me.

Then all hell broke loose.

The ground quaked, a sound like an oncoming freight train filled the air, and a cloud of dust exploded in the field next to the marquee as a stampeding herd of cattle barreled straight toward the arena. Wizards, magicians, musicians, and wenches shrieked and ran for their lives. Bill grabbed King Wilfred by the collar and flung him toward the royal gallery. Sir James and a brawny courtier heaved the king onto the platform. Sir Jacques shoved Mirabel out of his way, scrambled to his feet, and bolted. Bill turned toward Mirabel, but as the panicked herd burst through the fence, Edmond scooped the girl from the ground and ran with her to the base of the gallery. The damsels pulled her to safety and Bill gave Edmond a boost before climbing up behind him. Bill dashed to the side of the gallery, thrust his hand over the railing, and hauled me into his arms.

Five soldiers held their ground and fanned out across the arena, shouting and waving their axes. The challenge seemed to confuse the herd. The cows' forward momentum slowed, and suddenly, miraculously, they were milling around the arena, breathing heavily and bawling in protest, but perceptibly calming down. The soldiers circled them, talking softly, as if to reassure them, and the herd gradually came to an exhausted, shuddering standstill. The poor creatures looked as though they wanted nothing more than to munch on a bale of hay in the milking barn.

Mirabel, by contrast, was on the warpath. She'd left the gallery as soon as she'd spotted Sir Jacques nursing his bloody nose near the marquee. While the rest of us watched from beneath the canopy, she marched over to give the Dragon Knight a piece of her very strong mind. She kept her voice down, to avoid spooking the herd, but I could still hear every word she said—as could Edmond, who couldn't take his adoring eyes off of her.

"You coward," she began. "You bully. You sniveling, milk-livered *measle*. You kicked my poor Edmond when he was down, and you were so busy saving your own skin that you left me to die in the arena. You'll never be half the man my Edmond is. He was right about you all along. I was too caught up in"——she flung out a slender arm in a gesture that encompassed the whole fair——"all of *this* to see it before, but I see it now, and you can be sure that I'll tell other girls about you. You're a liar, a cheat, and a dastardly scoundrel, and I hope Perry thumps you the next time you sneak up on him after the joust." She raised a dainty fist. "Get out of my sight, maggot, before I blacken your other eye."

A rousing cheer went up from every damsel, noble-woman, and wench within earshot. Sir Jacques dabbed at his nose with a crumpled black dragon pennon and wisely retreated to the safety of the marquee. Mirabel spun on her heel and returned to the gallery, where Edmond was waiting for her.

"I'm so sorry, Edmond," she said, her hazel eyes filling with tears. "I've been *such* a fool, and I've treated you *so badly*. Can you ever forgive me?"

Edmond, still clutching his ribs, cupped her face in one hand and smiled down at her. "Do you know where the name Mirabel comes from? It's from '*mirabilis*'—— wonderful, glorious. That's what you are to me. It's what you've always been."

A sob escaped Mirabel as she placed her head, quite gently, against Edmond's chest. She allowed herself to rest there for a few brief seconds, then straightened her diminutive shoulders, dried her eyes on her apron, and put her arm around Edmond's slim waist.

"Let's get you to hospital," she said. "Someone needs to take a look at your ribs."

I think Edmond would have gone with her if she'd proposed a trip to the moon, so I was glad she'd made a sensible suggestion. As soon as he came down from cloud nine, he was going to need some serious medication.

"Do you think I should explain about the wench in his tent?" I whispered to Bill.

"I do not," he replied firmly. "It'll be good for Mirabel to believe that Edmond has a scoundrelly streak in him. It'll be good for Edmond, too, in the long run."

"By the way," I said, kissing his bruised knuckles, "I'm really very extraordinarily immensely proud of you. You put yourself at risk to save at least three lives, including mine, and as if that weren't enough, you vanquished the Dragon Knight. Where did you learn to fight like that?"

"I was captain of the boxing team at prep school," he said. "And the fencing team and the archery team. I was president of the chess club, too, so I know how to defend my queen."

"My hero," I murmured, snuggling against him.

"Uh-oh," said Bill, gazing out over the arena. "Horace Malvern has arrived and he doesn't look happy."

I raised my head in time to see Mr. Malvern cruise up to the arena on his red ATV. It was a sight to remember, since he was clad in the doublet, surcoat, gold chain, velvet hat, and manly tights of what was, presumably, his burgher costume. When he saw Bill, he drove over to the gallery. His mouth was clamped in a thin line and he looked furious.

"What happened?" Bill asked.

"Someone opened the gates between here and the south paddock, then let a bloody great Alsatian loose on the herd," Mr. Malvern replied grimly. "I don't know where the dog came from or who brought it here."

"I do," said Bill. "I know where the dog came from and I know who opened the gate. I know who sabotaged the parapet and the quintain rope. I know who stole the crown and poisoned your nephew. I know just about everything, now."

"Bill?" I squinted up at him in confusion. "What in heaven's name are you talking about?"

"Remember Horace Malvern's private investigator?" he said, gazing steadily into my eyes. "You're looking at him."

Twenty-two

$\mathcal{I}$ sat in King Wilfred's gilded throne and watched from the royal gallery as Horace Malvern and the five cow-savvy foot soldiers turned the herd around and got it moving toward the south paddock at an easy, shuffling pace. I hardly raised an eyebrow when it dawned on me that the five brave men whose quick thinking and stalwart actions had prevented the cows from wreaking further havoc on the fairground were the same five men who'd grunted and grinned goatishly at me in front of the black dragon pavilion. I didn't think anything would surprise me anymore.

My husband, the PI, sat in an ordinary courtier's chair, talking on his cell phone. I'd given up eavesdropping on the conversation because the only words he'd uttered so far were "Yes," "No," and "Good." It wasn't much to work with.

Calvin, who'd been frightened out of his wits by the stampede, had repaired to his motor home to quaff a cup of herbal tea and settle his nerves. Sir James and the brawny courtier, whose Rennie name was Lord Llewellyn of Llandudno, had gone with him. I had a sneaking suspicion that they were acting as his bodyguards.

The Rennies had straggled back to the encampment, and Mirabel had taken Edmond to the hospital in Upper Deeping, so once the cows were gone, Bill and I had the arena to ourselves. Bill had asked Horace Malvern, Calvin, Sir James, and Lord Llewellyn to return to the royal gallery in a half hour, at which point he would, presumably, dazzle everyone by explaining everything. I was forced to presume because he'd refused to explain a single thing to me.

"Why should he take me into his confidence?" I muttered glumly. "I'm only his *wife*."

"Did you say something, Lori?" Bill asked, covering the phone with his hand.

"Yes," I replied. "But you don't want to hear it."

"Okay," said Bill, and returned to his conversation.

I didn't mind that Bill had concealed his activities from me—much. I understood better than most people that it was sometimes necessary to skate delicate circles around the absolute truth. Now that his investigation appeared to be over, however, I would have appreciated a personal preview of his findings. I was dying to know if I'd gotten anything right.

My love triangle had fallen to pieces before my eyes. Mirabel hadn't been King Wilfred's plaything, she'd been infatuated by the classic bad boy, Randy Jack. If Edmond had wanted to kill anyone, it would have been the noxious knight, not the merry monarch. I was still fairly certain that I'd been right about the attempts on Calvin's life, but I had no idea who was behind them or what the guilty party's motivation had been. I seriously considered beating Bill over the head with his cell phone until he gave me the answers I craved, but decided in the end that it would be a poor way to repay him for saving my life.

Bill ended his mysterious phone call and asked me to help him arrange the chairs in a circle. By the time we'd finished shouldering the heavy throne into place, the others had arrived. Bill waited until the Malverns, Sir James, Lord Llewellyn, and I were seated, then took the floor.

"As you know," he began, "several unfortunate incidents have occurred recently at King Wilfred's Faire. The parapet on the gatehouse gave way and Calvin nearly fell twenty feet to the ground. The quintain's rope broke and a sandbag narrowly missed Calvin's head. Someone tampered with the cannon, then pointed it at the gatehouse, upon which Calvin stands during opening ceremonies. Calvin's favorite crown disappeared. After the royal banquet, Calvin became so ill that he had to be rushed to the hospital. Today, a herd of cattle was driven into the arena, where Calvin was rehearsing a brand-new routine with the knights. Do you detect a common thread in the aforementioned incidents, Calvin?"

"I seem to be the featured player in all of them," Calvin admitted, shifting his pudgy body uncomfortably on the throne. "But they could have been accidents, couldn't they?"

"They could have been," Bill allowed. "But they weren't."

"A jape, then," Calvin suggested. "A jest. A series of merry pranks gone awry."

"No one's laughing," Bill said firmly. "Your uncle was so concerned for your safety that he tried to persuade you to take certain precautions, but you refused. He asked you to report the incidents to the proper authorities. Again, you refused. As a last resort, he came to me. He asked me to use my contacts and my Internet skills to run background checks on your employees." Bill looked directly at me. "He also asked me not to talk about it, because he didn't want word of it getting back to you."

I gave him a small, grudging nod. I couldn't blame Bill for following Horace Malvern's instructions. I was well aware of my chatterbox tendencies. If he'd confided in me, I probably would have told Emma, who would have told her husband, who might have mentioned it to Mr. Barlow, who would have passed it on to . . . and so on. Since the village grapevine had sent tendrils into the fairground in the form of Peggy Taxman and all the other villagers who attended the fair, news about Bill's activities would have reached Calvin's ear faster than a flying sandbag.

Calvin frowned. "No offense, Bill, but I don't think I approve of you running background checks on my employees."

"I'm not seeking your approval," Bill said flatly. "I'm trying to save your life." He strolled to the railing at the edge of the gallery and looked toward Pudding Lane. "In many ways King Wilfred's Faire is more like a village than a business. Workers come and go as they please at all times of the day and night. They have easy access to all parts of the fairground and the encampment. No one questions anyone's right to be anywhere, because the fair is run on trust. If someone is working on the gatehouse walkway early in the morning, it's generally assumed that he has a good reason to be there, whether he's a builder or not."

"Can't have people punching time clocks at a Ren fest," Calvin protested. "That sort of thing doesn't work with artists. But everyone pitches in to get the grounds ready, because we're all in the same boat. If it sinks, we all go under, so when we need to, we put our hands to the oars and jolly well pull together."

"I understand the philosophy," said Bill. "Our perpetrator does, too. He was counting on it, in fact. He was free to commit his acts of sabotage and theft because he knew he could appear in strange places at odd hours without arousing anyone's suspicions."

Sir James spoke up. "The point Bill's making, Calvin, is that each of the fair's hundred-plus employees was a suspect. Background checks take time. It would have taken him months to identify the perpetrator if we hadn't narrowed the field of suspects."

"We?" I said, eyeing him curiously.

"Lord Belvedere, Lord Llewellyn, and I have experience in criminal investigations," Sir James informed me. "We retired from the Yard a few years ago."

"The Yard?" I said, my eyes widening. "*Scotland* Yard?"

"Correct," said Sir James. "We've participated in historical reenactments for many years, but when Calvin approached us, we decided to give the Ren fest idea a go."

"Why didn't you guys run the background checks?" I asked.

"We couldn't spare the time," Sir James replied. "We play high-profile roles at the fair. If we'd failed to show up for performances or rehearsals, we might have put the perpetrator on his guard."

"What's more, you would have disappointed our audiences," Calvin put in. "Rule number one at a Ren fest: Don't disappoint the punters."

"Be that as it may," Sir James said, with a slightly exasperated glance at his king, "Lord Belvedere examined the evidence and determined that none of the accidents had, in fact, been accidents. At the same time, Lord Llewellyn and I conducted extensive on-site interviews with employees. Those interviews repeatedly placed one person in the right places at the right times." He nodded at Bill. "Over to you, sir."

"With that person in mind," Bill went on, "I made inquiries, conducted online searches, spoke with friends and colleagues, twisted a few arms, bent a few rules"—he paused to take a breath—"and eventually unearthed several highly suggestive facts." He leaned against the railing and folded his arms. "Calvin? How did you come up with the money to pay for King Wilfred's Faire?"

"I used my inheritance to make a few investments when I was in America," Calvin replied proudly. "They paid off handsomely."

Bill nodded. "Did you also take out a life insurance policy when you were in America?"

"I did," said Calvin.

Horace Malvern groaned and put a hand to his forehead, but Bill pressed on.

"Did you make these decisions on your own, Calvin, or did you have a financial advisor?" he asked.

"I had an advisor, of course," said Calvin, with a genial, self-deprecating grin. "I've no head for figures at all."

"Do you know a man named Rowan Grove?" Bill asked.

I started, and my mind leaped instantly to a scene in my back garden and a voice saying: *A weedy child with a silly name learns early on to fight with words rather than with fists.* I stared hard at Bill. I felt as if he'd thrown a glass of ice water in my face.

"Never heard of the chap," Calvin declared.

"That's strange," said Bill, "because the name appears on many of the papers you signed. Rowan Grove controls your investment portfolio. Rowan Grove has access to your bank accounts. Rowan Grove is the sole beneficiary on your life insurance policy. You'll be interested to know that Rowan Grove is listed as your primary financial advisor."

"That can't be right," Calvin objected. "I've never met the fellow. My financial advisor is Jinks." He beamed at the rest of us. "Terribly clever chap, old Jinks. He was taking a postgraduate degree in finance at the University of Wisconsin. Gave it all up when he discovered Ren fests, of course, but he never lost his magic touch with money. Couldn't have done half so well without him."

"Calvin," Bill said gently. "Jinks's legal name is Rowan Grove."

"Sorry?" Calvin said, as if he hadn't caught Bill's words.

"When you die, Jinks will receive a handsome payout from your insurance company." Bill spoke slowly and carefully, as if he were explaining the situation to a child. "He'll also have complete control of your assets. It won't come as a shock to me to learn that he's been siphoning money from your accounts for years."

"Jinks told me he had no idea how much Calvin was worth," I said.

"He lied," said Bill.

"Look here," Calvin rumbled, eyeing Bill truculently, "if you're suggesting that Jinks has had anything to do with the confounded run of bad luck I've been having, you're quite mistaken. I've known him since I sold turkey legs at the Ren fest in Wisconsin. We've traveled all over America together—staying up till all hours, sleeping rough, getting up the next day to perform. That sort of thing forges a bond of friendship mundanes simply can't understand. Jinks is like a brother to me."

"He didn't drink to your health," I said, half to myself.

"Eh?" said Calvin, turning to me.

"It didn't mean anything to me at the time, but now . . ." I looked at Calvin's troubled face and forced myself to go on. "I drank a toast to you when I had lunch with Jinks on Sunday." I raised an invisible glass. "'To King Wilfred. Long may he reign.'" I let my hand fall as the significance of the moment struck home. "Jinks raised his glass, too, but he didn't drink from it."

"Perhaps he wasn't thirsty," Calvin offered.

"Toasts aren't about thirst," I mumbled, unable to meet his eyes.

"I'm afraid Jinks used you for his own purposes, Calvin," Bill said. "He gained your trust, then took advantage of you."

"See sense, Cal," Mr. Malvern scolded, peering sternly at his nephew. "Jinks will get a packet of cash when you pop your clogs. If that's not motivation for murder, I don't know what is."

Sir James nodded. "We have eyewitnesses who saw him fiddle with the parapet, cut the quintain rope, steal your crown, put rocks in the cannon—"

"Rocks?" I interrupted. "The famous 'projectiles' were *rocks?*"

"Mossy ones," Sir James confirmed. "They could have come from a local river or stream."

"Or from the brook next to our picnic spot." I could hardly believe what I was saying. I looked to Bill for support, but he'd turned his back on me to peer up Pudding Lane. "Jinks couldn't have poisoned Calvin, though, or started the stampede. He hasn't been here since the fair closed on Sunday."

"That's right," Calvin said, his cherubic face brightening. "He's been in Cheltenham."

"He came back," said Bill, still looking toward Pudding Lane. "If you don't believe us, Calvin, you can ask Jinks. Here he is now."

I swiveled in my chair to follow Bill's gaze. Lord Belvedere and Jinks had just emerged from Pudding Lane and were walking toward the royal gallery. Lord Belvedere was dressed in twill trousers and a plain, button-down white shirt. Jinks was wearing the same tie-dyed T-shirt and torn jeans he'd worn the first time we'd met, when he'd sailed over the stile and into the twins' sandbox, hoping I'd remember him.

"Evening, all," he called, smiling his crooked smile. "His Lordship rousted me out of the pub in Finch to attend this meeting, so it had better be worth my while."

"Finch?" Calvin said weakly. "I thought you were in Cheltenham."

"I was," said Jinks. "But I came back early. I get restless if I dwell among mundanes for too long." He hopped nimbly onto the platform. "So . . . what's up? Have you finally come to your senses and given me a starring role in the joust?"

"We've been discussing the fair's finances," said Bill.

"Not my best subject," Jinks admitted amiably, "but if you want a layman's opinion—"

"We don't," Bill interrupted. "We want your expert opinion . . . Rowan."

Jinks's smile froze and his green eyes darted from one face to another. Then he took his lower lip between his teeth and bowed his head, chuckling quietly.

"Oh, dear," he said. "The joke's on the jester. I've been caught with my hand in the cookie jar, have I?"

"I wish it were so simple," said Bill.

"Tell them it's not true," pleaded Calvin. "Tell them they've made a mistake."

"Ah, but they haven't," Jinks said softly. "You see, I couldn't let you waste your money on this ridiculous venture, old friend. Working a Ren fest is one thing, but running one? Do you have the slightest notion of how much you've spent already?" He lifted his head and met Calvin's beseeching gaze. "I don't have a pension, Cal. My knees are shot, but there's no golden-age home for broken-down acrobats. I was investing in my future as well as yours. I love you, Cal, but I couldn't let you waste my retirement fund."

"No," Calvin whispered.

"If it's any consolation," Jinks said, "I wasn't trying to kill you. I wanted merely to frighten those closest to you. I hoped they'd convince you to shut down the fair, not only to protect you, but to protect your fellow players and the paying public. Accidents are bad for business."

Sir James harrumphed impatiently. "You've explained why you staged the accidents. Would you be so kind as to explain why you stole the crown?"

Jinks threw his head back and laughed. "It's Cal's lucky charm. I was sure he'd give up the throne once he'd lost the precious, custom-made crown sprinkled with his mummy's jewels, but he soldiered on, regardless. Rule number one at a Ren fest: Don't disappoint the punters."

Lord Llewellyn lumbered to his feet and spoke for the first time. "Now, then, sir, if you'll come with me."

"Certainly I'll come with you." Jinks's eyes twinkled mischievously. "But you'll have to catch me first!"

Lord Llewellyn's brawny arm shot out, but Jinks dodged it, did a backflip off the platform, and sprinted down Pudding Lane. Bill took off after him, I took off after Bill, and everyone else followed me, with Calvin bringing up the rear. Jinks's laughter rang out ahead of us as we tore down Pudding Lane, dashed across Broad Street, and raced toward Gatehouse Square.

Bill reached the square before I did, but when I caught up with him, he'd come to a standstill. He signaled for me to stay back, then turned in a circle, scanning the stalls bordering the square.

"Jinks!" he shouted. "This may sound like a cliché, but we really do have you surrounded. You'll be caught the moment you set foot outside the fairground."

I looked over my shoulder at the retired Scotland Yard detectives, the middle-aged farmer, and the farmer's overweight nephew. All five were bent double and gasping for air, as if they'd recently crossed the finish line in a marathon. I didn't think they posed much of a threat to Jinks's bid for freedom.

"Police," Lord Belvedere managed, catching my doubtful glance. "Out front. All round the perimeter. Brought them with me."

I nodded to him, and as I turned to face the square again, a lithe figure darted out from the shadows between two of the stalls.

"Bill!" I screamed. "He's behind you!"

Bill swung around, but Jinks darted past him, hurled himself at the gatehouse, and began to clamber up the fake stone wall of the west tower. I heard the clinking of keys as Calvin jogged past me, but I didn't understand what the sound meant until I saw him open the locked door I'd tried to enter on my first day at the fair.

"Stop him!" I shouted, but I was too late.

Before anyone could react, Calvin had disappeared into the tower and slammed the door behind him. Bill darted after him and tugged on the door handle, but it wouldn't budge. He threw me a helpless look, then backed into the center of the square, peering upward. Lord Belvedere, Sir James, Lord Llewellyn, Horace Malvern, and I strode forward to join him, our gazes transfixed on the top of the west tower. Above us, Jinks pulled himself over the battlements, rolled onto the tower's roof, and sprang to his feet, with his arms outstretched.

"Outnumbered and undone!" Jinks shouted down to us, grinning. "Never fear, though. I have a new retirement plan!" He jumped up on the battlements and balanced on one foot, like a tightrope walker.

"Don't be a fool!" Bill shouted.

"But I *am* a fool," Jinks retorted, teetering precariously as he hopped from one foot to the other. "Just ask your wife. I tried my best to seduce her, but she couldn't stop laughing long enough to take me seriously. Women never do take me seriously. The story of my love life would fit on the head of a pin."

I heard a faint, whining creak followed by a thud that reverberated throughout the deserted fairground, and Calvin's bulky form suddenly appeared atop the west tower. He bent to close the trapdoor he'd pushed open, then stood straight and looked up at Jinks.

"I say, old man, come down from there," he said in a kindly voice. "You're going to hurt yourself."

"No," said Jinks, chuckling. "I'm going to kill myself."

"Don't be daft," Calvin chided. "Your sovereign majesty won't allow it. And *I* certainly won't."

"I'm sorry, Cal." Jinks's manic grin vanished as he locked eyes with Calvin. Then he let himself fall.

Calvin lunged forward and caught Jinks around the knees with both arms. Jinks struggled wildly to break free, but with the strength of a sumo wrestler, Calvin heaved him onto the roof, pulled him upright, and punched him in the face. Jinks crumpled into an unconscious heap at Calvin's feet.

Calvin looked down at him for a moment, breathing heavily, then leaned over the battlement and threw the keys to Bill.

"Be a good chap and pop up here," he said. "I'll need help getting the poor fellow down."

Twenty-three

The bonfire crackled and snapped in the cool night air. I sipped from my flagon of hot chocolate and listened to the sounds of the drowsing encampment—the indistinct murmur of voices, sudden outbreaks of laughter, the gentle notes of a harp. Beside me, Bill gazed reflectively at the star-filled sky. Unbeknownst to me, he'd arranged for Will, Rob, and Stanley to spend the night at Anscombe Manor, so we were allowed to stay out late.

Bill had attained celebrity status among the Rennies. He'd received so many salutes, bows, curtseys, and admiring looks as we crossed the encampment that Calvin had half jokingly offered to share the throne with him. Bill had politely rejected the offer, saying that he'd already found his Camelot.

Randy Jack had been given a somewhat less favorable reception when he'd crept back to his pavilion after the fight. The foot soldiers, as it turned out, took a dim view of the mistreatment of civilians. Their code of honor did not allow a knight to kick a handyman in the ribs.

The men had communicated their displeasure to the Dragon Knight, who'd promptly packed his bags, loaded Lucifer in his trailer, and taken off for parts unknown. Calvin was serenely untroubled by Sir Jacques' defection. He'd intended to sack the bounder anyway, he told us over dinner at the farmhouse, and replace him with a chap who didn't take the bad guy role quite so seriously.

A log fell on the fire, sending a shower of sparks into the air. Horace Malvern refilled his flagon, then passed the pitcher of ale to Sir James, who handed it off to Lord Llewellyn. Lord Belvedere was drinking mead. The hectic hours we'd spent giving statements at the police station in Upper Deeping were behind us. It was pleasant to sit peacefully around a bonfire, sipping our chosen beverages and reviewing the remarkable events that had brought us together.

"The fair is very much like a village," Bill continued, lowering his head and looking from Calvin's face to mine. "And nothing goes unnoticed in a village. Two food vendors saw Jinks near the quintain, with a knife in his hand, after the morning practice session on opening day. They didn't think twice about it, because . . . well, because he's Jinks."

I nodded. "That morning, when I heard the sound of the saw—I remember noticing how quiet it was on the other side of the stile. I thought Jinks was still asleep in his camper."

"He wasn't asleep," said Sir James. "He was up on the gatehouse, making fine cuts in the parapet's supports. A builder noticed him, but didn't ask him what he was doing. He assumed that it had something to do with the opening ceremony."

"A ticket wench saw Jinks come out of the motor home with the crown," said Lord Belvedere. "She assumed that he intended to wear it during one of his routines." He gazed into his mead. "We found it in his caravan, hanging next to his jester's cap."

"Mistress Farseeing, the crystal-ball vendor, saw him near the cannon," said Lord Llewellyn, "and the rocks in the brook near his picnic spot had definitely been disturbed."

"It's a moot point, in any case," said Lord Belvedere. "He's confessed to everything."

"I haven't read his confession," I said, "and I can't read your minds, so I'm still in the dark about a few things. Would someone please explain to me how he poisoned the king *after* he'd left for Cheltenham? I mean, did he ever go to Cheltenham, or did he lie about that, too?"

"He went there." Bill took a swig of ale, then placed his flagon on the ground and clasped his hands loosely around his knees. "But before he left, he presented Calvin with a bottle of Riesling, which he'd spiked with a tincture of aconite—also known as monkshood."

"We found monkshood growing wild near his picnic spot," Lord Llewellyn put in.

I recalled the pretty flowers dotting the sylvan glade and shivered.

"We had the wine bottle analyzed after Calvin became ill," said Lord Belvedere. "The dose of aconite in it was too low to kill anyone, but it would have incapacitated Calvin for several days, had he drunk the entire bottle himself."

"Fortunately, Calvin has a generous nature," Sir James went on. "He shared the bottle with me and three of the courtiers, thus sparing himself the full effects of the aconite."

"Okay," I said. "I understand how he managed the poisoning, but I'm still not clear about the stampede. Where did Jinks get the dog?"

"Liebling belongs to a gentleman who lives in a flat on Montpellier Terrace in Cheltenham," said Lord Belvedere.

"Jinks's friend?" I asked.

"They were at school together," said Lord Belvedere. "I followed Jinks to Cheltenham. I saw him put Liebling in his caravan. If I hadn't lost him in traffic, I might have prevented the stampede. However, I did lose him traffic, and he was able to travel back to Fivefold Farm and set Liebling loose on the herd in the south paddock."

"After he'd opened the gates between the paddock and the horse pasture," Mr. Malvern interjected. "Liebling's a fine, friendly dog, by the way. He'd just never seen a cow before, so he got overexcited."

A young woman emerged from the darkness beyond the pool of bonfire light and walked over to Calvin. I recognized her immediately as the tallest madrigal singer.

"Sorry to bother you, Cal," she said, "but I thought you'd want to know that Mirabel and Edmond are back from hospital. Edmond's ribs are bruised, not broken. He should be up and about in a couple of days. Mirabel's going to nurse him back to health."

"Of course she is," said Calvin, smiling. "Thanks, Kay. That's wonderful news, indeed."

"Mirabel also asked me to ask you if you would marry them on the last day of the fair," said the young woman.

"Tell her that I will be honored to preside at the ceremony," said Calvin. "It will be an idyllic conclusion to their romantic summer. Now, off to bed with you. I expect you to be in fine voice on Saturday."

The young woman bent to kiss the top of his head and he blew a kiss to her as she departed. I sat up straight and stared after her as a number of ideas began to spin rapidly in my mind.

"Calvin," I said slowly. "Who was that?"

"Kay Jorgensen," he replied. "My cousin."

"If you spot her in the crowd during the procession," I said, "do you blow a kiss to her?"

"I do, as a matter of fact." He laughed. "It's a family tradition. I've blown kisses to her ever since she was a small girl."

I felt the color rise in my face and hastily lowered my gaze to my flagon. I would never admit it to the men sitting around the bonfire with me, but I'd just solved another mystery. Mirabel hadn't been responding to King Wilfred when she'd curtsied during the procession. She'd been flirting with Sir Jacques, who'd been walking beside the king. King Wilfred's kiss had been aimed well over Mirabel's head, at Kay Jorgensen, his cousin, who'd reacted with composure because it was a family tradition, not a come-on. My mistake had been in assigning Calvin characteristics he simply didn't possess. Aunt Dimity had been right about him. Calvin was no lothario.

"Cal," Mr. Malvern said gruffly, "I wish you'd change your mind."

"You can go on wishing, then," said Calvin, with unaccustomed severity. "I'm not going to press charges against Jinks. He's spending the night at the station because the police insisted on it, but he'll be a free man tomorrow morning. The poor chap's had a breakdown. He needs to be looked after, not thrown in prison."

"He could have killed you," Sir James pointed out.

"Yes, but he didn't, did he?" Calvin retorted irritably. "And he never meant to kill me, so I don't see what all the fuss is about."

"He duped you into giving him control of your finances," said Lord Belvedere.

"I *want* him to control my finances," Calvin shot back. "He's done a bang-up job so far, and I expect he will again, once he's recovered himself. We'll make the arrangement all legal and aboveboard, naturally, but I'm going to ensure that he has his fair share of my money. If it weren't for him, I wouldn't have so much of it." Calvin peered at us in exasperation. "Can't any of you imagine what he's been going through? The poor fellow's been worried sick about ending up penniless, crippled, and alone. Is it any wonder he's a bit doolally?"

Mr. Malvern, Sir James, and the two lords shook their heads in bewilderment, but I caught Calvin's eye and nodded. I found it extremely easy to imagine what Jinks had been going through. It was, however, nearly impossible for me to imagine someone with a heart bigger than Calvin's.

"Once he stops fretting about his future," Calvin continued, "he'll settle down and be his old self again. When he's released from jail in the morning, I'm going to see to it that he has the very best of care." He raised his hand, palm outward, in a gesture signaling finality. "Let there be no more discussion. My mind is made up."

A period of silence followed his pronouncement. Finally, Calvin cleared his throat.

"I think you should have a knighthood for your valorous work on my behalf, Bill," he said. "What say you?"

"I'm sorry," said Bill, "but I can't accept. I've already sworn an oath of fealty to my family, so I can't swear one to you. My sons, on the other hand, are ready and willing to become knights of your realm."

"We'll have a horseback ceremony for them," Calvin

proposed, warming to the idea. "We'll do it in the arena, before the joust. The more pageantry, the better, I say."

"They'll love it," I said. "It might be a good idea to knight Thunder and Storm as well."

"An excellent idea," said Calvin. "We'll have to start thinking about Edmond and Mirabel's wedding, too. I want it to be a day they'll never forget."

"Leave it to Lori," said Bill. "She's good at weddings."

"Would you consider arranging it?" Calvin asked me.

"Would I consider arranging a full-out medieval, prince-and-princess, happily-ever-after, fairy-tale wedding?" I said in one breath. "Yeah. I think I might be willing to give it a go."

"Try stopping her," said Bill, grinning. "Are you allowed to marry people, Calvin?"

"Oh, yes," Calvin replied. "I got my minister's license on-line last year. It's perfectly legal." He sighed. "The wedding will be my last official ceremony at King Wilfred's Faire."

"Until next year," I said.

"I'm afraid there won't be a next year," he said. "At the end of the summer, I will close King Wilfred's Faire permanently."

For a split second we simply gaped at him. Then came the reactions.

"*What?*" said Mr. Malvern.

"*Huh?*" said Lord Llewellyn.

"*I beg your pardon?*" said Sir James.

"*Close the fair?*" said Bill.

"*Permanently?*" I said.

"*Why?*" said Lord Belvedere.

"I don't much like being king," Calvin replied thoughtfully. "Nor do I enjoy managing such a large enterprise.

I'll see it out to the end of the run, of course, but when it's over—and when Jinks is well enough to come with me—I'm going back to America. I'll work as a town crier or a lord mayor or a peasant." He chuckled. "Perhaps I'll sell turkey legs again. Anything to spare myself the dreadful burden of all this blasted responsibility."

"Uneasy lies the head that wears a crown," said Bill.

"Truer words were never spoken," said Calvin. "Clever chap, Shakespeare. Knew a thing or two. My head's so uneasy that I've decided to demote myself to the rank of duke for the rest of the summer. I've hired a new king. He'll start on Saturday."

I stared at him in utter disbelief. "You mean . . . King Wilfred is *dead*?"

"In a manner of speaking," said Calvin. "But a new King Wilfred will be born the day after tomorrow."

The men observed him solemnly for a moment, then got to their feet and raised their flagons. I hastily followed suit.

"The king is dead," said Bill. "Long live the king!"

"Long live the king!" we chorused.

We sat up past midnight, talking, laughing, and quaffing, but the day's intense emotions and dramatic events finally caught up with us and it was time to bring our gathering to a close. While Bill exchanged last-minute pleasantries with the other men, Calvin stepped to one side and beckoned to me.

"I have something for you, Lori," he said. He reached into his belt pouch and pulled out a folded slip of paper. "Jinks asked me to give it to you."

I unfolded the slip of paper and saw in the flickering firelight a handwritten copy of the honey cake recipe.

"Oh," I said softly, and felt my throat constrict. "Thank him for me, will you?"

"You can thank him yourself," said Calvin. "They encourage visitors in the place I've found for him. I'm going to make sure everyone goes to see him, especially Lady Amelia. She's had her eye on him, but she's been too shy to make her preference known. I think it's time for her to speak up, don't you?" He glanced furtively at Bill, Lord Belvedere, Sir James, Lord Llewellyn, and Mr. Malvern, then leaned closer to me and said quietly, "It's not just about money, you know. He needs to be shown how much he's loved." Calvin beamed jovially at me, turned, and strode away from the bonfire.

As the darkness swallowed him, I blinked back tears and whispered, "Long live King Calvin the Good!"

Epilogue

The invasion of Finch ended on a sweltering afternoon in late August. My peaceful English village had survived rampaging tourists, eccentric houseguests, and overcrowded evenings at the pub, but King Wilfred's Faire could not survive the unexpected death of its original merry monarch. At the end of the summer, the Mayne Entrance was closed for good, and all traces of the fair vanished from Bishop's Wood.

Merlot the Magician shocked Finch's wine connoisseurs by purchasing six cases of Dick Peacock's ghastly homemade wine to take home with him. Bill and I decided that his next trick would be to make his own tooth enamel disappear. Magus Silveroak graciously accepted Sally Pyne's going-away gift of lovingly hand-knitted sweaters, socks, and scarves, but no one believed that the wizard would get much use out of them. Peggy Taxman presented the jugglers with a bag of practice fruit when they departed, and the mime left without saying a word to anyone.

The village's traditional summer events flourished once Peggy agreed to hold them at the fairground. Grog the basset hound won the newly created Fancy Dress Award at the dog show, thanks to the dashing Robin Hood costume Sally Pyne had made for him. Grant Tavistock and Charles Bellingham took first place in the flower show with their stunning begonias, and the Anscombe Manor junior team won their portion of the gymkhana, which drew large and appreciative crowds to the joust arena.

Will, Rob, Thunder, and Storm were knighted in the arena by King Wilfred the Second, who conducted the entire ceremony on horseback. Bill wore his medieval dude garb to the festivities, but after wearing my costume for one action-packed day, I retired my role as Madame de Bergere and stuck to mundane clothes for the rest of the summer. I didn't want Alex or Leslie or Jim or Diane—whoever they were—to recognize me as the woman they'd seen crawling away from Edmond's tent. No bride wants to find out that her wedding planner was her fiancé's bit of fluff.

Calvin resumed the throne one last time, to marry Edmond and Mirabel in a daylong Rennie extravaganza that involved nearly every performer at the fair. The happy couple was escorted to the Great Hall by the soldiers, squires, and knights, serenaded during the ceremony by the madrigal maidens, and feted at the sumptuous wedding feast by beggars, gypsies, pirates, fairies, monks, snake charmers, Morris dancers, belly dancers, puppeteers, wenches, magicians, wizards, jugglers, acrobats, musicians, and the walking, talking tree. The wedding was the highlight of the summer, and a splendid way to say farewell to King Wilfred's marvelous, magical fair.

Afterward, the Rennies struck camp and dispersed. Some returned to their regular nine-to-five jobs, others moved on to participate in historic festivals and reenactments all over England, and a few traveled to America, to try their luck on the year-round Ren fest circuit.

Jinks spent seven weeks in the rest home Calvin had found for him, healing from minor knee surgery as well as a major nervous breakdown. Calvin didn't have to cajole his employees into visiting the rest home. Since the fair was very much like a village, the Rennies knew of Jinks's crimes before he was released from the lockup in Upper Deeping. They didn't condemn him because they were, on the whole, a remarkably nonjudgmental lot and because, like Calvin, they sympathized with Jinks's fears. Not a day went by without one or more of them showing up at the rest home to keep Jinks abreast of the fair's hottest gossip or simply to keep him company.

Lady Amelia was his most frequent visitor. The slim, raven-haired beauty taught him to play the lute and discovered that he had a fine singing voice that happened to blend exquisitely with hers. When he came to the wedding with her on his arm, he was no longer Jinks the Jester, but Rowan the Bard. The songs he'd composed to perform at the feast were witty and funny and wise, and they didn't require him to wear a belled cap or to do backflips.

"Lady Amelia reckons he'll be ready to go back to America in another week or two," I said. "He's asked her to go with him, which is just as well, because she's had her bags packed since July."

I sat in the study, with my feet on the ottoman and the blue journal open in my lap. King Reginald gazed down at me from his niche on the bookshelves with a satisfied glimmer in his black button eyes. He seemed to think that it was very good to be king.

Is Calvin aware of Lady Amelia's intentions?

I laughed as the question appeared on the page in Aunt Dimity's old-fashioned script.

"Are you kidding?" I said. "Calvin's done everything in

his power to encourage and support her intentions. He's hoping for a wedding by Christmas."

I'm pleased to know that Calvin continues to regard Lady Amelia with affection. It can be awkward when one's best friend finds a mate. I was afraid Calvin might feel excluded.

"Lady Amelia's way ahead of you," I said. "She's put Calvin to work arranging their schedule for next year. If a Ren fest doesn't want all three of them, he's to scratch it off the list and move on to the next one. He shouldn't have any trouble finding gigs, though. They're a talented and experienced trio."

I'm certain they'll do well as a team. I applaud Calvin's decision to give up his grand dream and return to his roots as a humble player.

"Why?" I asked. "Most people think he's going backwards—changing from a butterfly into a caterpillar."

Unlike most people, Calvin is at peace with himself. When his dream proved to be more than he could handle, he didn't become discouraged. He simply recognized his limitations and decided to live happily within them. I have no doubt that he'll make an exemplary caterpillar. Butterfly wings can be awfully hard to manage.

"Lord Belvedere and Sir James think he's a fool for letting Jinks off so lightly," I said.

I'd rather be his kind of fool than theirs. Where they see wickedness and demand punishment, Calvin sees despair and demands compassion. He won't tolerate cruelty—he would have sacked Sir Jacques if the soldiers hadn't beaten him to the punch—and to send a sick friend to prison would have been the harshest form of cruelty. Calvin is wiser than even he knows. He refuses to let bitterness poison his heart. He chooses instead to believe in the healing power of love.

"He certainly gives new meaning to 'Forgive and forget,'" I commented dryly.

The old meaning is potent enough. What would he have gained by holding on to anger and seeking revenge? A future shared with Lady Amelia and Rowan the Bard is brighter by far than one filled with regret and resentment.

"Calvin's smarter than I am," I said. "I'm still holding on to a sack of regrets."

Such as?

"I wish I hadn't pegged Calvin as a playboy," I said. "I wish I hadn't seen Edmond as a crazed assassin. I wish I'd noticed Jinks's attempt to seduce me. He would have felt much better about himself if I'd slapped his face. I wish I'd had more confidence in Bill's ability to defend my honor. I was so afraid that Randy Jack would knock the tar out of him that I couldn't bring myself to watch the fight."

What a strange and interesting set of regrets. Would you care to explain them further?

"It's my imagination," I said. "It's completely screwed up. The things I *could* imagine turned out to be false and the things I *couldn't* imagine turned out to be true. Calvin's not a playboy and Edmond isn't a crazed assassin, but Jinks was trying to seduce me, and Bill was perfectly capable of defending my honor. What's wrong with me, Dimity? No matter how hard I try, I can't seem to see what's in front of me."

How boring life would be if we could see only what's in front of us! Your imagination may lead you astray, my dear, but it takes you on fascinating journeys, and you always get off at the right stop in the end. Face it, Lori: You're not cut out to be a normal human being. You're meant to be better than normal. Take a page from Calvin's book. Recognize your limitations and rejoice in them!

"But—"

No buts! Dragons come in all shapes and sizes. Some need to be punched on the nose. Some need to spend time in a rest home. The dragons within us need to be slain. Stop doubting yourself, my dear. Don't try to be someone you're not. Let Emma be Emma. I vastly prefer you as Lori.

By the first weekend in September, Horace Malvern's cows had settled into their old pasture, and Finch had settled into its old ways. The village grapevine quivered with rumors about the wedding that would take place in two short weeks, and Peggy Taxman's gavel could be heard throughout the land. Nothing had really changed in Finch. Thank heavens.

I attended every committee meeting, not because I was afraid of being landed with an unpalatable job, but because I was eager to get to work organizing the Harvest Festival, the Guy Fawkes Day bonfire, the Nativity play, and the re-scheduled bring-and-buy sale. I'd had my fill of spectacle. I couldn't wait to bring out the frayed linen tablecloths, tarnished tea urns, and increasingly shabby, but soothingly familiar, decorations.

I was much too busy to dwell on the summer of the dragon. I looked to the future, and I let my imagination soar.

King Wilfred's Honey Cakes

Cakes

¹/₂ cup butter
4 cups sifted flour
2 egg yolks
1 cup milk
2 tablespoons superfine sugar
2 tablespoons honey
1¹/₂ teaspoons baking powder
pinch salt

Topping

1 egg white
1 cup heather honey
3 tablespoons ground almonds

Preheat the oven to 350°F. Grease the baking sheet.

Cakes

Rub the butter into the flour. Beat the egg yolks with the milk. Combine the sugar and honey in a small saucepan and heat over a low flame, stirring until well mixed. Then stir in the baking powder.

Add the sugar/honey mixture to the flour/butter mixture, alternating with the egg yolks/milk mixture. Mix everything together very well, add the salt, and mix again. Roll out gently on a floured board to approximately a ¹/₂-inch thickness. Cut into twenty-four rounds. Place the rounds on a greased baking sheet. Bake at 350°F for about 20 minutes, or until golden brown. Remove to a rack to cool. When cool, add the topping.

Topping

Lightly beat the egg white. Combine the honey with the almonds. Paint the tops of the cakes with the egg white, then spread the honey/almond mixture over the tops of the cakes. Bake in a very cool oven for no longer than 5 minutes, to set. Eat either hot or cold, and let your imagination soar!